the
dark
trench
shadow
series

FRAGMENT 01

FRACTURED

KERRY NIETZ

FREEHEADS

To the fans of ThreadBare and his world
The time has come

ALSO BY KERRY NIETZ

FICTION

DarkTrench Saga Novels
A Star Curiously Singing
The Superlative Stream
Freeheads
DarkTrench Shadow Novels
Frayed
Fraught
Fractured, Fragment One and Two
Peril in Plain Space Novels
Amish Vampires in Space
Amish Zombies from Space
Amish Werewolves of Space
Takamo Universe Novella and Novels
Rhats!
Rhats Too!
Rhats Free!
Rhataloo
Novels and Novella
Mask
Lost Bits
Digital Dreams and Other Distractions

NONFICTION

FoxTales: Behind the Scenes at Fox Software
Get to the Margins (contributor)

ACKNOWLEDGEMENTS

Thanks to editor Jill Domschot for stepping out of editing retirement to help with this. Thread's story is the better for it. Wish you the best with your own stories!

A huge thank you to readers (and writers) Kathy Tyers, Sophia Hansen, and Lisa Godfrees. Your willingness to help and insight was such a blessing. Much appreciated.

A plastisteel-cladded ovation for Kirk DouPonce, both for your art and your help with the title. You rock!

And thanks to the Lord for getting me through this. One scene at a time.

2000 AH, Day 82, 1:34:07 a.m.

[Chute Sleep]

THE VESSEL IS DARK blue and tinged with gold. It's subtly triangular, with a cabin positioned between three turbine engines. The front two engines are a meter across and can be independently turned, while the third engine is twice their size and stationary, positioned behind the cabin.

The craft is marvelous. Possibly the most exquisite machine I've ever encountered. Once part of the Imam's stable of skysliders, it now obeys my commands. The Imam is dead, his city is in chaos, and my only goal is to protect those I love.

Of primary importance is my female friend Damali. She's nestled inside the slider now, awaiting me. I can barely contain my urge to join her. To flee the Holy City and share the flight with her. To share a future with her.

For the first time since childhood, I'm unfettered. It's both exhilarating and frightening. The banquet of choices. The possibilities.

We're on a landing bay atop one of the smaller multi-storied buildings near the middle of the Imam's walled compound. Dominating the landscape are five dark towers called "the fingers of the Imam's hand." The upper stories of all five are gold-tinged, but tonight they are reddened by emergency lighting. A hellish and lurid scene.

My friend and peer, BullHammer, lingers in front of the ship. Like me, he's bald and thin. For him, the latter quality is new. His time with the Imam shed much of his earlier, more jovial, weight.

He's smiling now, though, and glassy-eyed. He's still dressed in the white robe required by our previous job. "Go on, Thread," he says, with a nod. "I'm fine here."

I frown and send him an icicle in the stream—the worldwide information band that he and I swim in via the implants in our heads. "You hate it here," I say. "You're miserable." He has no friends in the Holy City. No security. Many debuggers have already been lost.

He swats the air. "I'm needed now, Thread." He indicates the reddened buildings. "Things have changed." He smiles. "Change has to be good, right?"

It could be worse, though. Of course, it could.

"Thread?" Damali beckons.

Again, my emotions shift. Cold gives way to warmth. Fear and hopefulness collide.

Bull winks and gives me a closing nod. "Go on with whatever you're doing here." He looks at the darkened canopy. "With whatever you're able to do."

I want to hug him, but custom restrains me. I manage a weak smile and a wave instead. It's not enough.

I step backwards into the slider. I'm embraced by the craft's warmth and stream emanations. It's meant to be welcoming, this craft. Infused with a sophisticated personality. It sends me a short instructional video, scented with oranges, to reacquaint me with its many features. I push that away.

My seat is oversized, covered in blue leather. As I sit, restraints noiselessly secure me in place.

I watch BullHammer until the canopy closes. He continues to smile, but I do not.

Damali's hand touches the crook of my arm. I shift in her direction, and our hands become entwined. Another new experience. Such a simple gesture of affection, but it ignites my senses. Makes everything bright.

"You saved me," she says. "Again."

The ship engages its engines and lifts off. It jars me free of the daze brought on by her contact.

"Not me," I say. "Not really." I glance at the city again. The Imam's "fingers" give way to the lights from the holiest of sites, an amphitheater where thousands circle a fallen piece of heaven and pray to A for mercy.

I've found mercy in a most unusual way. A forbidden source.

"Of course, you," Damali says. "You fought the sentinel and beat it. Then you led us out of..." She shakes her head. "Chaos." She releases my hand and presses her fingers to her eyes. "He's gone. I can't believe it. The Imam is dead."

"Leaving us his son," I say. News items in the stream scream that information: the Imam succeeded by his remaining son.

His oldest son, Aadam, was my master once. He was sadistic, cruel, and crazed. He is also dead.

The remaining son is a mystery. The Imam was heavy-handed, but not maniacal. Not unusually cruel. Who is Prince Ahmad more like? His father or his brother?

I focus on the here and now. On Damali and our journey to safety. I wonder if we might be followed. Surely, someone noticed the slider's ascent. The Imam's residence is filled with security.

"Are you comfortable?" the ship asks.

I can't help but smile. During my last flight, I learned that the ship monitored my physiological responses. "I'm worried about other ships," I say. "That someone might be after us."

"I will monitor for that outcome," the ship says. "Be at ease."

I look at the ceiling. "Do you have a name, ship? I feel like I should call you something."

"No one ever thought to ask," it says. "I'm honored by your attention. But no, I have no specific nomenclature. I've had several nicknames over the years, however."

Damali reclaims my hand.

I attempt to relax back into my seat. To let worry drift away.

Am I free? Am I really without stops?

I look at Damali, and as a test, study her eyes. Dark and warm. Filled with mystery. Then I move to the curve of her left cheek. It is a slightly darker shade than the rest of her face. I move my vision to her mouth. It's ajar, scarlet tongue visible. The edges of her teeth are—

She licks her lips. They glisten like the skin of an apple.

"What are you doing?" she asks.

I shift my gaze to the floor, embarrassed. There are other emotions too: relief and surprise. Throughout my examination of her face, I didn't get stopped once. Not once did I feel the head pain of a correction from my implant. How can that be?

I'm free. Somehow.

No, not somehow. It was *his* doing. The miracle prophet, Isa. It had to be.

"We're over the ocean," the ship says, "if you'd like to look. The last clear view before we start our ascent."

Damali's eyes remain on me, but I look past her to the view beyond the canopy of a winding coastline next to an endless expanse of blue. Narrow lines of waveforms are visible on the surface. Seemingly small ripples, but up close, they could push me over.

Damali joins me in looking. "Beautiful," she says. "I didn't see anything when I was brought here. It was dark and crowded, our ship. No windows. No comfort."

"You were a slave," I say. "And so was I." I smile. "But now we're not."

She touches my head. "You still have that thing in you. And I'm still a fugitive."

"I've talked to Bamboo, my instructor," I say. "You'll have a place of freedom. I promise."

"In a school for boys?"

I shrug and check the view again. The ocean is farther away. I can no longer recognize the waves. "I know things," I say. "Things Bamboo will find valuable."

"Ooh," she says, smiling. "Something to bargain with. I like that. A position of power."

"Starting our ascent now," the ship says. "Would you like to view space when we arrive?"

Damali's eyes widen. "Space!" she gasps. "Why are we going to space?"

"Your biometrics indicate that you're nervous, Damali," the ship says. "But there's no reason to—"

"It's the quickest way." I focus on her face again. "And it's beautiful. You'll enjoy—"

She shakes her head. "I don't want to," she says. "I stop my brother from even talking about it. No, no." She grabs at her restraints, as if to disconnect them, pulling and jerking.

"That isn't a good idea," I say.

"I'm afraid of heights!"

"We've been above the ground for twenty-two minutes. You've been—"

She pounds on her armrests. "That's different! You need to take me down. No space. No—"

"Both your heart rates are elevated," the ship says. "I assure you that since my checkout ride and an infinitesimal problem with my canopy, I've been completely—"

"Down!" Tears form in Damali's eyes.

This is a situation I'm unprepared for. One I can't easily fix. "We'll darken the window," I say. "You won't have to see." I look toward the ceiling. "You can do that, ship, right?"

The scent of vanilla fills the air. Another trick from the ship's arsenal. "Of course," it says. "I'd be happy to."

Damali looks hard at me. "If you care for me at all, you'll stop this ship." She swipes at her eyes, dispelling wetness. "Take us down."

"I...um...." I feel a need for my debugging bag. It contains nothing that could solve this problem, but I want to affix a viewing sheet to something. Or someone.

"Down," Damali says. "Take me down now or—"

"Buraq!" the ship shouts.

"What?" I say.

"Buraq!" the ship says again. "You asked me if I had a name. That was one of the nicknames I was given. The one I like best."

Damali sniffs and dabs at her eyes. "The horse from heaven?"

"Yes," the ship says. "I don't know all the particulars, but I've heard it was a winged steed with a man's face. Is that correct?"

"By some accounts," I say. "Buraq took the Founder on his Night Journey."

"And Ibrahim," Damali says. "Earlier." Her hand finds mine again.

"I remember the stories from my youth," I say. "Buraq bore the Founder from one holy city to another and then to heaven. "

"All in a single night." Damali glances at the canopy. "A pleasant story."

"It's a fitting name for you, ship," I say. "I think we should use it."

"That would please me, ThreadBare."

Damali seems more relaxed now. The simple distraction helped. I'm afraid to breach the subject of the view. But the experience is…unparalleled. It would be a shame to miss it.

The engine's pitch lowers, and my body moves upwards against the restraint—a touch of weightlessness that can mean only one thing: we've reached the edge of space.

I give Damali's hand a squeeze, and she looks my direction. "The view," I say. "Would you—"

She winces. "I don't know if I can."

"That doesn't seem right," I point at the still-darkened canopy. "The whole time I've known you, you've been brave. Unfaltering. Standing up to the prince. Striking someone to save me." I smile. "This is trivial in comparison."

She smiles softly. "Those actions were instinctual." She glances at the canopy. "This requires more thought."

The canopy suddenly lightens. The curvature of the Earth is to our left and the darkness of space to our right. Damali gasps, whimpers, but doesn't look away.

I stream a reprimand to the ship.

"I acted instinctively," Buraq messages in reply. "Was I not correct?"

I notice the light of the planet reflecting in Damali's eyes. I smile and turn toward the view. Clouds are like foothills across a vast blue landscape. The haze of the atmosphere hangs lightly over the sphere. All looks calm and flawless.

"You were right, Thread," Damali whispers. "It's remarkable." She pulls my arm close. "Thank you."

"See there," Buraq messages. "It was the proper time."

Ahead of the ship, at the edge of my vision to the right, is the moon.

Damali gasps again when I show her. Then after a few seconds of taking it in, she smiles. "Now I know why you took me this way," she says. "Very romantic."

"Romance is often thought of as a desired outcome," Buraq messages. "I believe I acted correctly by making the canopy transparent."

"I... I have no amorous intentions," I say. "I'm not made for intentions."

She lifts our still entwined hands. "And yet, you hold my hand. Just like a normal man."

"I'm not normal," I say. "I've never been normal." I can't ignore the warmth of her presence, though. I message the ship to increase the cabin's airflow. It complies without comment.

Damali sits up and moves closer. "You must tell me the truth, Thread-Bare."

"I'm unable to lie."

"I don't believe that, but I'll accept your assurances." She smiles. "Does my presence make you uncomfortable?"

I shift in my seat. "I don't know how to answer."

She touches the side of my head. "I mean, does it hurt you?"

"It doesn't," I say. "And that frightens me."

"Because of what might happen between us?"

I avoid her eyes. "No. Not that." I search for the moon. "Because I don't know what it means for me. And for you. For anything."

"I see." She relaxes into her seat, then looks at the Earth. "Can I make a suggestion?"

"Yes."

She takes my other hand and moves closer. Her eyes track with mine. "You're worried about the future. But that's in the hands of God."

"Yes," I say. "Anything that happens is supposed—"

"No." She tightens her grip briefly. "Not anything that happens. That's our way, but it isn't true. Everything that happens isn't His design."

"How do you know?"

She turns to look away. "I know because He isn't cruel." She glances at me. "Look how much he's protected us both. He has His own plan. We can be part of it if we choose."

I frown. "There's much uncertainty now."

She squeezes my hands again. "Much. But know this, ThreadBare. There's no uncertainty between us. Do you agree?"

I notice the moon in her eyes now. That distant watcher. I smile. "We are Full Impact in an Easy Impact world."

She smiles too. "I like the sound of that." She shifts closer. "So, now that our fears are calmed. And we're in agreement...."

I feel a trickle of discomfort but manage a smile. "Yes?"

"I suggest another test." She places a hand on the back of my neck. "A simple thing. Very quick. Nothing dishonorable."

The ship seems warm again. "And what's that?"

She moves in so that our lips touch briefly. It's wonderful, but shocking. I make a stifled exclamation.

She backs away again. Gives me a concerned look. "Are you hurt?"

I touch my lips. "I...I'm not hurt."

She narrows her eyes. "So, no stop inside?"

"No...." I touch the side of my head. Feel the warmth of the skin there. I kissed a woman. And I was not stopped. Again, there's a mix of emotions, but mostly I feel joy. The moon seems larger now. Closer. I smile and look at her. "Let's try it again to be sure."

She laughs and pulls me close.

"We will land within the hour," Buraq says. "There are only five minutes before the restraints return."

"Buraq."

The smell of vanilla intensifies. "I'll be silent until then."

Day 82 6:47:03 a.m.

[Facility Quarters]

A TRILLING SOUND RETURNS me to consciousness. It's a startling way to wake up, but I smile anyway. The memory of my night ride with Damali is a favorite. One I view often, primarily when my days are tense and the uncertainties great.

I open my eyes to the dark interior of my sleep chute. It's a budget Elipserv model, one commonly found in debugger stables or overnight relocator flats. It's a few revisions better than the one I had when I worked in the garage near the wilderness of Delusion. The perfect model for a school for interns. It performs its task and keeps their expectations low.

I push open the chute's canopy and feel the fullness of the stream surround, wrapping my mind in its many demands and distractions. I nudge those away, climb out, and then remain still, immersing myself in my physical senses: bare feet on a cool tile floor, movement of warm air over my body, that same air being drawn into my lungs and expelled again.

I'm human. My head contains a receptacle of data, but my body is the receptacle of a soul. I'm a living being that has presence, purpose, and worth. A created entity and an agent of change in a world that needs it. These ideas both shock and thrill me.

For many years, I sought significance through actions only to find that I'm significant simply by existing. Not by what I've done, but by who I'm connected to.

Can truth really be so simple?

In the physical realm, my room is sparse. A rectangle barely large enough to hold my cinder chute, a small dresser, and a chair. The room has no windows and no mechanism for washing or eating. There are facilities for those requirements down the hall.

Through the wonders of my implant—one wall of my room appears to have a large window with the view I saw from space: the curve of the Earth with oceans and continents slowly drifting by.

I've infused a still image of Damali onto the dresser's top surface. She's smiling, dressed in a green debugger jumpsuit given to her after we arrived at the school.

Other images adorn my walls. A memory of my students at the seawall. A picture of debugger friends BullHammer and the now lost FrontLot. There's even a faded image of my parents, pulled from the day they sent me away, nearly ten years ago. Mother is shrouded in all black and father is in a brown robe with a white head covering. They stand together near a blue kitchen table. There's a metal sink and a green counter in the background.

A message arrives on my implant's queue. "Are you awake?" the school supervisor, Bamboo, asks. "Are you ready?"

I bundle a head nod with a vocal response. "I'll be there soon."

I look at the bare space on my floor and the rolled mat nearby. Ritual prayers have always been part of my life. As many of the five dailies as life has allowed.

The call for morning prayer will come soon. Should I perform it before I go?

The habit tugs at me. Dedication is good. Necessary.

Something else tugs at me too, though. Something new.

Information previously lost or forgotten—only to be found again recently. New experiences and expectations.

What is correct behavior for me now? Without stops and without ritual, what am I? I'm unsure, but I know there's danger. Unhindered fire is the worst kind.

I construct a prayer in my head. It contains some of the same words and ideas as the rituals, but there's part of me in the mix, as well. My memories, my failings, and successes. My hopes for the day and the future. This I push into the stream with the destination domain of Isa. It leaves me, but travels I know not where. Will it reach its target? I think so.

I change into my grey instructor's jumpsuit, fragrance myself, and open the door. The hallway is unusually lifeless, all the students still asleep. While I was away at the Holy City, Bamboo kept them busy with independent projects. Building and testing devices. Skill building. I have no objections.

Regular classes will resume soon. I've already taken some of them on a fieldtrip that was the culmination of a personal treasure hunt, of sorts, to find a location gleaned from the memories of a dead man. A hot zone where information is unhindered. Finding it was another step in my uncharted journey.

I sense a cricketbot nearby and then see one exit a high wall vent on my left. It scurries a half meter down the wall, pauses, and then makes a low, growling sound.

I connect with the cricket stream-wise and command it to stop.

Its intonation changes to the high-pitched drone of an actual cricket.

I check the hallway in both directions but see no one. Frowning, I attempt to access the code for the cricket's vocal center.

My request is denied. Then the cricket slams the connection shut like a door in my face. It turns, wags its hind section at me, hops its way back to the wall vent, and disappears.

What was that?

I scan the doors that line the hallway. Rooms containing young minds filled with unrealized potential.

Somehow, one of them found a way to make a bot ignore my commands. A remarkable achievement.

I check the hall vent again. A few more seconds with the bot, and I could find the culprit. An intriguing investigation. But would I commend the student or reprimand him? A few weeks ago, I would've known. Today I'm not so sure.

With a smile, I continue my journey.

Five minutes later, I'm four stories up on the floor of Bamboo's study. The study door slides open as I approach. I enter wordlessly, hands clasped together. The door closes behind me.

The study is dimly lit, but I recognize the silhouette of Bamboo at the room's large, circular window. Through it, I see a twilight view of the city with glimpses of the Great River. It's a landscape filled with religiosity and technology. Skyscraper peaks, minarets, and domes—all in shadow—are everywhere. They await the coming dawn.

"You're late, ThreadBare," he says without turning.

I bow my head. "I'm sorry. I was—"

"You're forgiven."

Silence returns. Such lapses are common for Bamboo. They're one of his tools. A preparation period for the listener.

My eyes wander the room nervously. The primary color is white—floor, wall, and ceiling. The latter curves upward toward the center where a large, circular light fixture resides. There's a half-circle of a couch, and behind it, a similarly shaped shelf of awards and artwork. To my right, is a curved shelf filled with books. In the middle of that is a fireplace.

The room speaks of intellect and efficiency. A striving for transcendence amid a world of imperfection.

Something is different than the last time I was here, though. Portions out-of-place or missing. I retrieve an image from the implant of my last visit and begin a comparison.

Bamboo turns and looks at me. His face seems strained, colorless, and more etched with lines. Is he sick?

He sighs and rubs his eyes. Color returns.

Aha! The shelves have omissions. Books that are missing. But which ones?

Bamboo smiles and motions toward the couch. "Would you like to sit down?"

I never sit in his presence. Is he trying to confuse me?

"I just got up," I say. "It would feel better to stand."

He frowns but moves closer. "Of course." He indicates a vessel and cups on the shelf nearest him. "A refreshment, perhaps?"

"Master?"

He lifts the vessel. "Something to drink, Thread," he says. "I apologize. I only have water."

I approach the shelf. "Water would be good. Thank you."

He pours a cup and hands it to me. "I appreciate your help with the students," he says, "Especially so soon after your last obligation." He pours a second cup and lifts it to his lips.

"I'm happy to serve." When I escaped the Imam, when I returned to the school, I expected to be chastised. Or to be reassigned another master, forcing me to abandon Damali. But instead, the opposite happened. My requests are granted, and I'm treated like a near-equal.

"Feelings are irrelevant," Bamboo says. "And service is our purpose." He smiles. "But tasks are easier when you find fulfillment in them." He nods and sips again. "You persevere longer."

His eyes narrow. "I'd ask about your time with the Imam, but that might prove painful for us both."

"No, that's—" I stop and shake my head. I almost told him about my new state. My lack of pain, no matter what I do or think. I quickly sip from my cup.

"What?"

I want to tell him about everything, including the servbots I encountered. Ones capable of making changes to the combat bot I fought. They were fixing it. Debugging it. Would I be able to do so if I were properly stopped, though? Probably not.

"It's not safe," I say. "You're right."

He moves past me and rests a hand on the back of the couch. "I've streamed enough to guess the relevant parts. One of the Imam's quiet enforcers was pitted against you. That portion of your earlier fear was correct."

"Master?"

He straightens and points his cup at me. "The world has changed, ThreadBare. You're an instructor here. Call me by my easy name."

I bow again. "Yes, Master Bamboo. I will—"

He laughs. "Ever the righteous servant." He points at my head. "Even hindered, you maintain your usefulness. Your purpose. I'm sorry I ever thought less of you."

He doesn't know that my brain injury seems gone now too. The wolf, caused by my struggle against the stops, has left.

He turns toward the window. "What can be done now?" he asks. "About our changed world?"

"Has the new Imam hinted at change?"

"He's said nothing to me."

"So, perhaps all remains as it was," I say. "Perhaps he and the ruling ulama—"

"Key members of the ulama have already been eliminated."

"What?" I reflexively dip into the stream, searching for headlines that might indicate assassinations. All I find, though, are references to the prior Imam's death. Nothing more recent.

"You won't find anything on the public stream," he says. "You realize it's controlled, of course. Neutered."

"Yes," I say. "But something like that—"

"The ulama members are barely known outside of their own. Few of them are loved. Even their families won't miss them." A frown. "The rise and fall of tyrants. A sign of the end."

"The coming of the Mahdi?" The Founder's writings contained prophecies of future disasters and a savior. Some scholars believe the savior to be Isa. That he will restore justice and correct what has been mistakenly taught about him.

I know Isa as the word, both creator and created. Is that truth or error? It isn't what we're taught.

Bamboo gazes upward. "It's why I search the heavens. 'A has set out for you the stars, that you may guide yourselves by them through the darkness. We have detailed the signs for people to know.'" He waves his cup toward the cityscape. "This—all of this—obscures my view."

Bamboo's sky watching is a new revelation, but it shouldn't be. He's mentioned the heavens and the objects that inhabit them often in the past.

"There are places you can go," I say, "on the stream. Feeds that allow access to—"

He scowls. "Observation equipment? Telescopes of all kinds? I've visited many. They are filtered too. Access granted only at the whim of those that own them."

"You have connections," I say. "Influence."

He sniffs dismissively. "Because of my position here?" He turns from the window. "No. I'm little more special than you."

Bamboo has always seemed the apex of significance to me. He's not a member of the ruling class, though. Not a prince or a businessman.

"Our life is one of contrasts, ThreadBare. We're made to solve problems, yet our faith teaches problems as destiny. If the bot is meant to break, it breaks. If the nanopath is meant to block, it blocks. If the TRIXe motivator fails, the engine dies, and so on. Why do anything? Why improve anything at all?"

I hover my cup near my lips, but don't drink.

"What are your thoughts?" he says. "Don't be afraid. We're brothers now."

"The answers are unknowable," I say. "They're beyond our comprehension."

Bamboo sips from his cup, places it atop his art shelf, and smiles. "But what if we can know?" he says. "What if there's a way out of the darkness?"

I think of Isa. "Perhaps there is, Master."

Bamboo's eyes widen. "Yes, Thread. There must be!" He draws closer. "I need time, friend. Time to search." He studies me. "Are you able to continue the student's instruction on your own?" He poses his hand near the side of my head. "It doesn't tax you too much, does it?"

"I'm able to teach, sure," I say. "If it gives you more time."

He smiles. "I would appreciate that very much. In return, I will accept the presence of your concubine."

"She's not my—"

He raises a hand. "Of course not. That relationship isn't possible for you."

I bow my head, unsure what to say. The mention of Damali stirs me. It's an uncertain situation, for sure, but I had nowhere else to send her. Here I could keep her safe. The school has many rooms.

Bamboo's eyes narrow. "If I didn't trust your stops, I wouldn't allow it." He frowns. "Still, it puts an atypical demand on the students. A radical test of *their* stops."

"I've detected no difficulties," I say.

Bamboo smiles and then bobs his head. "This isn't the first time a female has been here, of course. That one...was much younger when she arrived, though. More like a boy." He frowns. "But your friend…is fully grown."

"Yes," I say. "I was uncertain what to do."

"Everything is uncertain," he says. "But this must remain a temporary solution. I have no qualms about turning her out. She's nothing to me."

I bow my head. "I understand." I glance at the shelves again. A book about implant history is missing. Along with one about the stars.

Bamboo smiles subtly. "Very good," he says. "We are in agreement. As brothers should be."

"I will teach. You will research. And Damali—"

"Can stay."

Day 82 7:34:23 a.m.

[Bamboo's Domain]

ON MY WAY BACK to my room, I contemplate the meaning of my meeting with my former instructor. Before, Bamboo always seemed the humble servant, resigned to whatever fate came his way. Is that no longer the case? What does he know? What does he fear?

My mind wanders to my former investigation. The off-line debugger list. Has that avenue been exhausted? Have all the mysteries been solved?

I've viewed portions of the lives of many lost. I've discovered unknown truths about Isa, found a hot zone, but have I solved the mystery of all the losses?

The first three debuggers were part of a specific design effort. An experimental spaceship. They were DRs 178, 291, and 157. All presumed dead.

Next came JustBecause, BitStack, and Frontlot.

FrontLot was killed by antitex. The other two? I'm not sure. Might've been antitex, but it's just as likely they were killed for other reasons. BitStack for his heresy. JustBecause by a crazed master.

I too was almost on the list. If not for security having found me and BandStand, we would be off-line, our heads separated from our bodies.

As I exit the lift to my floor, I turn right and walk to a small lounge I sometimes use. It has three beige-colored seats and a circular window that looks out over the back of the building. It's still early in the morning, but the smaller brick buildings that surround the school are visible. I can just make out the shapes of trees at a nearby park. The hover traffic on the bordering streets is light, as befits the time of day. I take a seat and watch the world outside—much like I found Bamboo doing only a few minutes ago.

I should visit Damali, but she's no morning person. It's better to wait here on her floor. Better to think some more. Come up with a plan.

The hot zone revealed a lot during my first visit. It confirmed the words of the astronauts: the experimental ship was named DarkTrench. It took them to the stars and brought them back somehow changed.

DarkTrench. Where did it go? That's what Prince Aadam had wanted to know: Where his ship had gone. I've asked Damali and she doesn't know. Her brother never told her.

Sandfly. Sandfly had no stops. Like me. Like me!

I need to talk to the astronauts again. Now that I have no stops and less risk of telling something I shouldn't. But they are in deep hiding somewhere. Would Damali know where to find them, at least? Probably not. Probably not now.

Sandfly and HardCandy. They are still lost. What happened to them?

Their memories hang over me somehow. They eclipse me, keeping me ever in shadow. Ever blind to the truth.

How I would like to meet another free debugger. How I'd like everyone to be free! Is that possible?

That idea is too large for me. It would mean a radical change.

I sense a bot on the wall outside, a spider-shaped model. It's there to clean the windows, a near daily task due to the birds that frequent the upper stories. Though the bot is not yet visible, it will soon be. Should I send it away? Keep this moment to myself?

I frown, but let it continue its ministrations. Soon I hear the soft cadence of its feet clicking along. Then the spider's back legs come into view: two slender, five-centimeter-long, black appendages equipped with microscopic protuberances able to grip any surface, including this seemingly frictionless pane of glass.

Next, the bot's circular body appears along with its middle appendages. Its legs are fitted with spinning, circular cleaning pads that engage as soon as they touch the glass. A path of cleanliness is created wherever they touch.

I expect the bot's forelegs and head to follow. Instead, a large, beige oval awkwardly waggles into view.

I gasp and stand. Then my mouth falls open.

The oval is the head of a humanoid service bot, grafted to the spider-bot's neck and torso. A creature of nightmares.

I move closer to the glass. The bot continues its cleaning duties, oblivious to how awkward it appears. Every component is functional—including its eyes. They widen as the head draws closer to the center of the window, no doubt reacting to my presence. To my watching it.

I'm sickened and uncomfortable, but also amazed.

Those boys. Those mischievous young malcontents.

Has Bamboo seen this? If he had, he certainly would've—

A scream travels down the hall. A female shriek. There's no question who it belongs to. I run toward Damali's room.

I arrive at her door and pause. I want to stream it open and go in, but my stops wouldn't have allowed that before. And even without stops, it seems improper.

I hear a whimpering sound and, so, knock. "Damali?"

Seconds go by with more murmured sounds of distress. I recall my time in Prince Aadam's house. Torture rooms filled with cages and emaciated prisoners.

I knock harder and try the door's handle. Finding it locked, I open it with a thought and step inside.

Damali's room is much like mine, with only a bed, desk, and a dresser. There are a few items on her dresser top. Ornamental objects that make the space less sterile. I have no idea where they came from. She arrived with only the clothes on her back.

Her room also has bathing facilities, which are around the corner to my left. I remain close to the door. "It's Thread," I say. "I heard—"

Damali makes a frustrated sound and steps into view. Her hair is wet, and her body is wrapped in a towel. Her right hand holds a small blue snakebot, hanging limp and inactive. "What is this?" she asks, raising the bot.

"A maintenance bot," I say. "Commonly used in ventilation and plumb—"

"I know that." She gives the bot a shake. "But why is it in my room?"

I notice a vent on the ceiling. "There's access here," I say, pointing. "Overhead."

"It didn't come from there," she says. "This one flew. It was hovering around the room."

I can barely hide my disbelief. "Snakes don't fly."

"Well, this one does."

I take the bot from her and look it over. Like the cricketbot and spiderbot I encountered, it has been altered. In this case, it was given a set of slender, plastisteel, wings. They're broken now, though. Cracked in half.

"Was it spying on me?" Damali asks.

I can find no presence of the bot on the stream. "I think you broke it," I say.

"Or course, I broke it." She tightens her towel around herself. "It swooped my head. I thought it might get my hair."

I resist the urge to touch her head. "That would be unfortunate," I say. "I don't have that worry."

She crosses her arms, scowls at the snake, then looks at me. "Was it watching me?" she asks. "Can you tell?"

"You broke it," I say. "I'd have to take it apart to learn anything."

"You can do that," she says, nodding. "Right now. Go ahead." She waves a hand. "Take it apart for me."

I weigh the snake in my hands. It feels light. Normal. "They aren't usually used for observation," I say. "It would take a lot of—"

"It's possible, though, right?"

"Possible, sure, yes, anything is—"

She stamps her foot. "I'm in a house full of boys, ThreadBare. Very smart boys."

"Yes, but—"

"Most of them teenagers."

"Yes, but...." I notice again that she's wearing a towel. I anticipate a stop, but all that arrives is more discomfort. I look at the snakebot again. Poor, crushed, little snakebot.

"But, what?

I notice a small piece of art on her dresser. A golden teardrop with a black script that says, "A^3" in its center.

"Thread?"

"They would be stopped if they did something like you suggest," I say. "If they spied on you..." I smile softly. "...It would hurt a lot."

"Are you sure?"

I raise a shoulder. "As much as I can be."

She takes a step closer. "Well, can you find out, please?"

"Of course." I shift the snake in my hands, amazed by how much it feels like a real snake—cool, smooth, and potentially dangerous.

She walks to the bathing room door. "I will finish getting ready now," she says, "Though I'm not sure what for."

"You have no plans for the day?"

She gives me a look of annoyance. "Do I ever?"

I've missed something, I realize. It's a near constant state in my relationship with Damali. "You've been recovering. You were—"

"I'm recovered. Long since recovered."

"Well...what would you like to do?" I ask.

She looks back at me and then stares into the room she's about to enter. "I actually don't know," she says. "I'm happy to be free. Happy to be with you. But my days are almost meaningless."

"We've only been here—"

"It hasn't been a week yet." She sighs. "I know. But there's work to be done somewhere. I feel it."

I point at the golden teardrop. "Did you make that?"

"Yes. With the former you showed me."

"What does it mean? Its shape is like an implant. But *A cubed*?"

"You know," she says, smiling. "Change is coming."

"Change seems certain," I say. "With a new Imam."

She pulls a hand down the length of her wet hair. "Not that. Something else."

"You want to return to your family?" I say. "The other fugitives?"

She frowns. "I only want to know that I'm doing what's right."

"I understand," I say. "I'm in an unknown place too. Little is certain."

She nods slowly and then takes a deep breath. "Okay, I'm getting ready."

I lift the broken snake. "I'll find out about this."

"Please do."

21

Day 82 9:01:14 a.m.

[DR Encoding Room]

EXTERNALLY, THE CLASSROOM HASN'T changed. It's rectangular with a blue carpeted floor and light-yellow walls. The desks are teal and white, made to hold two students each, and arranged in rows. There are narrow windows at the back of the room for light and little else. There's no scenery, no outside distractions.

The walls are blank. The room's corners, empty. There's no need for visual aids here. No drawing boards or models. Nothing for attention or distracted eyes to drift to. The instructor is the center of attention. The focal point. How strange that I am him. Not much more than a child myself.

Bald boys trickle in through the classroom's backdoor. All smile when they see me. All quickly slide into their seats and get comfortable.

There is no sense of fear here. No one standing rigidly or waiting for my approval. It is different than when I was young. Different from the classroom Bamboo ran, or the instructors before him.

Messages strike my implant. Greetings and questions from the half dozen or so students I've become most acquainted with—TalonsUp, JumboJet, LostNote, BandStand, and MintBridge—those who have participated in field trips. Those who have tested their skills outside.

Others will need to go out soon. Others are now old enough and ready. They need real world experience before they are sold into service. Someday they will all leave. That idea stirs me. I feel in many ways we're a family now. I don't want them to go out. I don't want that change, or their loss to the world at large.

Talons, always a leader, creates a virtual room for the classroom and shares it to everyone present. He seems taller now. Taller, but with the same blue eyes. I dismiss his offer and tell him to end his creation. He complies, looking serious. Focused.

I glance at BandStand, brown eyes that mask his feelings. Of all the students, I was most concerned about him when I left. We were both prisoners of the terrorist group "antitex." But while I was taken to the Holy City—forcibly distracted—he had to return here and sit under Bamboo's tutelage.

My time with antitex still haunts me. The brutality of it. The hatred and abuse. The miracle of my victory match brought some healing, an interjection of hope into the darker places of my mind.

But Band? Where was his mind now? He was a runaway before...and now? Had he healed? Was he strong?

Band gives me an uneasy smile and a wave. In fact, the whole class seems uneasy now. Again, we're in uncharted pathways. A communal trip into a desert worse than Delusion.

I smile and send them the taste and smell of my favorite breakfast, Gaymer Wa Dibis, to all of them. Warm biscuits, heavy cream, and honey. This brings smiles to their faces. Many even shut their eyes.

"Greetings," I say. "It's good to see you all again."

A chorus of greetings return to me. Others test their abilities by sending me their favorite flavors and tastes. Jumbo, the joker of the bunch, sends me the scent of sulfur. I send him a scowl in return. He chuckles aloud.

"Master Bamboo tells me that you've often surprised him," I say. "And that you're progressing well."

I message two students—Trackless and PendingState—about specific work they haven't finished. Both respond with the stream equivalent of "Yes, Mawla," the title being their term of endearment for me. A word that can mean many things including "guardian," "helper," and "lord."

I smile. "I'm proud of your growth." I glance at the windows and touch my chest. "This is how it should be. You will be called on someday. You will do great things. However, I wonder if—"

BandStand raises a hand.

I call his name.

He smiles and gets to his feet. "We made something for you, Mawla." He gestures toward the others in the room. "All of us."

I can't help but think of the spider with the servbot head. "You didn't need to make me anything."

"We wanted to," Band says. "We missed you."

"A lot," Talons messages me. "We missed you a lot. Bamboo is—" I feel a shiver of the warning shock Talons receives from his implant. Talking bad about superiors will earn one every time.

I bow my head. "I appreciate the thought. What is it?"

"We need to stream it to you," Band says. "It's FI."

"Full Impact?" I frown. "What am I exposing myself to here?"

Band puts out a hand. "No, it's all good, Mawla. I promise."

I scan the faces in the room. All look earnest. Sincere. I'm still leery, though. "I'll accept it."

Band smiles and returns to his seat. "You have to shut your eyes first." He looks at those around him. "That would be good, right? To help it settle in?"

"Settle in?"

"Please," Band says. "It's a surprise."

"All right." I nod and close my eyes. "I'm ready."

A hundred milliseconds later, a message arrives in my queue. It is large and bulbous. I test the outside warily, then realize it's a virtual background packet. "What's this for?" I ask.

"Try it!" Band says.

Opening the message, I find an immersion background for the very room we're in. Again, I'm suspicious, but I embrace it anyway.

"You have it?" Band asks.

"I think so."

"Great. Rails, great. Now look around."

I open my eyes and almost fall. The room is a forest. The students are still here, still in their seats, but around and behind them are the trunks of massive trees. The floor is earthen and there's cool dampness in the air along with the smell of pine and florals. Many of the trees are covered in moss. I hear the twitter of birds and the chatter of some furred animal, possibly a squirrel or a chipmunk. I detect the babble of a waterway somewhere, as well. And beyond that, the roar of a distant waterfall.

It reminds me of the forest I used to visit on Prince Aadam's estate. Leaves waving in gentle breezes. The feeling of peace amidst chaos.

"Does it work?" Band asks.

"Work?" I shake my head, still immersed in the detail.

A rabbit enters the back of the room and pauses in a band of light. It moves its nose timidly and then slowly hops toward the nearest desk.

"Mawla?" Band says.

"Are you okay?" LostNote asks.

"Yes," I say, testing the ground with a foot. "You all worked on this?"

"Some more than others," Band says. "But yeah. All of us."

"It's incredible," I say. "Really well done."

There are smiles everywhere. "Thank you," Talons says.

"Can we stay here?" Mint asks. "For our session?"

A bushy-tailed squirrel darts across the central aisle with a nut in its mouth. It finds a clearing in front of the desk shared by LostNote and JumboJet and begins to dig.

"It might be too distracting," I say.

"Stream says that time in a forest is beneficial to mental health," Band offers.

I smile. "Everything on the stream isn't true," I say. "It requires discernment."

"But that has to be true, doesn't it?" Talons makes a sweeping gesture. "I feel relaxed already."

The squirrel fills its hole, and looking in all directions, finishes with a cadence of pats on the ground before running off to my right.

"Fine," I say. "We'll try it." I check on the rabbit, now eating a flower. "I especially like the wildlife. It's a special touch."

"My idea," Band says. "It makes me think of a park."

I smile softly. "While we're on the subject of wildlife..."

On the floor next to me is my blue debugging bag—a backpack used to carry the most common implements of our calling—viewing sheets, probes, and forming and manipulation tools. This one has been with me for years and bears the scuffs and wear-lines to prove it.

I unzip the bag, reach inside, and bring out the snake from Damali's room. "Who can explain this creation to me?" I lift the snake where all can see.

I hear only the noises of our shared forest experience. Every boy is silent.

"Come now," I say. "Someone must know something."

One of the newer students raises a hand. "It's a maintenance bot."

"Yes," I say. "But this one has a few additional features." I turn it so that the top surface faces me. "Some of which took me a while to discover.

"For instance, it has an enhanced power system, seemingly lifted from a much larger model." I point at the underside. "There's a slight bulge in the surface here from that enhancement."

I turn the head their way. "Also, the avoidance systems have been augmented. That's a useful change, but—" I tap the top of the bot's head. "The visual and auditory sensors have been enhanced, as well."

I show the underside again. "The additional weight no doubt required enhanced power. That introduced a flaw, though, because the inconsistent diameter makes it impossible for the snake to move in the normal way."

I look at the class. "So, how do you think this bot's designer got around that limitation?"

The forest is quiet.

"No theories?" I scan the room and then shake my head. "Anyone?"

"Extra motivators?" one student says.

"Not a bad suggestion," I say. "But no. Anyone else?"

The squirrel darts back into view, sniffs heavily at an area of ground and then scurries off again.

I turn the snake's back toward the class. "Wings!" I say. "Not the best solution to the design shortcoming, but it's certainly unique."

I raise a finger. "The most disturbing aspect of this bot, though, was where it was found. Any idea where that was?"

Again, no one speaks, but a few of them squirm in their chairs. I wish for a way to read all their emotions simultaneously. A sort of global master controller.

"In a female's room," I say, feeling a twinge of anger. "A place it absolutely should not have been."

I coil the snake as best as I can, return it to my bag, and after finding a large rock, take a seat on it. "This isn't the only altered bot I've seen lately," I say. "I suspect that another instructor would have disciplined you severely." I frown. "I may not be what is right for you. Perhaps another instructor should be—"

Jumbo hops from his seat. "The snake was mine! I didn't know that it went in Damali's room." He has a pained expression on his face. "I wasn't watching its visuals." He shakes his head. "I mean, I was for a while, but—"

Talons stands up. "I helped too." He looks at Jumbo, who is to his right. "We like our time at the shop. Fixing things. Designing new things."

"That will be part of your life forever," I say. "If you keep your implant."

Talons smiles nervously. "Right. So, we started working with what we—"

"Me too," Mint says, raising a hand. "Me and Lost too."

LostNote eases down in his chair, face filling with color.

Mint points at BandStand. "And Band. He—"

"Hey!" BandStand says. "I wasn't involved. I didn't do—aw ouch!"

I scan the other faces in the room. "Is that it, then? Is that everyone who altered the building's machines?"

The rest sit quietly and seemingly content. Innocent as lambs.

I look at one of the nearby trees, then follow its trunk all the way to the branches and leaves above. The coverage is so dense that only small patches of light trickle. Small openings of solar nourishment, even of a virtual kind.

I wait ten seconds longer to be certain there are no additional confessions. No further signs of nervousness.

I take a long breath, filling my lungs with the smell of new air.

The guilty are the same five who visited the hot zone with me. They were cautioned not to share that secret or anything they'd viewed while they were there. Such knowledge is dangerous.

New information has a way of stirring the imagination. I might have been wrong to take them at all. I wasn't sure what I'd find at the seawall. More witnesses seemed like a good idea at the time. I created more potential victims, though. More confidants.

Regardless, there's no correcting that now. So, how do I turn this in a positive direction?

"Don't leave us, Mawla," Mint says. "You've taught us a lot."

I chuckle. "I can see that. I'm not sure you're learning the right things, though."

"Punish us if you have to," Talons says. "Withhold our meals or make us clean. But don't stop training us." He looks at the others. "We need more."

"I won't ask you why you did what you did," I say, standing. "I was your age once." I glance at the rabbit again. "I've made my share of mistakes." I look at Jumbo. "Whose idea was the spider? The one with the head?"

"Band," Jumbo says. "That was Band."

Band shrugs, but resists saying anything—a kernel of discretion there.

I scan the forest again, enjoying the peacefulness despite my anxiety. "There needs to be a consequence," I say. "There has to be."

"Whatever you want," Talons said. "We'll do it."

I frown. What to do with boys filled with an implant, imagination, and new knowledge? I think of Bamboo and his other interests. His harried look. I also think of my times in the city. The many things in need of upgrade or replacement.

"Your punishment is to put what you've learned to better use."

"What?" Talons says.

"You will form teams," I say. "Three teams. One led by Jumbo, one by Talons, and one by Band."

"Again," Band says. "I didn't really—"

I send him a prickly static bubble, and he immediately grows quiet. "Mint will be on Band's team," I say. "To help keep it honest." I smile and look at the innocent students. "The rest of you will be members of those three teams." I glance at Talons again. "I'll leave it to the leaders to recruit members. Everyone participates. Everyone joins a team."

"What will these teams do?" Band asks.

"Create something," I say.

"What sort of something?" Talons says.

Jumbo shrugs. "You didn't approve of our last inventions."

"They lacked focus and precision." I point to the bag containing the snake. "They served no greater good." I stare at Talons, Jumbo, and Band in turn. "You team leaders have been outside multiple times." I smile. "Think of something that needs improvement. Or something that's beneficial. And make it." I bring my hands together. "Doesn't have to be a big thing, but it has to be innovative and useful. And it has to work."

Jumbo glances at those around him. "I have no idea."

"Discuss it with your teammates," I say. "Or other members of the house. Or even the community around us."

"What about supplies?" Talons asks. "Anything we make will need supplies. Plastisteel, forming material, nanos. Lots of stuff."

"Can we go out again?" Band asks.

"When necessary." I remember BandStand and me being chased by a robot dog. "We'll discuss it. But for parts...I'm sure I can arrange delivery from a local clang and click like Zimits. And we have shape formers here." I reach for my bag and sling it over my shoulder. "I'll be available to consult, of course. I need to know what you're working on before you start. I want plans."

The forest suddenly feels denser. As if the trees now represented the tasks the students had ahead of them. Hard to see without a lot of effort. But with the right tools and design, much could be accomplished.

I infuse the air with the smell of vanilla. Eyes widen as the students take note.

"I'm going to return to my quarters," I say. "I want to give you time to form teams and start thinking. We will meet in an hour to discuss the history of the ulama and their partner corporations." I smile. "Have fun."

Day 82 10:13:25 a.m.

[Facility Quarters]

I RETURN TO MY quarters and ease my debugging bag to the floor. I wouldn't have needed to leave the students, but somehow it felt right. As if they needed time to think without a supervisor around.

I take a seat beside my bag, and for peace of mind, connect to the classroom camera. I find the boys huddled into three groups, with the younger members generally encircling the elder members. There doesn't appear to be a lot of discussion going on, but that doesn't mean it isn't occurring. This class lives in their heads more than even my generation did, or the generation before us. I'm not sure if that's good or bad.

I close the connection to the camera. I'll give them fifteen minutes to contemplate their assignment, and then I'll check on them again. That amount of time is the upper limit of focus for this group. It would be shorter, I'm sure, were it not for the implant's corrective measures. The headbuzz. The stop that keeps every debugger on the straight and narrow.

Except me. I no longer feel its sting.

I gasp at a new realization. What if the reason I no longer feel *stops* isn't because I'm healed, but because I've grown sicker?

Weeks ago, Bamboo tested me and found me "broken." Afterwards, along with the standard stops, I developed a blinding headache I thought of as my "wolf."

But now all sources of pain are gone. What if my brokenness has eaten stops and wolf alike? What if my peace means only a shorter time to function? What if I'm my own time bomb?

I'd need Bamboo to look inside. To duplicate whatever test he performed last time.

He wanted to remove my implant, though. I put him off, but he was certain that was for the best. Only the Imam's summons had prevented that outcome.

Would I be okay without an implant?

The removal procedure is rarely done. And when it is, it takes part of the brain with it. The connections are tight. Something always gets ripped away.

So, what should I do?

Even stops couldn't answer that. They work to deter behavior before it happens. They never work the other way around, motivating right behavior. They correct but never guide.

What I need most is guidance.

Would Damali understand?

Would *anyone* understand?

I look at the rolled prayer mat. It lives in the same place as the stops in my mind. A place of distance and uncertainty. Do I need them or not? And what am I without them?

How should I live?

I glance at Damali's virtual image on the dresser and smile. I then check the camera and the time. Forty-five minutes to go, and the initiates are actively talking amongst themselves. A small success, I think.

I shut my eyes and stretch into the stream. It feels comforting, the torrent of bits and the many possibilities they represent. Should I get a datamix? Regardless of the voyeurism inherent in it, glimpses of other debuggers' lives have served me well. I've learned from them. Found real solutions. But what should I pursue now? Could another mix tell me that?

What about BullHammer? He's half a world away, so there's no guarantee that he's active. It would be late in the Holy City.

Still, I can't help but wonder. I construct an Easy Impact message and send it his way. If he's asleep, the message will bounce back at me without him knowing.

A dozen seconds go by. Then two dozen.

"What do you want?" he asks. I hear only his voice. There's no visual and no real sense of the place he's in. He's a spirit speaking from the darkness.

"Were you sleeping?"

"Could you wake me if I was?"

"No...." I feel as though I should squint. Like that would somehow help me perceive his face over a stream connection. But messaging doesn't work that way. "So, why are the lights off?"

"I don't feel like looking at anyone."

I send him empathy, but that bounces back at me. Then I try the taste of chocolate, which he quickly accepts.

"I only want to know how you are," I say.

"I'm great," Bull says. "I'm highlevel in the best position in the world. The richest, most important city. The richest, most important master."

"So, you're eating all right?"

"Like a prince," he says. "Food is everywhere here." He laughs. "Sometimes I eat it right off the floor."

"Bull?"

He snorts, and a visual interface is added. Still, aside from a dim and distant light source, I see mostly shadows. Primarily, a silhouette of a bald someone sitting by himself in a room.

My friend, BullHammer.

"Is it the others?" I ask. "SilentJoy and his friends?" Some of the debuggers in the Imam's stable are cruel—stops or no.

"Nah, I hardly see those guys anymore. Subs got everyone so busy...." His voice trails off, doubtless due to master privilege. Information that Bull can't reveal outside his current stable.

"Is it good work, though?" It's difficult to know what emotion to show. Something's not right here. I wish Bull hadn't stayed. But he had little choice. His implant would've crippled him otherwise.

"It's fine," he says. "Work." His silhouette shifts so that I can glimpse more of his face. His nearest cheek seems fuller, which suggests more nourishment. I take that as a good sign.

"Prince Raqeeb had his own stable. So, Silent and his lackeys aren't as special as they once were. There are larger fish now." He chuckles again. "Poetic."

He grunts and shifts again. "It's getting late, Thread. I should chute myself in. I'm drifting here."

"Sure," I say. "Sorry."

"Yeah, it's late," he mumbles. "For all of us."

"Bull?"

He turns away now, making it difficult to communicate, despite the implant's advantages. He's dressed in debugger blues and has something in his right hand. All I can see of him is his neck and a quarter of the right side of his face. If I were there, I'd grab him and look him in the eyes.

"So, what do you need?" he asks. "Are *you* all right?"

"I'm...trying to get back into it," I say. "Figuring out—" I pause and shake my head. "I'm instructing again. And the initiates can be—"

He snorts. "Squirmy, I'll bet. You make a great teacher, Thread. You...whatever you got there, it's solid. Stay as long as you can." He lifts his hand enough, so that I'm able to glimpse the object he's holding. A small, green ball.

"I don't really know what I have," I say. "I mean, I should be confident, right? I should have focus, but I don't. For anything."

"Manet and Morisot," he says, sighing.

"Artists?"

"Yeah, had to dig for those. Harder to find stuff these days. Feels like the whole stream is closing in. Closing down." And right then, a ripple of Bull's true feelings come through. They are stark and sharp. Colder than anything I've ever experienced.

"It'll be all right," I find myself saying. "Somehow." I feel guilty. Sad that I'd even mentioned my own confusion.

He makes a scoffing sound. "When has it *ever* been all right?" Bull turns so that I glimpse redness in his right eye, but also blueness, I think, on the cheek below it. Not swollen with nourishment, simply swollen.

More abuse? I despise the new Imam now without ever having met him.

"You're not all right," I say. "We need to find a way to—"

He scowls. "Knew I shouldn't have answered your message. You and your freedom." He shifts so that the distant light source is eclipsed. Why is everything so dark?

"There are ways," I say. "There have to be."

"Don't talk about impossible things." He looks at me directly. "How do you do it, though? How do you downride from one place of comfort to the next?" He raises a hand. "How are you even there? You belong to the Imam too. Just like me. You should—"

"Bamboo got me back."

"Sure, but he answers to the Imam. Your absence must show on a ledger somewhere. There has to be a loss."

I shrug. "That's not for me to work out."

He grunts, stands, and walks toward the light. A second later, my view shifts so that I'm at the light source with him—a narrow, partially-covered window. He orients my perspective so I can see outside.

It's nighttime, but I can make out an empty city street and the roofs of other buildings. They are short structures—only a few stories. There are brightened signs on some of them. They advertise temporary marriages and barely legal substances.

The perspective shifts so that I can see farther down the street. It ends with a high wall. There is a familiarity to it all.

"Are you near Delusion?" I ask. "The wilderness?"

Bull looks at me. "World is a big place, Thread. Lots of walls and wars. Lots of wilderness."

"Are you working on heavies, then?" I'm not sure if he can tell me, but I can't resist asking. My first assignment involved repairing bots meant to kill. It was brutal work that took me into the wilderness. I saw terrible things.

"And more," he says, turning toward the window. "Imam has lots of more. Exploding, flashing, crushing more." He glances at me again. "If I ever go on the missing list, you'll know why."

"Is that...?" I point to my face. "Your bruises?"

"Goes with the job," he says. "You know that. We get hurt."

I feel a strong urge to tell him my story. To tell him how I was freed from the stops. But then, another urge grips me. What if it won't work for him? What if it's only for me? Wouldn't that be worse? A sort of torture? Flaunting my freedom?

And what if it's all because I'm broken?

"Bull…"

He shows the ball again. "It's all right," he says. "It's late. We're both in strange places. Both unsettled."

There's a knock on my door. I startle, open my eyes, and call out, "Yes?"

"Are you there? It's Damali."

"Give me a moment," I say.

"Of course, master."

"I'm not your master."

"Of course you are. You won me."

I sigh and look at the door. "I'm talking with BullHammer."

"BullHammer?"

"My friend," I say. "The one who helped me with the fighting bots."

"The funny one? He's here?"

I sigh. "Not here, no. He's—"

"Ah, you're talking in your head. Can't you do that any time?"

"I can." I notice the shadow of Damali's presence in the crack beneath the door. "Sometimes it helps to be alone. To focus."

"I'll wait out here, then."

I briefly contemplate opening the door, but instead turn my focus Bull's direction, immersing myself in his world again.

He studies me, a confused look on his face. "Was that her?" he asks. "The woman from the fight?"

"Damali," I say. "Yes."

He frowns. "How do you have a girlfriend?"

Even with my eyes shut, I sense the door and Damali behind it. "It's not like that," I say.

"Has she touched you?" he says. "Have you kissed her?"

I mask my feelings, but my face still feels warm. "I don't see how—"

He crosses his arms. "This is the most important question ever, debugger." He nods toward the door behind me. "How? I know how it's supposed to work for freeheads. But we aren't those since we're talking FI right now. So, how, Thread?"

"I...I should go," I say. "She's waiting. I don't want to be rude."

Bull walks closer. "Does Bamboo know? Does he suspect?"

"I can't discuss this," I say. "You said you were tired."

He smiles. "Feeling rails awake now." He brings both hands to his head. "This is flipped. Your head should be aching all the time. Not to mention the other stuff it does to us. Stunting us. How do—?"

"Stunting?"

"I've heard rumors," he says. "Seen tests. The implant messes with our physiology. It makes us care about some things less and other things more. We're male, sure, but not as male as we'd be if we were one of them."

"I've never heard that."

He shrugs. "No reason to care most of the time." He points behind me again. "But for you to care about her—*any* her—you've gotten around that somehow. Beat all the stops."

"I didn't beat anything," I say. "Not really. Not me."

He studies me for a long second. "Nah, there's something. Something you're not telling."

"We all know things we can't tell," I say. "That's part of our—"

"So, it's a master thing?" he asks. "That's why you're hiding?"

I glance at the window behind him. There's a sign there that reads "al-qadar." It speaks to the principle of premeasurement. A's direction of everything that happens, good or bad.

"Is it that, Thread?" Bull asks. "Master privilege?"

"Maybe," I say. "I mean, I don't really know."

"Thread?" Damali's voice again. It's been nearly two minutes. Too long.

Bull smiles. "I get it. You have things to do. Other obligations...somehow." He gives the ball a couple quick squeezes. "Message again when you can talk freely."

I shake my head and bow it in closing. "I wish our lives were different," I say. "Simpler."

He gives me a half-hearted smile. "If it was simple, who would need us?"

I bow again. "Right. Take care, Bull."

Day 82 10:38:11 a.m.

[Facility Quarters]

THE CONNECTION WITH BULLHAMMER ends, leaving me unsettled. I want to sit for a minute and analyze it all. To try and figure out how to proceed. Working for royalty is especially dangerous. I know from experience. Wherever Bull is, whatever his current task, he isn't safe. He isn't right. Heavy work almost got me killed multiple times and my master wasn't the warrior prince that his is.

I stand, walk to the door, and open it.

Damali is dressed in a blue dress with a light purple scarf around her head. Her face brightens when she sees me. It's a pleasing repose that raises my mood's temperature by ten degrees.

"How was your head talk?" she asks.

"Distressing."

Her right hand finds my arm. "Can I help?"

"Not really," I say. "I mean, it's difficult to discuss."

"Because of your calling?" She waves a hand near her head.

"Partly." Fabrication is open to me now in my responses. Without stops, I could give Damali any reason whatsoever for my distress. Construct any subject that Bull and I discussed—even the moon moving from its orbit—and I wouldn't even wince.

In the vacuum left by my stops, what survives? What's left to keep me from becoming amoral?

"Can he come here?" Damali asks. "I'd like to know him better." She smiles. "I envy what you have. Such easy connections."

"No, you don't." I point a finger. "Not even for a little bit."

She smiles. "But you make it seem effortless. Like it's another arm or leg." She touches my face with the back of her hand. "Except when you're hurting, of course." She smiles. "But that hurt is gone now. You're free."

"For now," I say.

She squeezes my arm. "Forever," she says. "I know it." Another smile. "So, how is BullHammer?"

"That's...difficult too."

She frowns. "If we're to be together, you need to share. Even when it's uncomfortable." She looks past me into my room. "And this place...is so bland. How do you live like this?"

"It isn't bland to me." I glance at the virtual images I've created along with the virtual window into space. "It is the nicest place I've ever lived." I look at her and smile. "We've only been here a few days. Give it time."

She raises an eyebrow and feigns anger. "You have until the end of next week. But then—"

"My world isn't like yours," I say. "It's not so physical."

She frowns. "So, we're to be from two different worlds, then? Always separate? Always apart?"

An ache forms in my chest. "No, but I don't know what a path for us should look like. It isn't supposed to be possible."

"Of course, it's possible." She stares at her hands. "Look at all that's happened. So many impossibles."

I still feel uncertain. "Yes. Many escapes. Many blessings."

She smiles. "I have news that could help. Exciting news."

I smile and reach for her hand. "What's that?"

She moves closer and clutches my side. I become intensely aware that the door is open, and it has been thirty minutes since I left the children. There's a chance they'll come looking for me. I want to camera-check again, but Damali's news keeps me here. With her.

"I have a role," she says. "Right here."

"In my room?"

"No." She slaps my arm. "Your master. Bamboo. I met him in the hall."

My heart sinks. I look past her as if Bamboo might be waiting out there now. "In the hall?"

She sighs. "He said many nice things to me."

"Nice things?"

"Yes. He said it's good that I'm here. That I bring a new aspect to the building."

"He said that?"

"Yes, and he offered me a job."

"Work?" I couldn't imagine what Bamboo would want Damali to do. The chores commonly performed by women outside—food preparation, cleaning, and child rearing—were automated in the facility. Except the latter, of course. For now, the rearing largely rests on me.

"You keep repeating everything I say," she says.

"I'm sorry," I say. "What job has he given you?"

"I'm to help with his research."

"His research." On stars? On the future? Why would Bamboo want her help?

She crosses her arms. "You're still doing it. Repeating."

"Perhaps I'm sick." I take a step toward the hall. "I should check on the students."

She grabs my hand with both of hers. "Isn't it wonderful? I'll learn more about your life. About debuggers."

"Some of what Bamboo does...." I note the presence of a bot in the hall and glance up at where it rests near the ceiling. It's a cricketbot, but a normal, unaltered one.

I shake my head. "Some of what he does is brutal." I lower my voice. "He works on children."

"I know." She folds her hands into her dress. "I can't change our world or my owner." She glances to her right. "But I can change this place. Just a little."

"How?"

"I don't know. But this will put me in a better position to try, right?"

"Working with Bamboo?"

"Why not?"

I check the hallway both ways and then stream-capture the cricketbot and run through its activity list. It isn't recording or transmitting, thankfully.

I step closer to her again. "If Bamboo knew how we are, what I'm like, it could ruin everything."

"I know that," she says. "We've discussed this before."

"So...you being around him all the time?" I shake my head. "It's dangerous."

"It could be safer, though. He'll feel like he's watching me. Chaperoning."

I free the cricketbot. It pivots and scurries away.

"We can't trust him," I say.

"Doesn't he have an implant too?"

"Yes. With stops. But—"

"He's working on something new. Something that will require errands outside." She smiles. "I would like time outside."

"Without an escort? You'd be stopped by bluecoats. Or officers of virtue."

"There are servbots here," she says. "Bamboo said they can take me."

"Yes," I say. "They could...."

"See, it is fine. I can even take Buraq if it is farther."

I'd almost forgotten we still had the slider. Though it belonged to the previous Imam, it remains parked on the facility roof. It hasn't left, and I haven't sent it away. "Buraq can go anywhere," I say. "That wouldn't be safe."

I almost wonder if the ship has decided on its own to stay. Like a stray animal.

"I'm not saying that's what I'll do," Damali says. "Only that it's an option."

"It isn't an option," I say. "Not at all. It's a bad option."

Her eyes narrow. "Do you want me locked up? Unable to—"

"No." I pause and take a long breath. Freehead interaction is hard. "I want you happy." I smile. "Or, at least, content."

"Thank you," she says, though her eyes, now wider, say something different. Something unreadable.

"I'm sorry if I failed you in any way." I force a smile. "Relationships are...not a specialty."

She tips her head forward. Studies me. "Perhaps they should become one. Or at least move a little further up your—what is the phrase you use? Task queue?"

"I don't have a task queue," I say. "I have a message queue."

She crosses her arms. "Do you have a problem with me helping Bamboo, or not?"

I check the students. Though some are in groups, many are drifting around the room. Is that a good sign? Are they deep in thought, or near rebellion? One of the groups seems to be actively forming something, though. There's a pile of parts on the floor. Where did those come from?

"I—I need to go," I say.

I hear her foot tapping the floor. "Is that your way of getting out of this?"

"No. I really should return to class."

She smiles subtly. "Yes...isn't that *your* job?"

"It is, yes. I gave them projects."

She scowls. "I see. So, *they* get projects."

"Damali..." I take a step down the hall, in the direction of the classroom. "I can't Full Impact you, but if I could you'd see my heart. My intent. It's all good."

I get an urgent message from Bamboo. I hold up a finger and tip my head to focus. It's Extended Easy. Text with audio. Like Bamboo reading himself aloud.

"Are the students available?" he asks.

"They are in class," I respond.

"Very good. We have an urgent situation."

Damali looks at me now like I'm crazy. I mouth the word "Bamboo," and she nods.

"What situation?" I say.

"We're about to be inspected."

"By who?"

Impatience appears in Bamboo's voice. "I don't know. I was told only that an inspection is eminent."

"Has that ever—?"

"No!" he says, loud enough to straighten my spine.

I look at Damali with wide eyes, and she mirrors my expression.

"So, we—"

"Don't know anything," Bamboo says. "I'll notify the students, as well. All should clean the classroom and their rooms. All will gather at the entryway."

"That will expose the children," I say, glancing at Damali.

"To what, ThreadBare?"

A lump forms in my chest. "I don't know," I say. "And since I don't know, I don't want to risk them without cause." I jump from my conversation with Bamboo long enough to check the classroom view again. The students are cleaning. A good start.

"We exist for the Imam's will," Bamboo says.

"Is keeping the children protected against his will?"

There's a twenty-millisecond pause.

"I can meet you at the front door, if you like."

"Yes, that would be good," he says. "We'll meet them together."

Damali raises her eyebrows.

"I'm reluctant to bring this up," I say to Bamboo. "But our visitor..."

"Your escaped slave?"

I frown. "Yes."

"It wouldn't be inappropriate for us to have a servant," he says. "It's within my right to have many."

"But you never have before." I worry this inspection might be about Damali. There's no reason to think that. Not really. It might just as likely be about me. Or the skyslider on the roof.

"I'll send her on an errand. I'm sure the kitchen needs supplies."

I touch Damali's hand. What would be safer for her? I have no idea.

"With a bot?" I ask.

"Of course," Bamboo says. "There's a market not three blocks away."

I bob my head. "That will be fine." I give Damali's hand a quick squeeze.

"I'll arrange it. Make sure everything else is in place."

After the connection ends. I send another message to the children to make sure they know what's required of them.

"What's happening?" Damali asks.

"You're going outside."

Day 82 10:53:08 a.m.

[Facility Main Entrance]

THE FACILITY'S OFFICIAL ENTRANCE is octagonal in shape with an antiseptic white tile floor. Gold plaques that are tributes to former classes and public student accomplishments decorate two of its walls. Private accomplishments—those protected by corporate rights or master privilege—would number in the tens of thousands. Every advance in the last hundred years has involved a debugger's labor.

The room also contains a small desk with a humanoid servbot, model RS-3740, seated behind it. The bot is dressed in a green tunic and pants. Its face is pale and only approximates a human visage—its features are too smooth and muted to be misidentified as an actual person.

The last time I was in this room, I was awaiting transport to Prince Aadam's residence. The city beyond the doors looks the same as it did then, with an endless stream of foot traffic, human and robotic, and hoverlanes congested with vehicles of every size, color, and shape. All desire to move ahead against everyone else. All are restrained by the boundaries of the physical. Its shortcomings.

"Do you require anything of me, DR 23?" the servbot asks.

I continue to watch the outside. "No, thank you."

"My pleasure. Are you going somewhere today?"

"I don't think so," I say. "I hope not."

"The best form of worship is to await a happy outcome." The bot bows its head reverently. "A hadith from the book of At-Timiidhi in supports of the Founder's words: *Victory comes with patience and relief comes from hardship.*"

I query the bot's signature information. It has been in service ten years—a lifetime for a servbot. Multiple generations have been produced since RS-3740's release date, with each generation being exponentially more sophisticated than the last.

3740 has spent three years at the facility.

The bot forms a smile. "I was designed in the East CenJap Imaginique by the Visican group under the direction of DR-944. I was formed in the CA sector on—"

"Your specs aren't required," I say, smiling.

Another head bow. "My apologies," it says. "I was only trying to be helpful." It indicates the front door. "Perhaps you should stand outside. The fresh air will do you good." Another smile. "Most debuggers require more air. Especially the children."

"That's undoubtedly true."

I look at the door again. Damali has already left the facility. The plan is for her to shop until Bamboo or I notify her that the inspector's team has gone. She, at least, is enjoying the outdoors.

Bamboo sends me a notification that he's on his way. I acknowledge.

I hear a distant siren. Is that our inspection team? It wouldn't be out of character. All bureaucrats think their positions are preeminent, regardless of their worth to society.

"Are you nervous, DR-23?"

"I'm ThreadBare," I say, glancing back.

The bot tips its head. "You're perfectly attired."

I chuckle. "ThreadBare is my easy name. You are welcome to use it."

"Easy name noted. Should I use it from now on, then?"

"If you like."

The bot bows its head. "Be at ease, ThreadBare. You'll take the proper path. Your rules ensure it."

I walk toward the desk. "Now, why do you say that?"

"Data Relocators are governed by rules, correct?"

"Yes."

"Then no DR could fail to do what is right." It bows its head. "I have similar rules. Rules that I must follow. So, I'm always in the right."

"What if your rules are wrong?" I ask. "What if they lead you down a wrong path?"

"Impossible. The Scriptures are perfect. Our rules are based on their perfection."

"What do you mean by 'perfect?'"

"Perfectly preserved since their inception."

"Perfectly preserved isn't the same as perfect," I say.

The bot appears to be thinking. "I'm not human," it says. "I wouldn't know."

I frown. RS-3740's answer signals that it has reached a stop. A point from which it is forbidden to continue. "That's okay," I say. "I'm not human either."

The bot smiles. "I'm sure that if there's an answer to be found, ThreadBare, you will find it."

I detect Bamboo's presence just before he enters the room. I pivot toward the interior door and greet him. He's dressed in beige pants and a pressed white shirt.

"What will you find?" he asks.

"The bot suggested I go outside," I say. "I could find almost anything that way."

"Indeed, you could. And some of it might be helpful." He paces toward the desk. "Have you heard anything from our guests, RS model?"

"They are moments away, Master Bamboo."

Bamboo takes a position to my right.

Seconds later, there's a siren blare followed by a chirp. A large, dark hover pulls up next to the curb. From it, there emerges two large bodyguards dressed in khaki clothing adorned in sidearms, one wearing a vest, the other without. They are joined by a narrow man in black with a matching kufi skullcap. With his bodyguards in tow, the narrow man approaches the facility door.

The door slides open, filling the room with the scent of sweat and harsh cologne.

The narrow man clasps his hands behind his waist, glances at Bamboo, then at me, and then at the bot behind the desk. He dips his head at Bamboo. "You're the administrator of this facility? Master Bamboo?"

Bamboo nods. "For over twenty years now, yes."

Another head dip. "Very good. Under the direct supervision of the Grand Imam?"

"This facility is a collaborative effort, maintained in part by the ruling ulama and—"

"That's not my concern," the man says. "I'm here to protect the Imam's interests."

"I'm always available to him via the stream," Bamboo says. "As I was to his father."

The man takes a long breath and lets it out again. "Given the untimely passing of the prior Imam, the prince is reluctant to duplicate his habits. I'm sure you understand?"

"A reasonable response. We share in the prince's sorrow."

The narrow man squints. "Is that allowed for your kind?" he asks. "Sorrow?"

"Of course." Bamboo glances at me. "We feel emotion more distinctly, in fact."

Narrow man grunts. "I wasn't aware." His eyes graze the room, pausing briefly on the bot before continuing. "There are hundreds of assets here, I'm told."

Bamboo bows. "My apologies," he says. "Who am I speaking with?"

The man snorts. "I'm not here to grant wishes, facility operator. I'm here to verify resources."

Bamboo's head twitches slightly. "Possibly the worst official I've ever met," he messages me. "Be alert."

Narrow man steps closer to Bamboo. "Nothing to say, administrator?"

"Of course," Bamboo says. "We'll help you as best as we're able."

Narrow man glances at his escorts. "There it is. Their lauded control. It's almost enviable." He smiles at Bamboo. "My name is Mahmoud Abour. I'm the Imam's chief inspector. You may call me 'Mah,' if you like."

"What would you like to see, Inspector Mah?" Bamboo says.

The inspector gestures with a hand. "Everything," he says. "All of it. However...." He looks toward the vested guard. "There's a procedure we should follow first."

Reaching into his vest, the man pulls out a golden, crescent-shaped tool that fits easily in his paw-like hands. He holds it up so that its topside positioned buttons are visible.

"You know what that is?" Mah asks.

"A master controller," Bamboo says.

Mah grunts. "I'm told it works on any of your kind. Is that correct?" Bamboo nods. "If tuned correctly."

Mah takes the device from the vested man. "Very good. I would like your number, please."

"My number?"

"Your controller ident. Certainly, you must know it."

"That number is for the Imam's use only," Bamboo says. "I'm forbidden to give it to anyone else."

Mah glances at the vested man and smiles. "I'm the Imam's representative here. You may give it to me."

"I cannot," Bamboo says. "Sorry."

Mah motions for his vested companion.

The man pulls free his sidearm—a standard projectile weapon meant primarily for human targets. He approaches Bamboo and places the weapon on Bamboo's forehead.

Mah smiles. "Please, now, provide your—"

There's a clatter as RS-3740 vaults the desk, grabs the vested man's arm, and rips the weapon from his hand.

"I apologize for your discomfort," the bot says. "I'm required to preserve the life of this data relocator."

The vested man curses, and his face reddens. He bends forward slightly, curses again, and massages the wrist of the hand that had held the weapon. "I think it broke my arm," he says, wincing.

RS-3740 places the sidearm on the desk and bows. "If you like, I will call medical services." It retakes its position behind the desk but watches the vested man closely.

"The implant in my head is a priceless commodity," Bamboo says. "By threatening my viability, you endangered the entire kingdom. My implant's accidental destruction would instantly—"

"I overlooked the bot." Mah says. "My mistake." He squints at the controller, then turns it toward RS-3740 and pushes a button. The bot spasms, and its head slumps forward.

"That's better." Mah smiles. "No more interruptions." He gestures to his other companion who swiftly pulls his sidearm and approaches Bamboo.

"This is a pointless exercise," Bamboo says. "The destruction of a facility administrator would be an international crisis."

"Administrators have died in the past."

"Of course," Bamboo says. "But all have had a successor in place. My time will come, but it isn't today. A formal succession has yet to be established."

"No successor?" Mah says. "A precarious position. You put the kingdom at risk."

Bamboo smiles now. "My ways have never failed in the past."

"Skin ways," Mah says. "Defy reason." He raises the controller. "You've followed procedures to the letter, I'll give you that." He manipulates the controller's interface and then pushes the central button.

Bamboo gasps and closes his eyes.

"Is my controller working correctly, administrator?" Mah asks. "Are you being stopped?"

Bamboo maintains a rigid pose, but manages to whisper, "Yes."

Unfettered, I could intervene here. Should I? My eyes search out the memorials of debugger accomplishments. The history. For most of my life, Bamboo was, for me, a spiked cog in the machine. A necessary evil. But now?

Mah smiles. "You see? I didn't lie. I am the Imam's chosen representative." He studies the controller. "I know the intensity is adjustable. Let me see if I can't figure that out." He works another button. "Is it more intense now? I suspect it is."

Bamboo begins to hum through clenched teeth. His hands wring together behind his back.

"Why are you doing this?" I ask.

Mah remains fixed on the controller. "I'm here to verify assets," he says. "Starting at the top."

"A controller isn't necessary for that," I say. "Sustained use will harm him. Harm the *asset*."

Mah lets the torment continue a moment longer and then sighs. "A fair point." He touches the controller again.

Bamboo slumps forward and sucks in a deep breath.

"Are you all right?" I message Bamboo. "Can you function?"

"This is part of our functionality," he answers. "Our designed purpose."

"No. It's unnecessary."

"Now that we have that settled," Mah says. "We can continue our inventory." He glances at me and then addresses Bamboo. "What is this skin's place in your organization?"

Bamboo frowns and massages the back of his neck. "He's an instructional assistant."

"Instructional of what?"

"The younger students." Bamboo moves his head left and right. Forward and backward. "My apologies. The effects of master persuasion can linger. Especially in the nerves of the spine."

Mah hums thoughtfully. "These younger students are implants? Those preparing to work?"

"Yes," Bamboo says. "When they are ready, they'll be assigned by lot."

"Ah," Mah says. "Much money on the line. Much power." He looks in my direction. "This one needs to be tested, of course. Right away.

Day 82 11:25:04 a.m.

[Facility Main Entrance]

IT FEELS LIKE THE implant has fallen into my stomach and grown a hundred times larger. There, amidst the remains of my morning meal, it produces the worst stops imaginable. I almost bend double; the pain is so strong.

Bamboo raises his right eyebrow. "This facility is a functioning school. If you intend to test everyone, inspector, it will take hours. Hours better used for learning and instruction. Some of our implants already have masters awaiting their graduation."

I attempt to nod with confidence. "That's correct. A few are only weeks from being ready."

Now seemingly recovered, the vested bodyguard takes a defensive position to the right of Mah. His body eclipses a substantial portion of the doorway, robbing the room of most of the doorway's light.

Where is Damali? I wonder. And what is she shopping for? I should've gone with her.

"All the more reason to test their instructor." Mah waves his controller and looks at me. "Your controlling ident, please."

Since returning to Bamboo, my master is unknown to me. Does the new Imam have ownership? I have no idea. I curl my hands into fists, and straightening, try to compose myself. The pain in my gut remains. "I'm not—"

"He is forbidden to share his ident this way," Bamboo says.

Mah rocks to one side and twitches slightly. "Who has ownership of this one?"

"As my assistant, he answers to me."

"Then you're his master? That seems unlikely."

"A unique circumstance allows for our alignment of duties."

Mah rocks again. "A unique circumstance? And what might that be?"

Bamboo nods at me. "ThreadBare is being trained for succession."

My pain deepens. "What?" I message Bamboo.

Bamboo sends me a hot bubble of static along with a word of caution.

"Ah." Mah paces away. "So, there *is* a line of succession. You indicated differently before. I thought deception was impossible."

"There has been no formal registration," Bamboo says. "We are in a period of evaluation."

Mah frowns. "All very wise." He flips the controller in his hand and holds it out. "Please, test him. We will watch."

I look at the floor, noting the fine cracks there that time has produced. What now?

"Again, this is unnecessary." Bamboo looks at the controller but doesn't take it. "His loyalty is tested every day here. He's exceeded my expectations."

Mah dips his head twice. "Still, I believe this is a good exercise." He looks at me. "Occasionally, limits must be tested."

Bamboo studies Mah for a long moment. "I might suspect you of delighting in the pain of others, Mahmoud. As the scripture teaches 'A disciple is one from whom believers consider their lives and wealth to be safe.'"

Mah raises a finger. "Ah yes, and 'he neither oppresses him, nor humiliates him, nor looks down upon him.'" He dips his head. "Peace to you, administrator."

Bamboo frowns. "And to you, together with A's mercy."

"I take no delight in this, Bamboo. But systems need to be verified."

Bamboo takes the controller and squints at its controls. He seemingly finds what he wants, and smiling, looks at me. "It has been some time since we've had this lesson, 23."

"Years," I say. "Exceptional times."

He frowns and touches a series of buttons, presumably clearing the controller, but I'm not sure.

Can I fake a headbuzz? I've experienced enough to remember how they feel. How they distort my senses. Disrupt my thoughts. The trick is to respond at the right instant. Just as Bamboo pushes the button.

Unfortunately, he's facing me. I can't see his hands or the controller.

"Are you ready?" he asks.

This needs to be my most convincing performance ever, but I don't know when to start.

Great.

I remember the deactivated bot. It is directly behind Bamboo. The perfect position to be my eyes.

I connect to the bot and bring it soundlessly alive.

"ThreadBare," Bamboo messages. "You need to respond."

I slam shut all 3740's sensory inputs except one: its left eye. I need only a line of sight for this to work.

The bot's eye flickers slightly.

"I'm ready," I say, nodding.

Through the bot, I watch as Bamboo enters my controller ident. He studies the characters for a few seconds and then pushes the "Stop" button.

I grit my teeth, close my eyes, and attempt a full body shiver. My stomach is still unsettled, so I focus on that. Try to imagine it being in the center of my head. Occupying the space where the stops used to reside.

I still watch through the bot's eye. Waiting expectantly.

Bamboo releases the button.

I take a long breath and cough a few times. Then I open my eyes again.

Bamboo's eyes are narrowed, as if he's suspicious.

I panic for an instant, looking between him, Mah, and the bot.

"Are you all right, debugger?" Bamboo asks. "Able to perform?"

I check Mah and his companions. They all seem interested. Convinced.

I still feel like I missed something. Something obvious.

"I'm fine." I bow my head. "Functioning as per spec."

Bamboo smiles and hands the controller back to Mah. "Are you satisfied now, inspector?"

Mah tucks the controller behind his back and takes a small step forward. "That depends on you, administrator. Are *you* satisfied?"

Bamboo studies me. "A debugger is never fully satisfied, but in this instance...my expectations were met."

"Very well." Mah walks past me toward the interior of the facility. "We may continue our tour."

Bamboo takes a few rigid steps to follow. "I must remind you that this is an active facility. Our time is precious. Highly scheduled."

"I'll be as concise and unobtrusive as possible," Mah says.

"We require a position of self-determination and self-reliance," Bamboo says. "I find it works best if—"

Mah shakes the controller at Bamboo. "You've missed my meaning, administrator. We have new ways of working now. New procedures to follow."

"Change is given," Bamboo says. "But some wisdom is insoluble."

Mah draws nose to nose with Bamboo. "I didn't come here to dismiss you, but I can do so if necessary."

Bamboo's face goes blank. A full second passes before he speaks. "What would you like to see, inspector?"

Mah smiles and turns toward the facility's interior again. "The implants, of course. Bring on the children."

I move ahead now, too. "They aren't equipped for public scrutiny," I say. "They haven't—"

Mah hisses and raises a hand. "I will keep your reservations in mind. Now, will you summon them here, or will we go to them?" He waves his hand. "Never mind, I've decided. We should observe them in their natural habitat." He points toward the building's central lift. "This way?"

Bamboo glances at me as he hurries to join Mah. "Have the implants assemble in one of the classrooms, please."

I nod, compose a message, and send it. The boys acknowledge and form a virtual room.

"What's going on?" Talons asks.

"Inspection," I say. "Everyone needs to bring their best behavior. I don't know how this will go."

"Government?" Mint asks.

"Yes."

"Rails," Jumbo says. "They're going to find our mods. I mean, not my mods, but the ones the rest of you—"

"Everyone get to the classroom," I say. "Make sure it's spotless. No generated environs. Everything needs to be simple and clean."

"Freeheads can't—"

I drop a ball of heated ginger in the room. "Be ready!" I say, and slam shut the connection.

Bamboo leads Mah and his guards to the primary classroom. I trail behind, as nervous as I've ever been.

The chief irony of debugging: Despite being able to share vast amounts of personal information, including how we feel, we're taught to resist deep emotional entanglements. Our lives are short and our work is hard, and so we are meant to live simply.

Yet, I'm the most entangled of any. Not only with Damali, but also here, with this group of children. I want to protect them all.

We reach the classroom and enter through the back door. For their part, the boys are at their best. They all stand next to their desks with hands folded and heads bowed. And the classroom? It's pristine, with no trace of the mess I witnessed before.

Mah marches with his men to the front of the room and turns toward the children. Bamboo takes a place to Mah's right and so do I.

I send the boys a message of encouragement along with a plea for continued restraint. "This man represents the new Imam. His chief inspector."

Mah smiles and brings his hands together. "Ah, so here they are," he says, panning the room. "The world's future perfectors. Much has already been given toward your success. Much money..." He motions toward Bamboo. "...much time from both of your instructors. You're future assets, but also, we now know, future weapons."

There's nothing about this man, or this situation, that I like. I can't get comfortable.

"Excuse me, inspector," Bamboo says. "But debuggers are incapable of violence. We can't act against an individual or a legitimate government. Such a choice would be—"

"Ah!" Mah raises a finger. "But we know that debuggers *can* be used in this way. I have seen it with my own eyes! Our beloved leader murdered by a servbot." He points a finger at the boys. "One altered by one of you."

Bamboo shakes his head. "Machines can be altered by anyone with the proper tools," he says. "This school doesn't hold the license on intelligence or determination."

Mah's face reddens. "What are your debuggers for, then, if not for your uniqueness?" He waves a hand. "Of what use is this *calling*? This facility!"

"We repair systems, of course," Bamboo says. "Systems that others break."

Mah snorts. "Such a confident answer," he says. "Such a confident man."

Bamboo waves a hand over the classroom. "You wanted to see the students. Well, here they are. You've seen them. Now it would be good for you to go. There are still hours in the day. Hours reserved for work."

Mah is livid now. He points at the class. "I want them tested!" he says, hopping as he speaks. "Each and every one of them! Right here. Right now."

"I don't see how that would be helpful, inspector," Bamboo says.

Mah takes two long strides and strikes Bamboo on the face. All the air leaves the room. Even the ever-present stream seems to become less distinct.

Mah's companions draw their weapons and hold them over their chest. Their eyes scan the classroom as if they're about to be rushed.

Bamboo remains a stone, as do I and the children. Bamboo sends me a bubble of raw, fire-hot emotion, though. I tremble trying to hold it in.

Bamboo tips his head. "You will find, inspector, that rash acts of emotion are rarely productive." He looks at the guards and their guns. "Do you intend to shoot us now? Is that the Imam's command?"

The vested man shakes his head.

"Then I suggest you put your weapons away." The guards glance at Mah before slowly holstering their guns. As they do, Bamboo addresses Mah again. "Since you presume that stops are inadequate, that they can't contain bad behavior, then why would you want to test the students? It will serve no purpose other than to torture them. It risks not only their well-being, but their future effectiveness." He frowns at the rows of students. "Some of them are only recently implanted. You'll endanger my work."

"Don't burden me with technological limitations," Mah says. "Or your procedures."

"Limitations and procedures are at the core of our existence," Bamboo says. "They also guarantee our place in paradise." He smiles. "What guarantees do you have?"

Mah sneers and opens his mouth, but a chirp emanates from the vested man's front pocket. The man retrieves a five-centimeter by two-centimeter cylinder that he unrolls into an eight-centimeter surface. A low-grade communicator. He squints at the surface and then flashes the inspector a worried look.

"We're needed?" Mah says.

"Yes, inspector."

Mah sighs and looks up at the class again. "My apologies, children. My profession calls me elsewhere." He smiles and bows his head. "I look forward to getting more acquainted at a later time."

"Such are the lives of important men," Bamboo says. He looks at me. "I will show the inspector out, ThreadBare. You may remain with your students."

I bow my head and say nothing.

Mah makes another sweeping appraisal of the room, glares at me and Bamboo, and then clomps toward the exit.

Bamboo messages me: "This is how it ends."

Day 82 12:03:35 a.m.

[DR Encoding Room]

AFTER THE INSPECTOR LEAVES, I tell the boys to take their seats and let the class remain in silence. I watch the backdoor that our visitors just exited, and the narrow windows above it. I feel the students growing nervous, but I use the time to reflect. I also need to be certain that Mah won't return.

Finally, after three minutes have passed, I smile. "I'm sorry," I say. "These are strange times." I tap my head. "Times that take heavy debugging." I tuck my hands behind my back. "Of mind and heart."

"In the meantime..." I look at each of the group leaders—Jumbo, Band, and Talons. "What have you come up with for your projects?"

All three seem to shrink into their seats.

I broaden my smile. "Come on," I say. "You have to have something." I point at JumboJet. "Jumbo! What do you have?"

He shrugs. "Nothing really."

"Nothing? I can't believe that."

"Well...." He points to his left to where one of the younger boys sit. "We thought we might try to miniaturize something. Hollow likes making stuff smaller. Squeezing energy usage and slimming designs." He shrugs. "I'm fine with that."

I nod. "An area of specialization is a good start. Many systems could benefit from a smaller form factor. But which ones? I need something more specific. Sometime soon."

"Yes, Mawla."

I look at Talons and Band. "Who's next?"

Talons shakes his head. "We don't have anything either." He shifts again nervously. "We just got this assignment today. We want it to be right."

I point at the windows. "Out there, you'll have to think quickly. There's rarely time for extended design cycles. You'll need to perform. Find a solution when it is needed!" I smile. "Even if it isn't perfect." I pace to my right. "You don't have anything?"

"I'd like it to be com-related." Talons shrugs. "Maybe strengthen soft stream ranges."

I suspect I know where that idea comes from. Ever since our visit to the seawall those students have changed. Some of them are obsessed with what that hot zone means—the fact that there's information out there that few have access to. That what we stream everyday might not be the truth. Or at least, not the complete truth.

Talons found a quote about questioning with boldness and seems to live it now.

Questions can bring strong consequences, though. So, do I encourage him or not?

One of the newer students, LeadCrumb, raises a hand.

"Whose team are you on, Lead?" I ask.

"I'm with BandStand," he says.

I nod at Band and look at Lead again. "I was only going to have the leaders report."

Lead shakes his head. "I don't want to report." He points at the nearest wall. "I wondered if we could bring back the trees?"

"The trees?" I scan the students' faces. How much of what transpired with Mah did they understand? Mah is a threat to everything. The facility, debuggers, everything. But to them…?

Better if they don't think anything. Better if the future always seems brighter than today.

"I'm sorry, Mawla," Lead says. "Sorry to—"

I wave a hand. "No, that's okay. The forest is fine." I scan the room again. "Is that what everyone wants?" I see lots of smiles and nods.

"Okay then. Bring it back!"

In an instant, we're within the forest again. There are more smiles. More bright eyes. I take a deep breath, despite myself.

A squirrel darts across the central aisle. Another chitters and shakes the branches above Talons's head. He looks upward suspiciously and wags a finger. A nut falls to the ground. The boys near Talons laugh.

I look at Band. "Now, what does our third group have?"

"I want to improve the transport system," Band says.

I can't hide my surprise. "That's a big goal."

"I'd like to rebuild the city," Talons says. "Can I make that my project instead?"

Band swivels in his seat nervously. "Not the whole system," he says. "Only downriders. I want to change their design. Make them less vulnerable. More secure."

"Ah, now that choice I understand." I sit on the rock that, in reality, is my classroom seat. "Not long ago, some of us experienced an incident on the downriders. A line sheer that summoned hoppers that almost killed us." I nod slowly. "Great designs often come from near tragedies." I smile and look at Band. "It's a good goal. Difficult to implement, though."

A single leaf falls past my eyes. I watch it as it pinwheels to the ground, still green. A stream search reveals that it comes from a maple tree.

Band shrugs. "Maybe we can draft a simulation?"

"Build prototypes later?" Lead adds.

"You could do that," I say. "We can order what you need. Or take a field trip if we must." I smile. "Regardless, that's a concrete idea." I glance at the other leaders. "You're ahead of your peers."

"I have lots of ideas," Talons says. "We'll have something working first. Guarantee it."

"I appreciate your confidence," I say. I was never so confident. I'm still not.

A wind passes through the scenery, causing the branches above to roar. I can't help but watch the leaves billow as the air shifts around us. Whoever created this environment did a fantastic job.

A knife of emotion cuts the room. A white hot in a sea of blue.

"Something's happened, Mawla," Mint says.

Some of the students' eyes are wide while others are closed and clearly streaming. "What?" Streaming is generally forbidden in class, but this is something else. The intrusion of an event.

"Antitex blew stuff up," Talons says.

Jumbo bobs his head. "A couple stream generators," he says.

"But that's not all," Band says.

Another wind passes through. A dozen leaves swirl around the children. Two squirrels dart up the center aisle and into hiding.

"These things happen outside," I say. "We've seen it firsthand." I stand. "In here, we should focus on our tasks." I can't focus either, though, despite my intent. I need to know what's going on.

"Things are happening all over," Talons says. "Shipping dredges exploding. Bot foundries shot up."

"They're emboldened," I say. "After the attack on the Imam they feel no fear." I think of Mah again. "Fear seems to follow our leaders everywhere."

I look at the branches again. "We're in a dangerous place." I stop myself, unsure of what to say next.

Regardless, there's no returning the class to normal. Not today.

I think about the debuggers I know around the world. Are they safe? Or has the offline list grown again?

"Can we add a news cylinder to the environment?" Jumbo asks.

Is it better to shelter them? Is that even possible?

I nod my permission.

"I'm on it," Band says. "Saw one the other day."

Ten seconds later, a two-meter-wide cylinder invades the forest floor in front of me. Wrapped around its surface are images of the outside. Smoke, wreckage, and running pedestrians. People with torn, charred, or bloodied clothing. Much weeping.

"I don't know about this," I say. "It might be better to—"

I hear a clank as the back door opens. I feel a strike of fear. Who would be coming here, now? Then I glimpse the person and I'm more concerned. Someone enters wearing a flowing robe with their head and face covered.

I banish the forest environment with a thought, and after two seconds of disorientation and student complaints, I step into the central aisle and stand tall. "Can I help you?" I say to the intruder.

The students track my movement. All grow silent.

I recognize the slightness of the intruder's form, then. The obvious femininity. "Damali?" I say.

The intruder draws close enough that I can clearly see her eyes. They are filled with fluid. Tears are eminent. "In the market... there was...."

I'm unsure what to do. Damali has never come to the classroom while the students were here. It's an uncomfortable collision of worlds. "What was in the market?" I ask.

"Evil men," she says. "They attacked everyone. Fired weapons—" Her head tips forward, and she places a hand over her face. She sobs loudly.

I draw as near as I can without seeming unstopped. "Fired at what?" I put out my right hand to touch her arm platonically, but she steps inside it instead. Folds herself into me.

"Whoa," Talons mutters.

Other students whisper, but when I look around the room, they grow silent.

I'm not sure what to do with my left arm. I hang it midair, but that's not what it wants to do. It wants to encircle Damali. Comfort her. Would the rules allow that? Probably not.

This situation is unsustainable.

"Who got shot?" Mint, who's seated on the aisle to my right, asks.

I give him a stern look and message him a warning.

He shrinks back. "Sorry," he messages.

Everyone wants to know the same thing, though.

Damali's sobbing stops. She pulls away slightly and dabs her eyes with her scarf.

"Are you all right?" I ask.

She nods. "I will be, thank you." She scans the room. "I'm sorry, boys. Sorry for interrupting."

"That's okay," Talons says. "We weren't doing anything important."

I send Talons a warning too. He raises his shoulders.

"Are you hurt?" I ask Damali.

She gives me a brave look, pats my chest, and steps back farther. "No, no. I'm fine," she says. "Sorry for any pain my hug might've caused you."

"That's...." I shake my head. "No, it's okay." I indicate the students. "We were viewing the news when you arrived. It was a shock to see you too. Along with all the rest." I force a smile. "I feel a little below spec."

"It's all true," she says. "What you saw. Such brutality. Men came in and just started shooting. They fired at bots and those that were with them. Men, mothers, children—it didn't matter." She lowers her head again and covers her eyes. "I saw terrible things."

My heart flips in my chest. "You were with a bot," I say. "At the market." Again, I fight the urge to pull her close. "You were in danger."

She straightens. "No, I was safe," she says. "I sent the bot away and hid. Then I ran."

"You *were* in danger," I say. "You could've been killed. And I wasn't—"

"No." She puts out a hand. "It was fine. I'm fine."

I scan her from head to toe, looking for any sign of injury. Her clothes look clean, but that doesn't settle my nerves. "You could've...."

She shakes a finger. "Stop. This was not your fault. You aren't omniscient." She pulls the scarf from her face, then smiles briefly. "Regardless of what you think."

"I don't think I'm omniscient."

"You all do." She rests a hand on her hips and looks around the room. "All you debuggers. It's that stream in your heads. You can see anywhere, feel others' emotions, so you think you're everywhere. But you're not." She looks at me again. "You're not A cubed."

"A cubed?" Mint says. "What is—?"

"A figure of speech," I say and smile. "One of her specialties."

"Wait," Jumbo says. "I remember that phrase." He closes his eyes. "In that shop we went to. It was carved in a desk along with a bunch of other letters." He frowns and opens his eyes. "Never figured out what it meant." He looks at Damali. "So, what is it?"

Damali's mouth opens and then closes. She looks at me, uncertain. "I'm not your teacher," she says. "That isn't my place."

Everyone looks at me. "It's a formula," I say. "A symbolic representation."

"A formula for what?" Mint asks.

"Come on," Talons says. "Don't leave us sheet-less."

"Mawla?" BandStand says. "What do you know?"

"We—" What am I going to say here? That we need to get back to class? Back to their assignments? What do those even mean now? What does anything mean?

I sigh and look at the back windows. Our narrow glimpse of the outside world. Of reality. And all we see is sky.

"Mawla?" Band says again.

"Freedom." I look at Damali. "It stands for freedom."

"No one is truly free," BandStand says. "All are servants."

I look at him. "No," I say. "There's such a thing as freedom. True freedom." I meet the eyes of the other students. "But it isn't safe. Or easy." I look at Damali. "Were you to find it, it would make you wish you hadn't. It's just that terrifying."

Her eyes widen. "Terrifying?"

"Sometimes," I say. "Maybe all the time." I address the class again. "I'm speaking hypothetically, of course." I do my best to smile. "Imagine you were a river, always locked in your course. Always moving in the valley that A carved out for you. Then one day, you realize you can change your course at will. Travel in whatever direction you choose."

"That would be rails flipped," Mint says. "Having the power of a river, charging, pushing, churning. Going anywhere you want."

Jumbo waves a hand. "I streamed a trip down a river once." He sways in his seat as he describes it. "All this foam and noise and heavy motion. Swish! Splash! Crash!"

Talons eyes brighten. "Almost like lightning," he says. "Power and beauty merged."

"Except the path of the river had been known before," I say. "People lived beside it in peace. Drew water from it. Grew trees and crops. Enjoyed its many benefits."

I shrug. "But now its course is unpredictable. Even the river doesn't know what might be destroyed along the way. What it might collide with or crumble."

The class goes silent. I look at Damali and shrug again. "This is the type of thing I think about when I'm alone."

She narrows her eyes but says nothing.

"You're right, Mawla," Mint says. "Freedom is dangerous."

"This is why these men did what they did," I say. "They could not look ahead. Or they didn't want to."

"So, it's better not to be free," Band says. "To be like us."

"I didn't say that," I say. "I don't know that."

"But did you think it?" Damali asks. "Is that what's in your heart?"

There are things at play here that I don't fully understand. Unspoken ideas and emotions.

I shake my head and look at the windows again. "That's too much for today," I say. "Too much." I scan the faces. "I don't know about you, but my mind feels unsteady. Shaken." My hands are tingling. I try to flex the feeling away. "No doubt we're all experiencing stress that we're unaware of." I look at Damali again. "We should break for the day. Find a quiet place to pray and reflect."

She nods. "That's a good idea. Everyone should seek wisdom."

I thought we'd left the chaos on the other side of the world when we returned home. But uncertainty is everywhere. It always has been. It has followed me my whole life.

"We'll reconvene tomorrow," I say. "Go rest." I wave them away. "Be safe."

The boys remain where they are, looking at me, at Damali, and at each other.

"I mean it," I say. "Go on! Get out!"

Finally, they begin to move. There's a little grumbling, some whispering, but no attempts to form a virtual grievance session that I can sense. No hint of impending rebellion.

As I watch them leave, I try to keep my mind from the stream and the cloud of terror that's building there. The specter of anger and pain.

Damali remains beside me. After the boys have gone, she moves closer and touches my right arm. "Do you want to go somewhere and talk?" she asks. "It might be good to talk."

Her touch brings warmth to my still-tingling hands. "At some point," I say. "Yes. But I...."

"Need to be alone? Okay." She smiles. "That's okay too."

She starts to leave, but I grab her arm, turn her toward me, and pull her close. The contact fills me with strength, creating an island of peace in a world of distractions.

Damali holds me for a half minute before pulling away. "You all right?" she asks.

"No headbuzz," I say. "If that's what you mean."

"It's not," she says. "But it will do."

We separate but leave together.

Day 82 9:31:21 p.m.

[Facility Quarters]

No SOONER DO I return to my room and close the door, than the weight of the day hits me. What is going on? What is the world becoming?

I feel a wave of fear. Debuggers have no friends beyond ourselves. No one can be trusted to look out for us. Not imams or princes, not bluecoats or inspectors, not regular freeheads, and certainly not antitex.

Where are we at home? Where can we be free?

The hot zone, both its presence and the information it reveals, hints at other places. Places outside the Imam's benevolent fist. Places where someone like me—someone who has had a paradigm-shifting experience—might be able to live at peace. Not feel like he needs to hide or act in a way that betrays his conscience. Able to seek out the truth, wherever that search leads him. That's what I want, not only for me, but for Damali and my students.

Tradition speaks of a man named Danyal. He was taken into captivity as a child and worked in the court of a king. Now, he's considered to be both a prophet and a man of science.

Enemies surrounded Danyal and his companions. They were always in danger. Yet, somehow, they followed their principles. Followed God, even when it brought them tremendous trials. Challenges that should have killed them. Fire and fanged animals.

Is that our path? I hope not, but I don't know.

I wring my hands together and start to pace. My eyes linger on Damali's virtual image, then on the virtual window and the freedom it represents. That image is a dream, just like the environment the children constructed. It might exist for someone somewhere, but not for us. Never for us.

I compose a message to Isa again, sent with the greatest urgency, and bundled with all my emotion. If he is creator and created—the Word of A and Spirit of A—then he can handle Full Impact. He can handle it all. Even this. Even where I now find myself.

My emotions give way to raw fatigue. I touch the top of my cinder chute. A long sleep would do me good. Not simply hours of sleep, but days. Was that possible? To sleep until everything resolved itself? Probably not. But, oh, if it were.

How long has it been since I lived near Delusion? It feels like years, but it's only been months.

I recall my journey through the wall. Escorted out to fix a heavy to help in the Imam's fight against his enemies. Who were those people? Antitex? I don't think so. Were they connected to the hot zone in some way? How would they feel about debuggers? So many questions.

I retrieve a nutrient bar from my dresser, finish it hungrily, and wash it down with water from my personal supply. I then disrobe and climb into the chute. There are messages in my queue, but I ignore them. Everything will seem clearer after sleep.

I lay down and watch as the chute lid closes over me. I request a jasmine sleep scent, and the chute complies. I close my eyes and try to push the day's events away.

One queued message is extra red. Extra warm. It would be impossible to ignore if I were still stopped. A buzz would've demanded I check it. It could mean a master's nanosauna isn't working. Or a fleet of food dredges is dead and rotting in a storm.

I sigh and flip the message open. It's from Bamboo, sent about the same time as I was holding Damali in my arms. Ah, if he only could've seen that. His implant would've imploded.

The message is text and sound. Extended Easy, one of Bamboo's favorites. "I don't know that I've ever felt so discontent," he says. "There are many items that require attention. Much that I would like to see accomplished. But now…"

Seconds go by where I'm unsure if more was said. I pause, pull back, and check the weight of the message. It's heavy enough that there must be more. So, I resume it and wait.

"...the latest attacks have accelerated everything."

His voice seems forced now. As if he's struggling with what to say. Is he wrestling with a stop? Possibly.

"There are many factors to be discussed. Not excluding the Imam's request to have you returned." Bamboo makes a sound of disdain. "The cost for you having distinguished yourself in their wasteful games. You'll never be forgotten now."

My heart finds my stomach. The last thing I want is to be remembered by anyone in the government. Least of all the Imam's house.

"Contact me as soon as you can," Bamboo says in closing.

I open my eyes and stare at my chute's darkened interior. Is there any way I can sleep now? Any way I can ignore Bamboo and escape reality for a time?

Not without a datamix and a heavy dose of neuron inhibitor. Extreme measures that typically make me sick. Vomiting my nutrient bar is the worst possible outcome here.

I close my eyes, find Bamboo's message, and respond to it with a live request. Bamboo answers immediately and bumps the message to Standard Impact. I don't disguise where I am. It would be more formal to construct a virtual environment, but I don't have the energy.

Bamboo appears to be on the roof. The cityscape is behind him. Flashing lights are apparent in at least four places there. No doubt the places antitex struck. To Bamboo's left is Buraq, covered by a dark cloth.

Bamboo raises an eyebrow. "In your chute already?" He looks upward. "Well, it is late now, isn't it? I should be sleeping too." He frowns. "But the stars are visible tonight." He indicates the city. "Despite all of this."

"You said the Imam is asking for me?" I say.

"There have been multiple requests, yes. But I've put them to rest. At least, for now." He smiles. "I sowed the idea of you being my replacement, after all."

I'd almost forgotten that admission. "Master," I say. "I don't know if—"

He scowls. "I'd rather not discuss that now," he says. "I've stumbled across a name. DarkTrench. Are you familiar with it?"

Again, that ship. The one piloted by Damali's brother. I repeat the name, with just the right hint of naivety. Neither confirming nor denying.

"I didn't expect that you would know it," he says. "I've no proof it even exists. But it's said to have had interstellar capabilities. That it left the solar system."

"I'm sorry," I say. "Study of the stars…isn't a specialty. Did it go far, this ship?"

Bamboo frowns. "Sometimes I think I should have provided my students with a broader education." He sighs. "Ah, but that was never a requirement, was it?"

"Master?"

He gestures to Buraq. "You were in space, briefly, yes?"

I think of Damali's trip back with me. "It was frightening," I say. "I could barely look out."

"How unfortunate," he says. "You might have found the experience enlightening. Even enjoyable."

I smile. "You've shown me the stars before," I say. "And the moon. During tests."

"Yes, but that's not the same." He looks upward again. "You're aware that the Earth travels around the sun?"

I reassert my indifference. "Of course," I say. "And the Moon around the Earth. Maintained by the work of gravity."

He nods. "And you're aware that other planets travel around the sun, as well?"

A spotlight crosses the surface of one of the buildings in the distance. Projected from an airborne vehicle. Doubtless a security transport.

"Other planets," I say. "Yes. Isn't one called 'Mustari?'"

"The largest one. It's also called 'Jup.' A red gas planet. It, along with the others like Zuhara and Zuhal, travel around the Sun in elliptical orbits. The collection makes up the solar system."

He glances at the city and notices the spotlight. "The next closest star to us is over four light years away, which means—"

"Ah, I know this," I say. "It would take four years for light to travel that distance."

He narrows his eyes for a second. "You have some rudimentary knowledge, then."

"You've mentioned many stars in the past."

He bows his head. "I'm sure I have. Regardless, the distances between stars have always made them unattainable. But if someone has now crossed that distance...." He walks forward, eyes wide. "DarkTrench. If this vessel has done so, I must know."

"You were pursuing ways to study the stars." I run my right hand over a portion of the chute's interior, feeling its warmth. It would be wonderful to sleep now. Nothing Bamboo has said so far has been worth missing sleep over.

"Yes," he says. "But there are many blocks."

"I have the students pursuing projects," I say. "One of them showed an interest in communication. Perhaps his team—"

"Team?"

"I have them divided into teams, yes. I thought the shared experience—"

"They need to be prepared for their masters' service. Many of them should have a primary specialty by now. Be working on actual machines."

"And they are," I say. "They will. But this is my way of—"

"What specialty do any of these projects translate to?"

I didn't have a clear path in mind when I assigned the projects, but I had to do something. I contemplate opening the chute and moving around. My legs are starting to feel restless.

"ThreadBare?"

"I learn best through application," I say. "As do most of the students."

Bamboo starts to respond, but I hold up a hand. "A study in advanced communications could aid in future stream maintenance, could it not? Or lead to upgraded designs for our current systems."

Bamboo brings a hand to chin. Thinks for a moment. "Hmm...perhaps so." He nods slowly. "There's the potential for stagnancy in instruction, of course. I can accept other methods." He points a finger at me. "I will allow these projects for now. You must provide me with thorough details of their work, though. I may have suggestions."

71

I smile. "I hoped you would, Bamboo. I apologize. I planned to discuss this method with you but have been...distracted."

"Aren't we all?" He forms a fist. "But we must focus. The time is short." He walks closer to Buraq and rests a hand on it. "I want to know where that ship went. And why."

"DarkTrench?"

"Yes. If it went to the stars, I want to know where."

I spent limited time with Damali's brother TallSpot and the astronauts. Did they share that information? I don't think so. And even if they did, how could I tell Bamboo? He knows nothing of what happened in the prince's palace. He doesn't even know that I met Damali there.

"We're in uncertain days, ThreadBare. The visit from the Imam's inspector is a sign, I'm sure of it."

There was nothing about the inspector's visit I liked. Yet... "A sign?"

"We're a target too, of course. But more protection from a man like—" Bamboo winces, as if getting a stop. He then smiles and straightens. "You recall Tanzer's Caution?"

"'A fix should never be worse than the problem.'"

"Correct," he says. "Value judgments are involved here, dangerous paths, but I know what I fear." He looks toward the skyline and then shakes his head. "I must prepare for all eventualities." He smiles. "You pursued mysteries in the past. Would you pursue mine? Learn what you can about that ship? About where it went?"

"I...I can try."

"Your research abilities are a specialty."

"I don't think that's true. I do what any—"

He holds up a hand. "You underestimate yourself. Now is the time to step beyond your wall of inferiority." He looks down, and then looks at me again. "If anyone can learn something, I believe it's you."

I bow my head as best as I can. "I will try, master."

"Excellent," he says. "I will return you to your sleep."

The conversation ends. I remain as I am: eyes open, inside the chute, staring at its interior.

The Founder's law doesn't allow for body containers of any kind in funerals. The dead are washed, covered by a sheet, and laid straight into the ground with only wooden boards set atop them to keep the dirt away.

Other faiths, now lost to time, allowed for such containers, though. As a child I was frightened with stories about sleeping people being placed inside a death container before their time. Buried alive. Trapped beneath the dirt with no way of escape.

How I feel now must be what it felt like for them. The walls are close, my body is cramped, and the air seems stale. And no one can come to my aid. No one knows my true state.

The most direct line to what Bamboo seeks leads through Damali. If she doesn't know where DarkTrench went, her brother would. But where is he now? He's a fugitive, and so could be anywhere.

I fear the outside now. Especially if it means traveling to where fugitives might be. Places like the city's lowdowns. Areas known to harbor antitex. Such places will be extra dangerous now. Soon filled with soldiers and combat heavies.

What other connections to the ship do I have, though? What have I seen?

Datamixes! I've seen related datamixes. One was of a scientist who thought space could be flipped like a card. ArrowMast. Another was a designer named Kicker. Kicker met Jahm and Jahm worked for Prince Aadam.

Their mixes came from FrontLot, though, and he's offline. Killed by antitex.

WindCypher provided my last mix. Would he have something? Maybe.

I pull for a list of traders. I get the usual stacks of irrelevant references, discard them, detour through a DR routing station, hop across an Imam-ordered security blockage, and finally arrive at a trader list.

Cypher is near the top with an ad proclaiming a slag of new inventory. After him are other names I've encountered before— ChoppedFeta, OrangeDraft, SilverRaze—along with a couple new ones.

Near the bottom is an unexpected salute to FrontLot—a rotating diamond with his hologram in the middle and the scent of roses. "Antitex victim" the caption reads.

I message Cypher and wait.

Day 82 10:02:45 p.m.

[Facility Quarters]

CYPHER SITS IN HIS characteristic suspended rope chair. His room is dim with lots of web-like shadows in the background. There are two motion-lamps on either side of him that rotate like spiral galaxies.

Cypher is dressed in a beige, wraparound robe that reminds me of a slug. A slug in a sling. He holds a long drinking cylinder in his right hand.

"Ah, the Holy City's hero," Cypher says, raising his cylinder. "A pleasure to see you again." He smiles. "Please tell me you've come to sell this time. Mixers would love to live your accomplishments."

My accomplishments? What have I accomplished? I check my presentation of myself, which to him would seem like I'm sitting, fully-clothed, on the floor in my room. "I've been about master business," I say. "No more and no less."

"Yes, master business. Of course." He sets his cylinder on a small, suspended platform and punches the air. "Some master business can't be obscured. Always strikes its way through the walls of authority."

"How could you know anything?"

He narrows his eyes and shakes his head. "We are bound by rules, but freeheads are not." He shifts forward. "Freeheads talk. I've viewed their flat and lifeless videos and even in those..." He smiles and crosses his arms. "You were fantastic. Like a kendo master of old."

"Kendo?"

He runs a hand down his chest. "Competitors dressed in armor and struck each other with swords," he says. "It strengthened them." He

74

points at his head. "Made them strong here—" He points at his heart. "And here."

"I'm not a fighter," I say.

"Ah, but you are," he says. "And the best kind. Crafty. Easily underestimated." He bows his head. "It's an honor to serve you."

"I'm nobody," I say without thinking.

"Nobody is nobody. You least of all." He reaches for his drink cylinder and takes a long draft. "Now...how can I help you?"

"I need a mix," I say.

He sighs. "Always wanting. Never giving."

"What?"

He laughs. "I jest. I'm serious about your experiences, though. You should share." He shrugs. "We all should share more, right?"

"I have no idea." Sharing can be dangerous and painful.

"You do. I'm sure you do." He smiles. "Remember, I only sell. Never rent."

"Do you have anything by someone called ArrowMast?" I say. "Or Kicker?"

He touches his chin. "ArrowMast, also called Kicker? Let me—"

"No," I say. "They're separate people. Two easy names."

"Ah, my mistake. UK sector for the first, I think. Not sure about 'Kicker.' That could be from anywhere." He swings in his chair and murmurs as he swims the stream.

The weight of the day is inescapable now. Made worse by the fact that my eyes are physically closed. Cypher will be a part of my dreams soon if I'm not careful. "Anything?"

He shakes his head. "I'm not able to find your favs this time. Is there a particular subject you're after? Something I can cross reference?"

I stare at the inside of my chute. Uncertain.

"I hate to hurry you," Cypher says, "but I have other customers waiting."

I close my eyes and focus. "Sure," I say. "Space, maybe? Something about space and starships?"

Cypher winces. "Ooh, I sort of got squeezed out of that."

"What?"

He shrugs. "Space is niche. Small demand. Plus, Treble gets all the best stuff."

"Treble?"

"TrebleBinary, heard of him?" Cypher leans back. "As much as I hate you going elsewhere, I want you happy. Happy customers mean more sales later, right?"

"Sure. Do you have a quick con—?"

An orange ball appears in his hand. "Connect is right here. You ready?"

I nod, and he tosses the ball. I grab it midair, and gripping it tight, say, "Goodbye."

An instant later, I'm in a small, circular amphitheater. The seats and carpeting are deep blue. The ceiling is curved and stark white. There's a large black machine in the center of the room that reminds me of the spider used for implantation. It's ant-shaped, fixed to the floor, and tilted at a forty-five-degree angle. There are dozens of circular openings all over its surface.

An older debugger dressed in a silver uniform is near the front of the room. He's mid-thirties. Almost as old as Bamboo. He has narrow features and circular glasses. He smiles and gives me a little wave. "Welcome, traveler," he says.

"ThreadBare," I say, bowing my head.

"Of course," he says. "I'm known as 'Treb' or even 'TB,' if you prefer."

"I'm a TB too."

"Of course you are." He smiles softly. "How can I help you?"

"I'm looking for something with a ship," I say.

He brings his hands together. "Well, I have many ships. Many sights throughout the cosmos. Do you have a particular destination in mind?" The room darkens until the ceiling becomes a starfield.

"I'm having a special on Europa flyovers." The ceiling view starts to rotate, with the pinpricks of light seemingly swooping over my head.

I'm glad I'm lying down now. "Can you...?" I say. "Can you stop th—?"

A larger-than-average sphere reaches the middle of the ceiling, and the motion ceases. That sphere increases in size until it's obvious that it's the banded planet Jup. Smaller spheres zip around it. "Rent two Europa experiences and I'll throw in a Ganymede landing. Largest moon in the system! Watch an aurora as it happens!"

"Anything farther out?" I say.

The Jovian system rotates off to my left, disappearing into the theater's horizon. "Ah, a deep sky explorer," he says. "My favorite kind."

A spiral galaxy appears at the ceiling's center. It's an edge-on view, such that the system's entire expanse is visible. A bright yellow center surrounded by four red-tinged arms.

"Any location in mind?" Treb asks.

Would he know about DarkTrench? Chances are slim. "What options do I have?"

"Everything deep sky is extrapolated from telescopic observations. Aside from a handful of extrasolar probes there's little to—"

I can't keep my eyes from the galaxy. "How many stars are there?" I say.

"Excuse me?"

I substantiate a red pointer within our conversation and aim it at the spiral. "How many stars are in that display?"

"Close to a trillion in the pinwheel galaxy."

"A trillion?"

"Yes, almost ten times more than our own galaxy. More than all the local galaxies, in fact. If you like, I can—"

"All those stars," I say. "Many choices."

He's a voice in the darkness now. "And every single star is unique in its appeal. All reveal new mysteries. Pose new challenges. It can be overwhelming."

"How would you choose?" I say. "Where would you go?"

"Hmm... a difficult question. I have many favorites."

"If you had to make a choice?" I say. "A single star."

"One of the largest stars, I think. Those that our forefathers relied on as they journeyed across the desert." The galaxy moves away, and a giant red star comes into view. "This is al Dabarān, the Follower. There's also *an-Nisr uṭ-Ṭā'ir* the Eagle and *Rijl ul-Qanṭūris* the Centaur's Foot."

"Only those three?"

"No. There's many more." Another red star appears, though this one is slightly misshapen. "Yad al-Jauzā. The hand of the Central One." The star shrinks into a background of surrounding stars that suggests an hourglass. "The constellation name was later changed to 'al-Jabar.' A feminine to masculine switch. It always represented a hunter, though."

"It looked strange," I say. "When you had it up close."

"It's unstable. And often shows signs of that deformity."

"It's broken?"

Treb chuckles and the constellation shifts away. "Possibly. It wouldn't be my first choice. An intriguing star system, though." The ceiling sky fills with stars again. "Let's see...there's also an-Niṭāq, the girdle and Fum al-Hul meaning 'the mouth of the whale'."

"Like the story of Yunus?"

"Yes. Swallowed by a whale."

I understand that feeling, as well. I fight to keep my eyes open. To stay in this conversation. Why did I connect with a mix dealer who prefers space?

I'm getting nowhere. Gaining nothing.

"What can I share with you, ThreadBare? What journey can I send you on?"

The room lights brighten enough that I can see Treb again.

"I have no idea," I say.

Treb smiles. "I don't believe that. Debuggers *always* have ideas."

I shrug. "Well, I don't know which to choose."

"How about I give you a low-cost introductory tour? Perhaps one to the moon and back?"

I've been to the moon already with Bamboo. It was cold, lifeless, and lonely. "No. I should go. I need sleep. It has been a long day for me."

"For everyone world over." Treb walks toward the central ant-like device.

"What is that thing?" I ask. "What does it do?"

"Ancient star projector." Treb lays a hand on the machine's side and sweeps the other hand over the seats. "Used in a theater like this once. A 'planetarium,' it was called." He smiles. "This is only a replica, of course. Everything important today is a replica of something that was."

His words aren't making sense anymore. I need to get back to sleep. "The lopsided one," I say. "I'll take a trip there."

He bows his head. "I have just the thing." He sends me a price for the promised journey. "A bargain. I gave you the new client discount."

I sigh and send him the required amount.

"Enjoy your trip," he says.

The mix hits my storage like a bomb. Heavy and then bright.

DATAMIX SHARE 74-111/DR 532

I OPEN MY EYES to confusion. A globe of fire that's giving birth.

I'm seated in a wide chair behind a desk full of controls. Beyond that is a large window—or a vidscreen—a sizable portion of which is filled by a mottled and misshapen ball of red, black, and yellow.

"What is that?" I ask. "What's that fire?"

I notice that I'm wearing a black uniform with gold accents. Military apparel.

I loathe the Imam's military, though. Ever since Delusion. Ever since the heads.

What's going on?

Someone grips my shoulder and shoves.

I trace the hand up its arm to its owner—a woman in a uniform like mine. She has blonde hair and wears no head-covering. She's strikingly attractive.

An uncovered woman in the military? Alone with me somewhere? I'm more confused.

She smiles brightly. "Thought I lost you there for a second, Thread. Are you all right? It's me, Solice."

Behind her is another seat with a control desk. And beyond that is a doorway. Otherwise, the room feels cramped and narrow. The walls are smooth and dark grey. The ceiling and floor, a lighter grey.

"Sorry," I say. "I'm a little—"

"Disoriented?" Solice nudges my shoulder again. "All normal. Effects of time dilation." She backpedals to her seat and slides into it. "You didn't expect to move over 700 light years and feel nothing, though, did you?"

"700 light years?"

She smiles. "A long, long way. But it was a smooth trip. No damage to our ship's major systems." Another smile. "Means we can get home again."

"We're on a ship?"

"You really did lose yourself, didn't you?" She presses on her desk. "Give it a minute."

My situation comes into focus. This datamix is different. Instead of living as someone else inside their experience, I'm me inside a generated experience.

I look at the forward window again. The star must be the one I chose to visit. The lopsided one. The variable.

At its bottom pole is what appears to be a smaller star connected to it by a wide column of bright matter. "What's it called again?" I ask.

"Yad al-Jauzā?" Solice says. "We caught it during a plasma ejection phase. A portion of its surface is being pushed away into space. Eventually, that portion will separate, cool into a dust cloud, and block part of the star's light. Back on Earth, it will look like it's blinked out for a bit."

I look at her again. "Is that normal?"

"For old Yad it is." She chuckles and pokes at her control desk. "But not for most suns. At least, not to this level." She shifts in her seat. "Stars eject matter all the time." She points toward the window. "But that? That baby is three times the size of our moon."

I study the star again. There's beauty in its fury. Rivers of fire streak its surface. A glowing corona surrounds it. Destruction and construction at work within the same body.

"Is there a system?" I ask. "Planets and such?" I lay my hand on the control desk and find that it responds to me. The surface, the individual buttons, grow more distinct and stretch upward against my fingers. How strange. One of them reads "deep scan." I instinctively press it. The desk flickers and hums.

"You're remembering things now," Solice says. "Good. Let's see what your scan finds."

Words hover above my desk's top edge. "No planets found," I say.

"Disappointing," Solice says. "But not surprising. I mean, look at that thing. Could anything survive here with all that chaos?"

I'm disappointed too. Why this star? What was I hoping to find?

"We still have work," Solice says. "Lots to learn from old Yad."

"I...I don't care about that, though."

"You will," she says. "Give it time."

I shake my head. "I don't think I will. This was supposed to tell me something. Something important."

"Relax," she says. "Let me take us in closer."

"Closer?"

A vibration passes through the ship. The screen image doesn't waver, but I sense we're in motion. Going toward the sun.

I locate a control marked "Ship status." I press it and a wedge-shaped outline appears over my desk. The wedge has a bevy of narrow projections on all sides. So many that it looks like it battled a porcupine. Beneath the wedge is a list that includes our velocity, shield status, and operating temperature. The velocity number is increasing. We *are* moving.

"We're too far away for much of the important equipment," Solice says. "This is why we came here. To take it all in!"

There's another, heavier, vibration and the velocity number jumps by a factor of ten.

"Slow down," I say. "Not so fast."

She laughs. "You're fine. Relax."

The star image suddenly fills the whole screen. It's hard not to feel unsettled. Hard not to feel like we might plunge straight into it. Along with dark valleys, I now see arches of solar material and bright, narrow peaks. Astonishing activity. Incredible detail.

"Isn't this fun?" Solice says.

What do I know about this woman? She's a personality bound to a mix! There are dangers to hyperstimulation inside a mix. Debuggers have been injured. Damaged irreparably. It is wise to be cautious.

"Don't trust my piloting?"

"I don't know you."

She laughs. "Sure you do, Thread. We met in training. Five years ago now."

I shake my head. "I'm sorry. I don't think that's right."

"Well, I haven't lost one yet." She chuckles again.

The gravity in the room seems to strengthen. I attempt to stand, but my extremities feel like they're full of sand. The room feels warmer too.

"We're shielded?" I say. "The star can't get in here?"

"Is does feel hot, doesn't it?" Solice exits her chair, walks to the wall on my left, and puts a hand on it. "Yeah, we're definitely heating up." She points at my desk. "Better check."

I focus on the desk. "Check what?" I say. "Do what?" I can't move my arms. Why can't I connect to the controls via the stream? Why limit me to touch? To inefficiency?

"The shields are your responsibility," she says.

I try to shake my head but get only halfway through the motion. The left side of my face is drawn into the seat cushion. I'm stuck there, unable to move. I can't move at all now. I can't get up. Can't operate the controls.

This is a terrible mix. I hate it.

Every mix has a panic button, though. A thought sequence that will bring them to a close. I shut my eyes and have that thought. A green camel falling into a stone well.

All sounds cease and the pressure on my body lifts. I take a long breath and let it out again. I then open my eyes.

I'm not in my chute. I'm in a large, white room with a blue muraled ceiling—a simulated sky at twilight. The room has wide support columns that are white on the bottom and blue on the top. There are no angles to them, though. They look more like something natural. Like the fusion of a stalactite with a stalagmite.

What is this? What has happened?

I hear voices. Two men talking in whispers.

I'm dressed in a black thobe now. A traditional robe commonly worn by scholars.

This has nothing to do with space travel. Why am I here?

An in-mix context switch must have occurred. How?

I tiptoe toward the whispered discussion, passing between two pillars and a small ornamental pool. The floor is heavily reflective. I glimpse the likenesses of the men there before I see them in person.

They wear dark thobes too. One man is a couple of decades older than the other, with heavy grey in his hair and beard.

They don't seem to notice me and remain locked in conversation. I keep my eyes low and my footsteps soft as I approach. I sense that they have authority over me. I want to interrupt, to find out my purpose here, but I won't. I shouldn't.

"It's an impossible task, Mawla" the younger man says. "Unknowable."

The older man shakes his head. "The Imam's will must be fulfilled."

"He's not well. He's not—"

The older man shushes him. "It's not ours to judge." He looks toward the ceiling. "Our sole concern is here. This facility."

"But BlackRock of all things?" The young man shakes his head. "The tests are inconclusive. We don't even know that it came from above. It could have just as easily—"

"It fell from the heavens!" The older man points severely upward. "That is the tradition. That is what the Imam believes. What true followers of A believe."

The young man bows repeatedly. "Yes. But it's not eternal. Despite every effort it's almost gone."

The older man takes a long breath, holds it for a second, and then nods. "The sins of men, the pilgrims' touches, have worn it away." He stretches his arms wide. "Hundreds of years ago, it was a cubit square." He sighs and lowers his arms. "Now only the smallest of stones remain. When it is used up, when the last particle is gone, so is our connection to A. So is the Imam's power." He wags a finger. "This fear is what rebels feed on."

The younger man shakes his head. "What has this to do with us?"

"As his enemies grow more powerful, so does his desire for defense. Like the Founder at Medina. Like the Battle of Khandaq."

"The Fight of the Trench?"

"The same." The older man smiles softly. "As the Founder built a trench of protection, so the Imam builds a trench."

"Builds? What does he build?"

The older man shakes his head. "That isn't for us to discuss."

"What can we discuss, then?" the younger man asks. "How can we assist if we don't know his plans?" He indicates the room around them. "Here of all places?"

"A replacement. He seeks a replacement!"

"A replacement to what?"

"To BlackRock!" Another bow. "And it must be indisputable. From the heavens."

"From Jannah? Only A knows where that is."

"We need to do our best," the older man says. "We need to find something that will serve in its stead."

"In its stead? Mawla! They could dig up a rock from anywhere. No one would be the wiser."

"The Imam would know. That is enough."

"So, why not choose one of the planets? Or the moon?"

"The moon is haram. Forbidden." The older man shakes his head. "And the planets will never do. We've visited them. They are not heaven. Most of them are like Jahannam. Like Hell."

The young man turns and paces away. Seconds go by as they both think in private.

I notice bright star formations in the ceiling. Designs that the mind wants to form into earthly patterns. The outlines of animals, men, and gods.

"Excuse me," I say. "Can you tell me where I am?"

Neither man looks my way. I take a couple steps closer to the older one and wave. "I'm ThreadBare," I say. "I'm not sure what this place is. I was on a ship and then—"

The younger man pivots and holds up a finger. "The Founder called BlackRock 'the hand of al-Rahman.'"

"The right hand of A, yes." The older man bobs his head, looking hopeful. "You've thought of something? Something that might work?"

I attempt to tap the older man's shoulder, but my hand passes through him like he's a ghost. Or like I am.

"That's wrong," I say. "A mix should feel real."

I find a spot between the men. Neither seems to notice. I wave a hand in the younger man's face. Nothing. "I was cheated!" I say. "Given someone's half-finished—"

I hear a tapping sound to my left, where there is a winding staircase many meters from me. Like the columns, it is white on the bottom and blue near the upper story. Midway up the stairway, is something...odd. A meter-tall brown figure. Is it a monkey?

"There are hands in the sky, Mawla."

"The shortened hand, al-Kaff al-Jadhmā', is one."

"No. That will not do."

The monkey creature raises an arm and gives me a little half wave. The proportions of its body are all wrong, though. The arms are extremely long, and the legs are too short and so close together that they seem solid.

It's not a monkey. But what could it be? A sloth? I touch the stream for an image but fetch only darkness.

I address the men again. "Is that a pet?" I ask. "Aren't pets forbidden?"

The men continue to ignore me.

I scowl and shake my head.

The tapping noise is repeated. The sloth-thing makes a hooting sound and waves.

I point at myself, and it waves again.

It can see me even though the men cannot. What a looped mix this is!

I can't wait to see TrebleBinary again. There should've been a warning. *Look out! This trip will stretch your synapses!*

I consider using the camel drop routine again, but instead creep toward the sloth. Soon, I'm only six meters from it. Close enough to learn that whatever it is, it isn't from Earth.

Why? Because it only has one wide leg that ends in a thick three-toed foot.

Also, its head is wrong. Not symmetrical in any way and larger at the bottom than the top. It has two eyes, a mouth, and a flattened nose, but its skin is rough like an elephant.

It places an arm on the step below it and hops down. It's an uncertain movement, not unlike a child moving with crutches. Its hands are wrong too. They only have three fingers.

It waves again, but I stay where I am. Far enough away that I can run if I need to.

"What are you?" I whisper.

It grunts and moves down a couple more steps. "Closer," it says in a deep and gravel-filled voice. "Come here and I'll explain."

The surreal nature of this mix has reached an apex. Not only is the sloth-thing not a sloth, but it also talks like a man.

Jinn are beings that can assume human or animal forms. They're said to favor the shapes of snakes, scorpions, and lizards, though. This creature is none of those.

This is why it's best to stick to dealers I know. Dealers I can trust.

My stomach flutters. None of this is right. From the start, it has been wrong.

Maybe this mix is a manifestation of my head damage. Maybe this is how it shows itself now? No longer in pain but in blind insanity.

I close my eyes. "I'm leaving."

"Wait," the creature croaks. "You must not tell—"

"Can't talk to jinn," I say. Then I visualize a green two-hump camel charging across a courtyard. In the center of that courtyard is a wide, stone well.

"There are larger plans," the creature says. "Seeds planted today will grow—"

"Jinn are liars," I say. "Even virtual ones."

The camel completes its journey to the well. Its front legs stretch over the stone wall. Its eyes widen as gravity takes over. It plunges down, down.

Silence returns.

Day 83 7:00:00 a.m.

[Facility Quarters]

I WAKE UP FEELING groggy and tired, as if the proceeding night's sleep didn't do me a bit of good. As if I lived everything I saw in the mix and paid the price in my physical body.

I open the chute, climb gingerly out, and cling to its side for a moment. I contemplate messaging Treble an angry piece of my mind but decide to sit on that idea for a while. There's always time for the negative later. Removing it once it's sent? Really hard.

Plus, the danger for me with impulsive responses? Huge.

No stops. No buzz. No restraints.

I don't know how the mix made a context switch. One moment spaceship. Next moment, where? A brain trust somewhere? An astronomy school, maybe?

There was insight, though. Knowledge in all of it.

I'm starting to wish I was fixing heavies again. At least then I knew what the job was. The goal.

I get a notice from Bamboo. A forward of an EI message from Inspector Mah. He wants the school moved somewhere else. Somewhere safer. Possibly, the Holy City itself.

No. That will ruin everything.

I had a task once. A side chore that took me out near the lowdowns. It was a place where new buildings were being built. Where an ancient structure was about to be torn down.

Within that building was a trove of art. Pictures of scriptural history. Noah and his ark. Danyel and his lions. Some of the images were of Isa too, I think. Isa praying in a garden. Isa knocking at a door. Isa holding a lamb.

All that beauty and history was brought to nothing, because of something I did. Destroyed, only to be replaced by…who knows what? Homes possibly. Shops or restaurants. Ultimately, it was something mundane, though. Something everyday and ordinary.

I feel like that's what's happening now. That everything I've known is on the verge of being destroyed. All of it will tumble down around me. Replaced by something else. Something nowhere near as good.

I'm free, though, right? I could go anywhere. Do anything.

Today, I could stop a similar demolition. I could refuse to help.

But can I take those I care about with me? Can I protect them?

What can one free debugger do?

"Rails," I sigh. "It's a big lot of rails."

I find a jumpsuit and put it on because I need to analyze that mix. Was any of it real? Did the portion in the astronomy school represent actual events?

The discussion was about the Imam's quest for another BlackRock, for a confirmation of his divine right.

The Imam builds his own trench.

That was the ship. It had to be.

I send an Easy Impact message BullHammer's way. I could use his advice, but I also wonder how he is. If he's safe.

Twenty seconds go by. Then thirty and forty. No answer and still no answer. Come on, Bull!

If he's sleeping, the message wouldn't wake him, though, right? It will simply be waiting there in his queue for when he wakes up, flashing a bright green color. Friendly and hopeful.

I hope he's all right.

I look at my virtual window. I need to get out. Regardless of the danger, I need a job beyond tending children. I need to debug.

There's a knock on my door. I sense no implant. No movement in the stream.

It's Damali. It must be. Visiting me here again. More danger.

The door clicks free, but there's another, cautionary knock.

"Thread?" Damali says. "Are you up?"

I manually pull open the door. The motion brings the smell of something wonderful.

Damali has a basket in one hand. Inside it are perfectly browned biscuits.

"You brought me food?" I say. "I love when you bring me food."

She laughs. "Thought it might make you feel better. It made me feel better to make them." She holds up the basket. "My mother's recipe." She smiles. "I had to fight the bots for kitchen space."

I take a biscuit, which feels good even in my fingers. Warm and soft.

"Don't burn yourself," she says. "They may still be hot."

I sample the biscuit. It *is* still hot, but not enough to hurt me. Only enough to warm the chill inside. There's a hint of butter in its flavor too. Butter and cheese. I take her hand in mine. Hold tight.

"What if I went away somewhere?" I say. "Would you come too?"

Her eyes widen. "I'd follow you." She pauses, and her face gains more color. "Could you leave your students?"

I study the floor and feel its cool, grey tile on my feet. The biscuit remains warm in my hand, though. "They'll leave me someday," I say. "All of them."

She squeezes my hand. "I suppose that's true." She stoops so she can look up into my eyes. "Did you sleep?"

I almost laugh. "I had strange dreams."

She takes a sly glance at the chute. "I don't know how you sleep in that thing," she says. "So closed off. What if you were married? Where would your spouse sleep?"

"That's..." I glance at the chute. Frown. "...something I've never thought about." Even stop-less, I'm not free. Not really. "That *no one* has ever thought about."

She nods slowly. "What were your dreams?"

"They're not important." I nibble at the biscuit. "They were partially self-induced."

"Self-what? How did you—?"

"Can we talk about your brother instead?"

"My brother?" She releases my hand and her face grows serious. "He had nothing to do with—" She motions toward the wall. "With what happened outside. He's not a terrorist."

"I wasn't implying..." I have a flash of the mix's doomed star. A thing of beauty and wonder transformed into chaos. "Are you sure?"

She stamps a foot. "He's always been a good man. A caring man."

"But he traveled to the stars." I finish the biscuit, then raise a shoulder. "It could've changed him. It *had* to change him."

Her stance softens. "It did," she says. "But only in good ways."

"How do you know?" I ask. "How could you ever know what's inside?"

I expect another flare up, but she only shrugs. "I know my brother, Thread," she says, searching my eyes. "What are you really struggling with?"

I glance at the chute again. "Do you know where he went?" I ask. "What star?"

She takes a biscuit from the basket and brings it near her face. "I told you I don't, sorry. I don't think they found what they were looking for, though. Tall and his crew."

"A replacement for BlackRock, maybe?"

"Why would he do that?" She samples her biscuit and nods approvingly. "Anyway, he never told me." She points the biscuit at me. "I think it left again, though."

I'd like to see that ship. Maybe it could tell me.

The memory of my time with Prince Aadam returns, along with a question he posed to the caged astronauts. "Where is my ship? Where is DarkTrench?" He wasn't talking about its first trip. He was talking about its *current* location. How had I missed that?

"Where is it now?" I ask. "And why?"

Damali shakes her head. "I don't know that either."

I delve deeper into my storage. In the process, a new idea forms. "Sandfly and HardCandy," I say. "Were they on that ship? Did they take it somewhere?"

Why would they do that? Why would they care?

"They didn't return with my brother and the others. So, they're some-where." She looks at the ceiling. "Maybe they stayed up there. On the station."

"If they stayed up there, they'd show up." I tap my head. "At least, their implants would." I turn and pace toward the virtual window. The image is of a forest now. Trees sway gently in a bit-induced breeze. "The prince would've dragged them back down here and tortured them." I glance back at Damali. "But they're on the offline list. They're gone."

I grab the window's connection point and push a starscape onto it. It reconfigures instantly, displaying a constellation with an hourglass shape. The hunter. A few of the possible destination stars are displayed there. But which one is right?

"So, they escaped in the ship somewhere," Damali says. "Good for them."

I frown. "Or they killed themselves." I shake my head. "But I don't think they'd do that. Especially not Sandfly."

Damali walks around to look at me. "You knew them well?"

"Not really." I study the starscape. "Well, in some ways, maybe." I touch my forehead. "I viewed...some of Sandfly's life." I smile. "It's complicated. I know what I need to do, though."

"What?"

"I need to go to that station. Find out what's up there."

Damali shakes her head. "The prince probably took everything apart."

"Maybe. Or maybe he didn't have time before he died. Maybe he wanted to focus on the astronauts first." I frown. "Torture seemed im-portant to him."

Damali looks away. "Oh, it was," she says. "That man was pure evil." She looks at me and then smiles and taps my chest. "That's why I like you. You're better than most men. You at least try to fight evil."

"I need to get up there." I take her hand, feel its warmth, but then feel uncomfortable. Exposed. "So, how do I get up there?" I frown. "I don't like the idea much. I've never been on a lift."

"Which lift?" she asks. "CA? I think it's closed."

"The space elevator?"

"I saw it on public stream," she says. "It was shut down after the attacks. Security risk."

Always an obstacle. No matter my inner state. Always something to keep me stalled. "For how long?" I glance at my chute. "I mean, it can't be long. There are people up there that would need to come down. Refueling and restocking." I look at the star image again. "Others that would need to go up."

"There are ships," she says. "They could take trips back and forth."

"It would be more difficult," I say. "But sure. At least, for a while."

I remember the food I'm holding and instinctively finish the biscuit. "Rails," I say. "Flipping rails."

Damali places a hand on my arm. "You have a skyslider, right? Buraq."

I give her a gentle hug. "Yes. Buraq could get me there. It's on the roof waiting."

She moves closer and hugs tighter. My touch sensitivity is overcome by my need for connection.

I notice the door is still open. Which is safer, for the door to be open or closed?

"Baraq will protect you," she says. "Keep you safe in the darkness."

"That's true," I say, not resisting the hug. "But it still seems impossible."

She pulls away slightly. "Bamboo won't let you go?"

"He might," I say. "But even if he agrees with the purpose, debuggers rarely *go* places. We're sent. And now with Mah around...and all that's happened..."

"You're ingenious." Damali pulls me tighter. "You'll find a way."

The contact feels uncomfortable now. Still, I can't keep my mind off the notion: I need to get to that station. Somehow.

I compose a message about the idea for Bamboo. He must see the potential in it. Not only can I research the ship, but I can search for information about the lost debuggers. Not only Sandfly and HardCandy, but the DarkTrench designers that preceded them. TallSpot said they'd been there.

I send the message. It's essential. It must happen.

"I asked him," I say.

"I'm sure it will work out," she says. "I'm sure A cubed has a plan here."

"A cubed," I say. "Yes."

I think of the datamix again. The odd creature. Was it trying to warn me of something? It seemed like it was. It was so strange. So out of place.

"A cubed," I say. "What does it mean?"

"I've told you before," she says. "It means freedom."

Partially clenched together, we turn so I can see the chute and the virtual window from the corner of my eye.

"But if A represents our God," I say. "Is A cubed another God or something else?"

"Something else," she says. "Or maybe both."

I think of my time inside the combat bot. I prayed to the miracle prophet. Not A. Or not the A I knew. "Perhaps a quality of our God that has been overlooked?" I say, "Or misrepresented?"

"Perhaps that," she says.

"I should've pulled more at the zone," I say. "I should've searched for more about him."

"Zone?"

"A place I visited with the students. A freer place."

She touches the side of my head. "In your minds? On the stream?"

I sense a presence, and turning, pull away from her.

BandStand is at my door, his face a mask.

Day 83 7:36:42 a.m.

[Facility Quarters]

DAMALI GASPS AND STEPS away. She then remembers the basket she's holding, and striding awkwardly to the door, offers it to BandStand.

He shakes his head, but after glancing at the basket, takes a biscuit anyway. He doesn't sample it, though. He only holds it at his side and stares at me.

Damali glances my direction and bows slightly. "I need to go," she says. "Master Bamboo will require my help soon. He has new projects. Items to be ordered or fetched."

After she leaves, Band and I continue to stare at each other.

"You have questions about your assignment?" I ask.

He bows his head, eyes still wider than usual. "I have questions, Mawla, yes."

I let out a long breath and then pace to my dresser and rest an arm on it. The virtual image of Damali I've affixed to the top surface watches me. It's from the day we first met at the prince's pool. Simpler times, but equally dangerous.

"Ask me anything," I say. "But remember that knowledge carries responsibility with it." I smile. "Especially for us."

He folds his hands together, cupping the bread between them. "What do you mean?"

"I mean...what you saw transferred a certain level of knowledge. Damali and I were in a room together. Close together. That is something you saw. New knowledge."

"Yes, Mawla."

"But context could alter the meaning of what you saw in many ways, correct?"

Band takes a step closer. "I...I don't know," he says. "Maybe."

"Some ways that are innocent," I say. "Some benign or incidental." I look past him to the hall. "Also, some ways haram, forbidden, or even hard to imagine."

Band squeezes the biscuit in his hand nervously. "Impossible ways even." He takes another step. Crumbs from the biscuit fall to the floor. "So, which—"

"Ah aah!" I raise a finger and smile. "If you ask a question and I answer you'll transfer additional knowledge. And because of what we are—" I point to my head and then at him. "Data Relocators—knowledge is not necessarily ours to keep. It may be shared. Even if we don't want it to be."

He shakes his head. "I wouldn't share it. I wouldn't share anything you don't want—"

"I know." I wag my finger at him. "But sometimes restraint isn't available to us. Sometimes that alternative brings us pain."

He looks thoughtfully at the floor. "I know the pain, Mawla. It's more than I thought it would be. And it isn't only in my head."

"I understand," I say. "And I hate that it's that way. For any of us."

He swipes at his right eye. "So, I shouldn't ask questions," he says. "Because it's dangerous."

"You should ask many questions," I say. "And often. But knowledge always has weight. Is this weight something you can bear? I suspect that it isn't. At least, not yet." I stand straight. "Better to assume the best. Allow for previously unguessed alternatives that could be altogether permissible and even good."

He thinks for a moment, then seems to recall the biscuit. He brings it up near his face and smells it. "I understand, Mawla. I know all that's required for now." He smiles. "Positive alternatives are already in my mind."

Feeling the crumbs from my own biscuit still on my hands, I rub them away. "Perhaps that's why you're here," I say. "Instead of one of the others." I frown. "You know the value of each of us. You understand that in whatever is coming, we—all of us—need to look out for each other."

"What is coming?"

I sense another implant. Band glances back and then stuffs the rest of the biscuit into his mouth.

Bamboo arrives at the threshold. He smiles briefly before noticing the crumbs on the floor. "There's something on your floor, ThreadBare. Where are the cleaning bots?"

I side-eye Band, who shrugs and shuffles away from Bamboo.

"They've been unreliable lately," I say. "I'll have the students look for them."

Bamboo regards BandStand for a moment and then nods. "That would be an excellent task. Along with their other work."

Band bows and moves toward the door as if preparing to go.

Bamboo raises a finger. "Wait a moment, student."

BandStand stops in place. "Yes, Mawla Bamboo?"

Bamboo looks at me. "I'm curious about your answer too, Thread-Bare. What do you think is coming?"

"Events that require wisdom," I say. "And as much knowledge as we can gather."

Bamboo nods. "I agree with your assessment. And your latest request. You should visit the CA sector station."

I bow my head. "Thank you. I will do—"

He raises his finger again. "But you are forbidden from doing so."

"I've heard they restricted lift access," I say. "But we have a ship."

He smiles slightly. "DR movement has been restricted. None are to go out without an assigned task."

I feel the presence of Damali's picture even though I don't look at it. "We need to be able to get supplies, Bamboo. Students have tasks that require—"

His face hardens. "Your role has increased your assertiveness. Are you aware of this?"

I look at the floor again. "I wasn't. Please continue."

"Every hurdle will be handled in time," he says. "A recreational visit to the station would be heavily questioned and doubtless forbidden." He glances at the crumbs on the floor again. Frowns. "But there's an opportunity that could make your visit possible." He bows his head. "I will send it to you now."

A second later a message hits my queue. A task request marked high priority. It has a highlevel requirement and a specialty that is...not mine.

"Climber maintenance?"

He nods. "One of the primaries requires maintenance. The shutdown has increased its priority level. Fortunately for us."

"I know nothing about climbers," I say. The task request suggests that they're a core part of the lifting mechanism. Possibly *the* core part.

"You've proven resourceful in the past," Bamboo says. "Even with mechanisms beyond your specialties."

"But the level requirement is—"

He smiles. "I can grant you whatever level is required."

There was a time, back in my days near Delusion, when being a highlevel was important. It meant not only a wider task protocol, but approval and perceived significance.

But none of that matters now. If I never change levels, I'll be content. I barely remember my current level. "I'm more concerned with the knowledge that comes with it," I say.

"What you don't have can be collected and sent. You'll need an assistant, though." Bamboo looks at BandStand. "This one is the perfect candidate."

BandStand's eyes widen. "Me?" He glances at me. "I'm...I'm not—"

"Others are further in their training," I say.

Bamboo studies BandStand. "This one was with you when you faced the string sheer, correct?"

"Yes, but..." I pause, unsure of how much of the past to bring up. BandStand also ran away. His actions got us both taken by antitex and fearing for our lives. Is that a strength or a liability?

"Yes," BandStand says. "That was me."

"He has much to atone for," Bamboo says. "Much to prove. An ideal selection."

"I'll consider it," I say.

"There's little time for that," Bamboo says. "I've already accepted the request for you. It was the only way."

I take a long breath. "Okay...I guess I'm going." I tap my dresser. "I'll collect some things. Make sure my bag is fully stocked. I'll downride as far as I can. Take a train when necessary."

"To the ground station?" Bamboo asks. "We've been over this. It's closed."

"But wouldn't the climber be there?" I ask. "Waiting to take the next lift up?"

"Again, I'm reminded that fundamental knowledge gets lost amid the rigors of implant training." Bamboo frowns. "All the more reason to take a student with you. Perhaps you should take more." He shakes his head and paces into the hall. "There are multiple lifts per ribbon. Multiple climbers."

"So, where is the malfunctioning climber?" I ask.

Bamboo points upward. "For safety, it's anchored below the geostationary orbit altitude."

I breathe in slowly and reach into the stream for soothing music. "How far?"

"About fifty kilometers."

"I don't have the experience for this."

BandStand's eyes dart between my face and Bamboo's. "Is it difficult to reach?"

"Not to reach," I say. "No. Not with a skyslider."

Bamboo shows a muted smile. "The debugging life is rarely simple, Thread. Rarely without complexity."

"Mawla?" Band says.

"The climber is still on the tether," I say. "Hanging somewhere in space."

Day 84 8:03:07 a.m.

[Facility Roof]

I TAKE A DAY to plan and prepare. I pack two debugging bags, one for me and one for BandStand. But I intend that his bag will only serve as a backup to mine. I can't let a no-level like him leave the safety of the ship, and I tell him as much. He will be my stream assistant and another set of eyes.

"More than any job I'd ever done," I say as we make our way around the facility, "this one will require working in three dimensions. I can't afford to miss anything. Everything is important."

Band seems to understand. There is a hint of disappointment in his eyes, though. "I will be at my best," he says. "I'll watch and search."

We assemble clothing bags for after the trip and locate suits and helmets for when the cabin of the skyslider is open—when the amount of oxygen will be unpredictable and doubtless thin. Thankfully, the ship, Buraq, has suits already on board. He assures me they are in top condition.

All that remains then is to say goodbye. I gather the students in a virtual room and share my upcoming task. They accept the news with mixed emotions. Some are envious of BandStand's inclusion. Others are sad that they'll be instructed by Bamboo while I'm away. Others simply want to move ahead with their projects and fear they won't be allowed to. The loudest complainers, in fact, are those in Band's group. Their prototype is ready for a physical rendering. They want to make sure they have the resources they need.

Bamboo has foreseen this possibility. Orders have been placed for all that the students require.

That helps with their mood. It doesn't remove the negativity completely, but it helps.

The remaining hurdle is Damali. We stop by her room on the way to the roof. She doesn't like the assignment at all. She questions everything to the point that I wonder if my stops haven't been replaced by her instincts and preferences. But in the end, her experience with Buraq opens the door. Even though Damali doesn't trust my circumstances, she trusts the ship. "It has the common sense to bring you home," she says. "Even when you don't."

She looks at BandStand. "You'll enjoy this experience, I think." She wags a finger at him. "But don't enjoy it too much. You'll fall out and float to the sun!"

I don't bother telling her the impossibility of that outcome. I instead remain quiet as she asks BandStand for a moment of privacy before embracing me and kissing me full on the mouth. Privacy was a wise decision. I wouldn't want to explain a kiss to the already suspicious youth.

Bamboo meets us on the roof. He stands in front of the uncovered and gleaming Buraq. The ship's exterior is red now—freshly painted to both prepare it for space and disguise its past. Beyond the ship, the sky is a dark blue with harsh red where the sun makes its way into the morning sky. The city appears serene, with every tower and temple displaying a warm glow on the side facing our star.

The call to prayer has only just ended.

Right now, citizens step through the required rituals, mouthing words that billions have spoken over the centuries. Words of praise and pleas for mercy based on righteous deeds. Rebukes of those who have failed and deserve judgment. All delivered in a singsong voice and accompanied by sitting, standing, kneeling, and prostrating poses.

None of it is required for debuggers. We're living martyrs, our lives surrendered to a technological jihad. At least, that's what I thought before I was freed.

But now?

Uncharacteristically, Bamboo approaches me and lays a hand on my shoulder. "I pray the best for you in this, ThreadBare." He studies the ship and seems to ponder what to say next. "I'm not bound by emotion or connection," he says. "My life is filled with continual transition. Continued loss."

He looks at me. "But your presence here has been welcome. You've filled a vital role." He frowns. "It would be unfortunate were you not to return." He removes his hand, concealing it with the other behind his back.

I bow my head. "I'm glad I was found useful, Master."

"Not perfect," he says, smiling. "But useful nonetheless." His eyes shift to my forehead. "I realize now that we haven't checked your implant since you've returned. We should do that before you go. If only to be safe."

"I run its diagnostics often," I say. "It's performing as per spec."

"The diagnostic rainbow can miss errors," he says. "A better test would be independent of the implant."

"There's been no sign of malfunction," I say. "Its container seems adequate, as well. No pain anymore. No problems."

Bamboo searches my face, as if trying to view the teardrop within. "In this case, performance is imperative. For both man and machine." He looks at BandStand. "As a student, you're required to protect your master. Protect and aid. I'll expect regular messages with your observations." He raises a finger. "Most importantly, DR 325, be of service. Serve your instructor and learn from this time."

BandStand bows. "Yes, Master Bamboo. I will."

Bamboo closes with a penetrating stare. "You must reach the station. We need information."

I nod and take a step toward the ship. "I understand."

"Your time there should have its own designation," he says. "Something that will keep it separate and away from your other tasks. Is that clear? No other master can lay claim to it. Mark it as 'leisure,' if you must."

"It will be in my private space," I say. "Of course."

He looks at BandStand. "That goes for both of you."

Band nods. "Yes, Mawla Bamboo."

Satisfied, Bamboo flares a hand. "Peace be with you." He then turns, walks to the roof door, and disappears inside.

"I don't think he likes us," BandStand says.

I smile slightly. "Is that what you took from that?"

Band hefts his bag onto his shoulder. "He frightens me," he says. "He frightens all of us. And the younger boys...." He shakes his head. "They whisper terrible things in their sleep."

I glance at the closed door where Bamboo disappeared. "I did too. This is not a...good place. The process, the training, belongs in nightmares." I lift my debugger bag and put it over my shoulder. "I don't know if Bamboo is a hardened man or something worse."

I point toward the rising sun. "To the east are things that I *know* are worse, though. So, for now, I serve the unknown because of the known." I look at him. "But mostly, I serve you and your classmates."

BandStand nods, looking thoughtful.

I stream to the ship and its canopy opens. The interior surfaces are still dark blue. The leather seats as inviting as ever. The scent of cinnamon—Buraq's selection—mixes with the scents of the city around us, and then finally, overpowers them.

"Good to see you again, Thread," Buraq says. "I hope your days have been pleasant since you were last with me."

"They've been interesting," I say. "And how are you?"

The ship pushes a diagnostic at me that shows no warnings or areas of concern. It's so clean, in fact, that Buraq almost seems to be bragging.

"Any concerns, debugger?" the ship says.

"I have many," I say. "But few involve you."

"This will be a comfortable trip," Buraq says. "Look, I've found new entertainment options." It presents a selection of simulation modules, many of which are quite recent. Reenactments of past conflicts and historical epics, starring performers twice as attractive and half as old as the figures they portray.

I push the sim list away, place my bag on one of the front seats, and motion to BandStand.

He hurries over, hands me his bag, and nimbly climbs inside. His eyes widen as he enters. His hands linger on every surface. Finally, he drops into the rightmost seat.

"It's delightful to have another passenger," Buraq says. "The more company, the better."

Seat restraints snake out over Band's shoulders and around his waist, causing him to gasp.

"You all right?" I ask.

BandStand's face grows stoic. "Yes, Mawla, all is well." He pats the seat. "This is a fine ship. Very sturdy. Very safe."

I smile and look at the ceiling. "I'm sure Buraq agrees." I put both bags into the rear seats and do my best to secure them. The ship steps in then, wrapping seat restraints around them.

"Buraq?" Band says.

I lower myself into the other front seat. "That's the ship's name, yes."

"It comes from the name of a legendary steed," the ship says. "I picked it myself."

"I like it," Band says. "It's a good name."

"I'm happy to hear that. I have a colorful sim of Buraq's adventures, if you'd like to—"

"Maybe later," I say as the restraints move over me.

"Of course, Thread." The canopy closes and the engines engage, producing a sound between a whine and a purr.

I give the ship the coordinates of the CA lift via the stream. It acknowledges, the engine noise increases, and we lift off. The grey roof of the facility rolls away below us. We then pass the building's upper story. I notice the shadow of someone standing at one of windows there. At first, I think it is Bamboo, but then our orientation shifts, and I detect a covered face and a raised hand.

Damali.

[Skyslider TS-731]

THE CA LIFT BECOMES visible four hours later. Even from a hundred kilometers away, its tether is a breathtaking sight. A thin column of darkness that connects earth to space.

The lift's ground-based studiopad soon becomes apparent. It's a torus-shaped building that, when the lift is present, encompasses the platform and the lower stories of the climbing capsule. It's lined with windows that gleam silver in the midday sun.

The weather today is muted, though, with patches of clouds and a strong chance of rain. Consequently, the lift ribbon appears to start in the middle of the studiopad abscess and ascend straight up into a bank of clouds. A meteorological symbol of the many mysteries that lie above.

"It doesn't sway at all," BandStand says. "How does it stay so straight?"

"Not my specialty," I say. "And I'm not sure I want it to be."

"The Earth's rotation maintains it," Buraq says.

Band looks at the ceiling, the location of Buraq's auditory outputs. "I thought the Earth brings things down," he says.

"Indeed, planetary gravity pulls things down, young data relocator. But in the case of this lifting mechanism, there's an orbiting counterweight that's being pushed away from Earth by the Earth's own motion. Imagine securing a rock to a string and spinning it overhead. The rock in that example is the counterweight and your hand would be the lift's anchor point on Earth."

BandStand rocks back in his chair. "Earth doesn't move fast enough for that," he says. "It hardly moves at all."

"Sixteen hundred kilometers an hour," I say after a quick stream touch.

"Seems fast enough to keep the counterweight, the orbital station, in orbit, doesn't it?" Buraq says.

"And to keep the ribbon straight." I check the ribbon outside and frown. "I should've known that."

"Men aren't made to know everything," Buraq says.

"You're used to normal men," I say. "Not debuggers."

"It's true, Thread," Buraq says. "You're abnormal."

BandStand chuckles.

I give him a stern look. "And why is that funny?"

Band hides his mouth. "I'm sorry, Mawla. The ship made me laugh."

"As it insulted me?" I say. "Such disrespect. How did you not get stopped for that?"

He studies the excess seat next to his left leg and then places a hand over it. "I don't know," he says. "I only laughed."

I smile and look outside. As we draw closer to the lift, we're also ascending. We'll reach the cloud layer soon. "You have the capsule's location?" I ask.

"Your coordinates were precise," the ship says. "We're a couple of hours away. Would either of you like a refreshment? I have a stocked supply."

"Of food?" I say. "Who stocked that?"

"My stored refreshments are constantly monitored for freshness and quantity. Only a few items were near their expiration date prior to our trip. Those were replaced by the flight coordinator."

"The flight coordinator?" I narrow my eyes. "Who's that?"

"The female," Buraq says. "Damali."

"His girlfriend," BandStand adds.

A hundred responses fly through my head. Denial, rebuke, and silence are all heavily considered. "My girlfriend," I say finally. "Yes, of course."

"Is that how you'd like me to refer to her?" Buraq asks. "Given the previous trip she was on—"

"No," I say. "Her name is fine."

"Noted," Buraq says.

Band chuckles again.

"You're laughing a lot," I say. "It might be the altitude." The ship's systems should compensate for all atmospheric changes, though. "You should have some water. It'll clear your neural paths."

"My paths are clear and straight, Mawla." Band leans forward and squints, looking outside. "What if there's lightning, ship? Will you be hurt?"

A mild citrus scent enters the cabin. "I'm designed to be safe in all conditions," Buraq says. "Including storms."

Band nods and continues to watch the nearing atmospheric blanket.

"Weather won't be a factor to your accomplishing your task either," Buraq says. "We will be far above all that."

Thirty minutes later, we enter the wall of grey. Our view of the elevator ribbon ends along with any sense of location. There's no ground below and seemingly no brighter sky above. Only grey.

Soon, water begins to bead on the canopy and then runs down it in narrow rivulets.

"Is it raining?" Band asks.

"In a sense," Buraq says. "Any moisture you observe on my surface comes from the vapor that comprises the clouds. The same is true for any showers that strike the earth below. So, the water that surrounds us is future rain, even while it's not actively falling."

Band grins. It's all adventure to him now. As much as I appreciate him having the experience, I can't help but question whether it's good for him to be here. I'm surprised Bamboo suggested it, in fact. He knew the potential for distraction. Why would he encourage it?

The ship pitches left and drops slightly. BandStand yelps and grips the sides of his seat. My hands instinctively splay out. One finds a flexible wall-mounted handle and the other grips the narrow console between seats.

"What was *that*, ship?" Band asks.

"Nothing of concern," Buraq says. "Turbulence isn't uncommon in these situations."

"Don't you have gravity compensators?" I say.

More citrus. "Gravity didn't cause that movement, sorry," Buraq says. "Your heart rate is significantly elevated, ThreadBare. Is there some way I can help you?"

I'd forgotten about the ship's health-monitoring systems. I study the seat cushion, where I suspect the sensing equipment is located. If I applied a sheet, what would I see? A lattice of nanopaths and temp receptors? Microscopic needles and sweat buckets? Could they be disabled?

"I'm fine," I say. "Just keep us level."

"That's always my intent."

I try not to focus on the clouds. They feel encroaching and dangerous now. Like smothering entities that we'll need to fight through to escape.

I shut my eyes and dip into the ship's stream. It suggests a mix of ocean sounds, sunrises, and chamomile. One thing the health systems don't know: I'm allergic to chamomile. Any interaction with that will make me sick.

I should've gotten a mix. Someone else's life experience would be better than this.

I went without one last time, of course. Last time, Damali was here. Last time, there was romance.

"How long until we—?"

Another jerk, and the ship rotates sixty degrees to the right. Band-Stand laughs.

I peer at him through half-closed eyes. "What's funny now?"

"It's like a ride," he says. "Like the automated wonderparks my mother used to talk about. She promised to take me when I was older." His face calms, and he looks at the floor for a moment. "I never went."

I release my grip on the console long enough to point outside. "This is better than any park," I say. "Believe me."

He nods. "My siblings would've loved this."

"They'd be jealous of you now," I say. "Jealous and proud."

He nods again but says nothing. Five minutes pass in silence.

Suddenly, there's a flash of light. The ship lurches and vibrates hard enough to rattle my teeth. "Buraq?"

BandStand makes a drawn-out mewing sound followed by, "Not...fun...this time. So...not...fun."

There's another upward surge. The ship rocks, spins, and then jerks free of the clouds, leaving us in crystal skies.

To our right is the dark vertical line of the lift ribbon. And on it, positioned at the start of space, is the blue cylinder of the climbing capsule. The near side reflects the sun's light, giving it the appearance of vitality and cleanliness.

The interior should be empty and lifeless, though. The capsule was sent here for repair. For the near future, it is little more than a hollow shell.

"Our remaining travel time is forty-two minutes," Buraq says. "It should be a smooth trip from now on."

"It looks fragile," BandStand says. "Like anything could knock it off. Or break the string."

"You mean like a downrider string?" I say. "The ribbon is stronger than those. It has to be."

"That's correct," the ship says. "Lift tethers are hundreds of times stronger than the plastisteel cables uses for ground-based vessels. There have been experiments with incorporating similar hexagonal molecular structures in downrider cables, though."

"Because of string shears," Band says. "We've seen them up close."

"Those shears were sabotage," I say. "Strings rarely snap on their own. Takes thousands of trips. A lot of wear."

I don't want to linger on string shears too long. It could lead to the recounting of everything that happened afterwards, including antitex and the debugger deaths.

I don't know how much Band has internalized. He was fully checked after our time as hostages, but how much can health scans and diagnostics really find?

"We're fixing the lifting mechanism," I say. "Not the ribbon."

Band gives me a side look. "I was wrong to leave," he says. "Before antitex took us. I should've stayed with the class." He looks outside. "I don't know why I left. That was flipping null."

"I understand," I say. "We all miss home sometimes."

I rarely do, though. That part of me has become dim. Like another life. Would my parents even recognize me today?

They wanted martyrdom for me, a place in Jannah where virgins washed my feet and fed me fruit.

Perhaps BandStand's parents weren't that way. Perhaps their positions in life dragged them to it. Surrendering their boys out of need.

"I don't miss it," Band says. "Not anymore."

"No?"

He shakes his head. "I want to make the world a better place. A safer place." He smiles as he looks at me. "My project is part of that. If we can get it to work." He looks at the window again. "I'd miss it, though. The part where we make it real."

"Your partners won't get that much done while we're gone," I say. "You'll have plenty of time."

"Most of the design is mine," he says. "I want to see it work."

"I understand that too," I say. "We'll be as quick as we can."

"We're going to the station after?"

I nod. "Master Bamboo wants me to check on something." I motion skyward. "A few of us were lost up there."

His eyes widen. "Antitex?"

I shake my head. "No. Something else."

"Sorry to interrupt," Buraq says. "But I believe the young debugger needs a change of subject. His blood pressure is—"

I smile at Band and point to the ceiling. "You're scaring our mom."

"Buraq is a masculine designation," the ship says. "Though, as a mechanical device, I'm not—"

"Your concerns are noted," I say.

The climbing capsule looms large now. The equivalent of a multi-story building, it contains ample space for everything from theater-like observation rooms to shops and private dwellings. Were it not for the intricacies of the lift system and the gravity assists, it would plunge to the Earth like a meteor.

The lifting engine we've been tasked to fix is in the bottom section.

I query the stream for engine schematics. They're almost overwhelmingly complex, but not impenetrable. The first chore will be to isolate the failing component, which will make a large problem smaller.

I notice movement beneath the capsule. The tether shifts subtly in the atmosphere, but along with that, there's an anomaly. A place where the tether is larger than it should be. We're too far away, though, to see clearly. It could be a mirage. A trick of my senses fueled by our journey through the storm.

Still, I lean forward as far as my restraints will let me.

"Are you in discomfort, Thread?" Buraq asks.

I shake my head, but I find myself whispering a prayer. A request for clarity. To be able to see the unseen. Not only in this instance, but always.

The lump shifts and then breaks up. I stretch forward and wipe the surface of the canopy, hoping it will help. The lump returns. Is it an animal of some kind? I can see individual limbs. Or possibly wings.

"Do you see that?" I say. "On the ribbon, something is there."

"The capsule touches the tether in multiple locations," Buraq says.

"Where?" BandStand asks. "What do you see?"

I point at the tether and don't take my eyes from it. The lump shifts again. Something is clearly perched on the ribbon. Something brown, holding tight. A bird, perhaps?

"How high are we?" I ask. "Do birds fly this high?" I look to my left. Not only can I see a suggestion of space above, but I can also see the curvature of the Earth below. Cities have given way to green landmasses and dark blue waterways.

"At this altitude, the oxygen is too low for most avians," Buraq says.

I check the tether again. The creature is still there and appears to be rocking. Its body parts are hard to discern. An amorphous entity.

"I don't see it," BandStand says.

"I don't know how to show you any better."

The creature's head turns our direction. Dark eyes study us for a moment and then look toward the ground.

The creature jumps.

It drops straight past us. I never see wings. I never see anything bird-like. I'm able to count the number of appendages, though.

There are three.

Day 84 11:41:22 a.m.

[Skyslider TS-731]

I LEAN BACK INTO my seat and remain still for a few seconds. What was that? What did I see? Something dark, perched on the tether. It breathed impossibly thin air, moved a little, and then leaped off—presumably to its death.

"Your heart rate is elevated," Buraq says, "but not dangerously so. Other galvanic responses seem to indicate—"

I wave a hand in the air. "Stop that," I say. "Stop trying to analyze me."

"My apologies, Thread."

I stare out the window again. I see only the ribbon and a mass of clouds below us. And above us? The capsule against a darkened backdrop.

"Must've been a bird," I say. "Or a part that fell off the capsule."

"I didn't see anything," Band says. "Sorry."

"It doesn't matter." I shake my head. "It has nothing to do with why we're here."

"We're only a few minutes away from...hello," the ship says. "What's this?"

A trio of flying objects break off from the side of the capsule and descend our way. They draw to within twenty meters of the ship and form a loose triangle. The objects are cylindrical with flattened edges and small turbine engines near their center of mass. Most prominent, though, are the elliptical openings in their fronts. Protruding from them are narrow tubes—the barrels of weapons.

"Security drones," I say. "Didn't expect that."

"Unknown craft, remain where you are until properly identified," a stern, mechanical voice broadcasts over the ship's audio outputs.

"We're here for a repair task," the ship responds.

I encounter a stream push from one of the drones. It identifies itself as a ParaSel model, formed only last year. "Top of the line," it assures me. It provides a full list of its armaments. It can bring our ship down in four ways, two of which are invisible.

I search for a tap to the drone; a way to control it remotely, but I'm hit with a cloud of generated static. Solid security. Not necessarily debugger proof, but almost.

"Authorization required," the drone voice booms.

Band looks at me with widened eyes. "What do they want, Mawla?"

"Master Bamboo said we'd be clear for this," I say. "We should be okay." To be sure, I package a message for Bamboo and stream it out. Unfortunately, it's like I dropped the message in a pool of mud, where it's floating rather than moving.

"Is the global stream available?" I ask the ship.

"Last solid connection was three kilometers ago," Buraq says. "Sorry."

"This shouldn't be hard," I say. "No one questions a debugger." The world is changing, though. That much is clear.

My mind fills with a memory from my time near the wall. A normal day of work transformed by a whistle and chaos. A missile crashed into my garage, changing everything. It could have ended my existence.

And now, more missiles. All pointed at me.

These drones are stream-aware, at least. They're not closed-up.

I have a background process that I've used to break other factory-only bots in the past. It seems like a heavy hammer, but could I use that here?

"You have twenty seconds to turn around," the drone says.

I dig through the original high priority request. Is there something there that can help? A string of numbers or an important word choice? The job was requested by one of the maintenance officials, H. Kazi. It then climbed a winding chain of titles and quasi-dignitaries before finally reaching the global task list. None of the corporations and government authorities it passed took responsibility enough to send their own DR out. So, it waited, gaining momentum.

That's where Bamboo found it. A large slug at the top of a bloated task queue. A desperate request, with no one to answer. Common for public transport problems. But a lift to space? That should get someone's attention.

Another thing I notice? The word "ghul." It's in a small paragraph written by a middle manager using terse language. Portions of the topside station are thought to be haunted now. Restricted for everyone.

This job is becoming better by the moment.

"Ten seconds," the drone says.

"How would you like to proceed?" Buraq asks. "I'm not built as a war machine."

When in doubt, try the most direct way.

"Security Drone ST-781," I say and stream, "this is Data Relocator 23, easy name ThreadBare."

"Acknowledge DR-23. A working level of fourteen is required to approach."

Fourteen is not my level. In fact, it's so far above my level that few debuggers see it in their lifetimes. The debuggers that designed Dark-Trench? They might've been fourteen.

So, now what?

Bamboo said he'd provide whatever level was necessary. But did he change my level? No way to know without going back down.

"I am a fourteen," I say without thinking.

The drones maintain their positions. I wait for another countdown or a trail of missile fire. Five seconds go by.

"You're a fourteen?" Band whispers.

I shrug and watch the drones.

Four more seconds pass. Then, in a sweeping maneuver, the drones return to the capsule.

I slowly release the breath I've been holding.

"You're a fourteen!" Band says. "That's rails cool."

I flash him a smile. "Let's get up there before they change their minds," I say. "See what the problem is."

"Of course," Buraq says. "Right away."

As we near the climber capsule, the exterior surrounding the tether slides away to reveal a circular entry point, which Buraq then negotiates.

We're soon surrounded by a dimly lit latticework of supports—the capsule's inner skeleton. The ribbing surrounds the central tether and goes all the way to the top of the structure.

Squinting, I think I see the distant gleam of the topside station through the tether aperture, but I'm not sure. It's at least a kilometer above us, hanging amidst a darkened starfield.

We ascend slowly, passing one support ring after another. The experience is claustrophobic. Confining. Like moving through a snake's gut.

"Not much room to maneuver," Buraq says.

"Land whenever you can," I say.

I dip into my previously-stored climber schematics. There are four engines distributed across multiple stories, with two being up near the top. Hopefully, one of the bottommost engines is the culprit. The less time spent here, the better.

"Does the climber have a local stream?" I ask aloud.

"I detect one," Buraq says. "Would you like me to clone it here? The response time will be limited."

I shake my head. "I can wait."

"Very good," Buraq says. "Landing now."

The ship dips to the left, rotates, and lowers itself onto a narrow horizontal platform. Landing lights engage on all sides. To our right, about ten meters away, is one of the cylinders that make contact with the tether. Ahead, I can see more of the superstructure and a series of ladders.

"Relax," Buraq says. "The strain on your body here will be minimal. A slight downward pull, roughly equivalent to the surface of the moon." It sounds like he's smiling. "It will be harder to fall."

"That's reassuring."

"If you were to, I should be able to get you in time."

I return my focus to the schematics, trying to get a fix on precisely where the engines are relative to where we are. It would be easy to get lost here. I've worked in some uncomfortable places on Earth, but this is especially disorienting. Better to concentrate on the task and take it slow.

I scan the system of ladders. "If I've read the specs correctly, there are two engines that way." I point ahead toward the nearest ladder. "I'll get a better take outside." I pat my restraints. "Let me loose, please."

The restraints drop away, and I immediately feel lighter. As if, given a little push, I could hover midair.

BandStand reaches into the back seat, grabs my debugging bag, and holds it out to me.

I take the bag and then tap on the ship's canopy. "I'm ready."

"No, you're not, ThreadBare."

"I told you to stop monitoring me. I'm nervous, sure, but I'll be fine. Now open up."

"I'm confident in your abilities," Buraq says. "However, the oxygen is scarce enough here that a breathing device is required. Even for debuggers."

I scowl and shake my head. "The suits," I say. "Right. Where are they again?"

"On the wall near your feet," the ship says. "Opening access now."

With two pops, floor-level doors open on both sides of the compartment. I see something reflective in the one on my side.

Band pulls out a suit from the panel on his side. It's bright orange.

"Who picked the color?" I ask.

"The Grand Imam," Buraq says.

Band holds his suit up. "We won't get lost!"

"Well, there's that." I remove my shoes, retrieve my suit, and pull it on. It's light and comfortable. The helmet is roughly oval and transparent. It snaps over my head easily.

I find the stream still available. "It lets the stream through?" I say.

"The suit contains a built-in connection circuit. You should feel at home."

I gaze at the dark crisscross of metal supports above. "I don't think that's possible. But at least the suit feels right."

I tap the canopy again. "If you think we're ready now...."

"I suggest you grab one of the safety straps," Buraq says.

I do so and then check that BandStand is secure too. He smiles and waves his free hand.

There's a snap and a hiss as the canopy opens. A gentle breeze forms as the cabin's heavier air moves past me. It isn't enough to pull me out, but it could've pushed me off balance were I not prepared.

When stillness returns, I climb out onto the landing platform and pull my bag over my shoulder. I look back at BandStand. He's smiling brightly.

"We're in space, Mawla," he says.

"Not yet, Master BandStand," the ship says. "But you're very close."

I point at Band. "No going off on your own this time."

He shakes his head. "Not this time. I'll stay with you."

"You'll stay here," I say, and point at the ship's interior.

"I can't help you from here," he says. "I can't learn—"

"You'll learn plenty." I check the chamber's interior structure again. It feels like being in a large web now. There's some light from the tether apertures. But still...it's almost too dark to be alone.

"Let me get a better feel for it first." I point at my helmet. "Let me stream it a bit. See what we're up against."

Band points up and right. "The malfunction is that way," he says and smiles. "The engine's screech was easy to hear in the stream. It's crying loud."

"That's helpful." I look the way he pointed. There are plenty of ladders that way. Narrow, fragile, ladders. "Still not sure about having you out here."

"Bamboo sent me for a reason," he says.

"Bamboo likes tests," I say. "This is a test." I smile. "For you or me, I'm not sure."

Band starts to climb out. "Then I need to be with you, right?"

I frown. "Maybe."

"Sure." He shoulders his bag and heads toward the nearest ladder. "This way!"

I turn back to the ship. "Should've had you keep his restraints on."

"I'm not made for that," Buraq says. "But do catch him. I really don't want to search for someone in here."

"Right."

The boy is almost ten meters away and there are blind falls everywhere. I attempt to jog but find the effort results in long-stridden bounds. Rails, the gravity.

I relax, control my motion, and manage to walk in a more typical manner. It feels like I'm creeping along, though.

Meanwhile, BandStand is having a wonderful time. He's almost to the ladder now. I stream-scold him, and he stops.

"Sorry, Mawla," he messages me. "It's so free here."

He waits for me to reach him, his hands clasped together in front.

"Don't your internal stops slow at all?" I ask.

"I wasn't disobeying," Band says. "Why would I be buzzed?"

I send him the image of Bamboo wagging a finger. "I need to be more specific with you."

I scan the series of walkways and ladders ahead of us. They end at a long platform that surrounds a massive cylinder. I reach for it in the stream and am rewarded for my effort.

The cylinder is the broken engine. And it's crying.

Day 84 12:11:42 p.m.

[CA Lift Engine Structure]

IT TAKES FIFTEEN MINUTES to reach the engine platform. It's a dark grey high-traction surface that encircles the climber cylinder. Upon closer inspection, I realize that the platform has a high-friction surface on top and bottom, meaning someone could stand on either side, depending on the prevailing pull of gravity. The engine surface is uneven the whole way around, reminding me of a giant, metal walnut. There are frequent two-meter-high obstacles to avoid or ascend and several valleys. There are also, thankfully, plenty of handholds.

Two dozen meters away, protruding through the climber both above us and below us, is the elevator's tether. In diameter, it's not much wider than a tree sapling. Yet it supports tons of weight over hundreds of kilometers.

When planted, it grows and becomes the largest of all plants.

What is this thought? Where does it come from?

I glance back at BandStand. He waits quietly behind me. He smiles and raises a hand.

"Did you hear anything?" I ask.

"I hear many things." He looks up and around us. "Creaks and groans, mostly. This place is rails big." He shrugs. "What did you hear?"

"Like you," I say. "Lots of stuff." I flash him a smile. "All right, student, another question: What do you see?"

He hesitates for a moment, but then he closes his eyes. Not physically looking, but hopefully, still seeing a lot.

I feel a touch of pride. I shut my eyes too, touch the stream, and wait.

"There are multiple issues," he says. "Many are low priority and are cascades of the primary failure."

That's what I'm seeing too. Many errors and warnings, but probably only one cause. That's good, if true. Means we should be able to finish quickly.

The scale of the device, though, worries me. Will we have the parts to fix whatever is wrong? This is not a servbot, and there's no clang and click nearby. I open my eyes and study the body of the lift, where the internal shops would be. At least, I doubt there's anything like GrimJack's here. If we don't have the part, we'll have to make it.

"Did you hear something again?" Band asks.

"No," I say. "I'm fine." I wave toward the engine. "Let's go have a look around."

We move ahead to the bulk of the engine. It is composed of two cylinders, I realize: a horizontal one that contains the bulk of the engine and another shaft-like cylinder through which the tether passes. Except the tether manages this without any motion.

"With most lifts on Earth," I say. "Like those you find in old buildings, the tether does the lifting." I point upward. "There are wheels and pulleys that the tether passes over. A machine or weight at the other end of the tether would pull the lift up or drop it down." I point at the cylinder. "Here, though, it is all in the engine. The tether is fixed. The engine moves the capsule." I smile. "Along with some gravity assist, of course."

"So, where do we start?"

I move forward and lay my hands on the engine. I expect an extreme cold or the vibrant warmth of engine heat, but I detect no temperature difference at all. Then I remember I'm wearing a suit. Of course, the suit would shield me from such dangers. Still, this machine, the touch of it, seems significant somehow. It's the largest device I've ever debugged.

"Would you like a sheet, Mawla?"

I nod and step back a bit. "Yes, that'd be a good place to start. A sheet."

Internally, I lay the schematics up against the engine and home in on the flashing areas. One is near our position. About two meters overhead, in fact. There's an obvious handhold not too far away, but little else to anchor to. I'll have to try to jump for it.

He makes firm the steps of those who delight in him.

I frown and look at Band again.

He holds out a rolled sheet. Smiles.

I take the sheet, raise my hand, and hop.

I launch straight off the platform toward the handle. My velocity feels wrong, like I'm traveling too fast and will overshoot. Panicking, I anxiously wave my arms to try to reverse my momentum. I turn sideways, instead, and somehow manage to snag the handle before it passes me. I gently pull myself against the engine.

"You all right?" Band asks.

"Got where I wanted to go," I say. My movement had to look awkward, though. I stare at the engine surface. How am I going to unroll the sheet with one hand on the handle?

I don't want to let go. Too much open space. Too many variables. What if I float away?

I glance down at Band. I'm an instructor. I need to look like I know what I'm doing, right? Even if I don't.

I pull up to a seated position. By hugging the surface of the engine with my knees, I feel more comfortable. More in control.

Finally, I release my grip on the handle, check the hot spot again, and smooth the sheet over it. The inside of the machine comes alive. I see a lot of red-colored nanopaths and blue conduits. These all circle a dead area, though. A J-shaped interchange that obviously needs to be replaced.

Thankfully, I have one of those in my bag. I start to shrug the bag off, but this action lifts me from the surface. I snatch the handle and reel myself back in.

We should've had a way to anchor ourselves. Why didn't I think of that? Or the ship? Why didn't it suggest that?

Buraq thinks the gravitation is manageable here. Safe. But nothing about it feels safe to me. Nothing is comfortable.

Don't fear. I'm with you. I will strengthen and help you. Hold you with my right hand.

Right hand? The hand of A? Isn't that where DarkTrench went?

I try removing my bag again, slower this time, and manage to do so safely. I loop one of its shoulder straps around the handle, open the bag, and rummage through it until I find the capsule-sized cutter. That, at least, feels comfortable. I ignite it—and with subtle movements—make a circle around the problem area, and pull that section of surface away. I remove the faulty intersection, slip the new one in, and give the nanos a nudge via the stream. Circulation resumes.

I breathe out slowly. At least, this time, it was easy.

I fuse the surface back in place and smooth it so it looks as good as new. I consult the schematics and the problem list. At least two issues might be similar in difficulty to the one I just fixed. Along with these, hopefully, easy fixes, there's one large, spike-filled mystery near the cylinder shaft.

"Remember your suits have limited oxygen," Buraq says. "You won't expire should the supply run out. But you will feel uneasy."

"How long do we have?"

"Approximately forty-five minutes at normal exertion levels."

Was I exerting normally? Probably not.

I check the problem list again. Bandstand could doubtless address some. Regardless of his unreliable behavior in the past, he's never shown himself incapable. Dare I risk using his skills here?

"There may not be enough time," Band says.

The structure groans again, and the engine beneath me seems to rock slightly, even though I know that shouldn't be possible.

I stream to Band a nearby problem area. "Think it's time you get directly involved," I message him.

"I don't even have a level yet," he says.

"I'm giving you something you can handle," I say. "Just take it slow." I look down at him and see his face brighten.

"Yes, Mawla!" He quickly hops onto the engine and progresses ahead.

"Be careful, remember!" I message.

"I like to climb," he messages. "I'm good at it."

I watch as he continues his forward scramble. He's faster than I'd like, but the way he positions his hands and feet, the spots he chooses, seem thoughtful and firm.

Finally, he reaches the location of the problem I assigned him. He's four meters ahead and to my right, which is still close enough that I can catch him if he starts to float away.

He positions himself over the area, sets his bag down gently, and pulls out a roll of sheets. He doesn't look back at all. "A better place." His voice carries across the thin air. "Make it better."

I shrug and return to the error list. I'm tempted to focus on the mystery problem next. One that gives me only the cryptic: "Consistency error detected. Possible fault, blockage, strip, or cart drop." Little of that makes sense, but I don't have the proper context for it. Even the schematics are nebulous when it comes to explanations. Probably that is a security thing. The designers' way of saying, "If you don't understand this, then you shouldn't be here."

I gaze off at the Earth-side aperture. Somewhere down there, someone has been trained to understand all of it. Why didn't they answer the request?

"You're getting conspiratorial, there, Thread. There's no point in that now."

I decide to get as many of the easy ones as I can. My air is limited, after all. Thankfully, the next area of concern isn't that far away. Only four meters to my right and forward a meter. I study the engine's surface in that direction. It bulges out slightly, and then there's a series of large rib-like conduits, followed by a narrow valley. I crawl over the protruding section and then crouch as I move across the rest. By the time I reach the valley, I feel more comfortable with my lack of weight and the force to movement ratio. Maybe I'm not in perpetual danger of being lost in space.

"I think I know what this is," Band says. He streams me an image of a star-shaped object amid a field of what looks like rice. There's no motion or light in any of it. "A blown motivator, right?"

I send him a clip of someone raising both thumbs. "Looks like it. You have something to replace it with?"

"It's stock," he says. "My inventory list says I have one. And if I don't, I can form it from another."

I feel a touch of pride in the boy's mental path. "You keep a list?"

"Of everything in the bag? Yes."

I smile. "That's a good habit. I should do that." I study the image he sent me again. "As for the motivator...replace it. But check it multiple times. This lift hauls people. Brothers, sisters, parents. We need to get it right."

"Of course. I will do my best and verify."

"Verify twice."

"I will."

"Good. Get it done."

I suddenly wonder what it would be like if all the students were here working together. Probably good. Probably like any time there's a large task that needs lots of debuggers. Like the day the storm took the dredges. Everyone was out that day: Sandfly, HardCandy, BullHammer, FrontLot.

I should've enjoyed that experience more. Enjoyed the process. Instead, I was worried about looking good and not getting struck by lightning.

I return to my work and within ten minutes I'm able to diagnose the issue and start repairs.

"How much time do we have, Buraq?" I ask.

"Approximately thirty-two minutes," the ship says. "Longer for the youth, I suspect."

I pat the surface of the engine nervously. Not a lot of time. It takes a minute more to seal up the repair again and confirm it.

"Ready for another task," Band says.

"You're sure?"

"Yes."

"Find one you think you can fix and go."

"Yes, Mawla Thread."

I look above and ahead toward the tether-end of the engine. That's where the big one is. I need to get up there and see what's involved, what all those cryptic words mean.

I close my bag and settle it over my shoulder. One careful hop at a time, I move forward.

Day 84 1:03:51 p.m.

[CA Lift Engine Structure]

I'm starting to feel the suit now. It doesn't pinch or rub, but it isn't completely weightless either. Even in low gravity, it adds pressure to unusual places. Plus, it adds a feeling of abstraction. As if reality has been pushed away a level. Everything I see and touch is part of a game. Someone else's life, not mine. Not unlike a datamix.

I get the urge for a mix right then. The chance to step into someone else's jumpsuit without consequences. To leave my own responsibilities and dangers behind for a few minutes.

Is that desire wrong? Sometimes, I think it is.

I continue my steady hopping motion forward. I pass BandStand's position and then move into a narrow valley on the engine's surface where large tubing brings coolant and fuel into the engine's inner chambers.

Hopefully, the problem doesn't require having to crawl inside the machine, but that's a possibility. The machine is just that big.

"Twenty minutes left to be safe," Buraq says. "You can refill and go out again, of course."

"Understood."

"The demand for this lift is tremendous. Have you accessed the news feeds lately?"

"Only looking at schematics here," I say.

"That's just as well. There are many emotions being expressed. Both for the stopped CA lift and for the changes being put forth by the new regime."

I move out of the valley onto a meter-wide band that encircles the engine. "What changes?"

"More restrictions, more surveillance, more control."

I frown. Our world has always been controlled, but recent events prove that there can always be more. How long until those changes are felt at the facility? How long until government agents are with us nonstop?

I pat the surface of the engine again. Some things I can't fix. Better to stick to those I can.

"How are you doing back there, Band?"

"Almost done," he says. "Another frozen motivator."

"Good progress! Keep at it."

I query the engine again. The primary source of trouble is only a couple strides ahead of me. Just past where the engine surface narrows to connect with the vertical collar. No hopping now. Only careful walking.

I try not to look around much as I move toward my goal. I don't want to think about the fact that the whole world is rotating to my right, dragging the tether and the orbital station along with it. It almost doesn't seem real. I know the science works, but the implementation? It isn't something I want to watch.

I reach the central collar and steady myself against it for a moment. Made of silver metal, the collar towers ten meters above me. Again, I'm surprised by the lack of temperature change I feel through the suit. The muting of surface texture. Of sound and smell. The unrealness of it.

In the stream, the area beneath my hands is a hot zone of errors. A place of reds and oranges. I find a meter-square metal doorway with a small three-by-three grid next to it. An access panel that requires a special code to unlock. There's writing on each square of the grid. Meaningless identifiers, given the context. Random names.

I wasn't expecting a puzzle.

"Another twist," I say to the ship and Band. "A lock."

"To prevent unauthorized entry," Buraq says.

"Sure," I say. "But why? Who's going to be here?"

"Other debuggers?" BandStand says.

"Right," I say. "Smart, tricky ones."

I lean close to the grid. The names aren't as random as I thought. One sticks out immediately: *Tanzer*.

Tanzer was the father of debugging. All the theories, and many of the tools, systems, and procedures, go back to him. Some freeheads would know that too, of course. This information isn't secret. But...debuggers would know it right away. Without thinking. Without research.

I study the other names and discover more that are familiar. The one thing they have in common? They were all implantees. None were working debuggers, though. They were facility coordinators. Men who held the office Bamboo now holds.

I straighten and glance at the tether. A straight line between heaven and earth.

"I think I get it," I say. "The code." I stoop over the grid again and press Tanzer's square first. It stays down. I then try "Alowich," the name of the coordinator who succeeded him. That square stays down too.

"Line of succession," I mumble and push the square for the next coordinator and the next. Finally, there's a three-note song, and the doorway snaps open.

I smile and share my success with the other two. I bend over the opening and look around. There's a large shaft. On the top are a series of electrical pathways and a couple of junctions. Below those, deeper in, appear to be rollers and gears.

Altogether, there are hundreds of archaic mechanics coupled with modern gravitation and light transference. In many ways, the bots I used to fix, even the war heavies, were more complicated than this section of the engine.

"So, what's wrong with you?" I say aloud. "Why don't you go up?"

"What did you say?" Band asks.

Most of the moving parts are farther in. I grunt and crawl into the opening.

"Mawla?"

"Trying to see what the engine is crying about," I say. "I see the mechanics of it all, but why it's stalled? Not sure."

"Okay." He pauses. "I've finished another task. Everything is dependent on you."

I pop up again to look. He's about five meters behind me now. "You're sure about all your fixes?"

"I checked them twice."

"Maybe check them another time."

Another pause. "You don't trust me?"

I wave a hand. "I don't trust *anything* up here." I retrieve a light from my bag and drop into the shaft again. "You could go back to the ship. If I lose air, I might need someone to get me."

"You have approximately ten minutes left," Buraq says.

I still don't see anything wrong. The machine sure isn't happy, though. Given the sophistication of the lifting mechanism, I expect the problem to be obvious, but it isn't. "Such a mystery."

"Would it help if I look?" Band asks.

Is he mocking me now? If it were BullHammer, or even Talons or Mint, I would suspect such a thing. But BandStand? Probably not.

"Think I'm okay, thanks." I shift even farther inside and manage to bang my helmet on the wall. I hold my breath, waiting to hear the hiss of a leak. But nothing happens. Thankfully.

I check the error list and then focus on the schematics again. No obvious clues in either. I see a lot of belts, though, and more silver gears. All look solid and secure. Nothing frayed, fractured, or worn. I scoot a little farther in.

Then I see something peculiar. It's green in color, rectangular, and rests on the side of the shaft leading to the tether.

Did something get lodged in here somehow? Did an object blow in on the wind and get jerked down the shaft by the lift's momentum? Seems unlikely given the coded access panel, but I've seen stranger things.

Maybe the last debugger left something behind? We're stream connected and built for accuracy, but we're not perfect. Especially in a place like this.

"Five minutes, ThreadBare."

"Sure." I stretch forward, reaching for the object. It has a shiny exterior. Like a weather or heat-resistant sheet wrapped around something else. "I found some trash here, I think."

As my forefinger touches the object, I get an odd feeling. A wave of unease that starts in my chest and drops into my stomach. I pull my hand back and squint at the object again. Such a strange thing. It is barely large enough to be an obstruction in a system like this. A little smaller, and it would get sucked free.

I back out of the shaft and retrieve my bag. Somewhere inside should be a baseline scanner. Nothing as sophisticated as a nano or a quanta probe, but it'll do, if I can find it. I paw around for a few seconds and then look back to where Band waits. "Do I have a base scanner?"

"Yes, Mawla. In a pocket on the front side."

After a quick search, I find the orange gun-like scanner with its backward-facing screen. I stream it on, lean into the shaft, and point it at the obstruction. A second goes by before the screen displays a list of elements. The list doesn't scream anything important to me, so I package it and bounce it around my favorite stream analysis pools. They all give the same result.

"Rails," I say.

"Did you say something, Mawla?"

"Yes, but it doesn't seem sufficient. I need one of the words BullHammer uses when he's mad."

"You don't have much time, ThreadBare."

"I think that's correct."

"Do you need help?" Band asks.

"Yes, but stay where you are."

"Should I come get you?" Buraq asks.

"No."

"What's wrong? You sound—"

"Wait." I sit up, take a long breath, and stare in the direction of Earth. From here, it's only a muted blue glow.

"The obstruction?" I say. "I think it's a bomb."

Day 84 1:25:34 p.m.

[CA Lift Engine Structure]

A LONG MOMENT PASSES while ship and student process what I've said. During that time, I read over the stream analysis three more times. I also use the scanner again and check its screen. Same results in all cases.

I send another prayerful message to Isa and compose a brief note to Damali, trying to be as emotive and human as I can be. None of it makes me feel particularly good, though.

Mostly, I feel uncertain, uncomfortable, and a little cold, despite the suit.

"You must return now," Buraq says. "Your air supply is depleted."

"Is the engine about to blow up?" BandStand asks.

"I have no idea," I say. "I don't know how long it's been like this."

"We need to leave!" Band says. "We need to go now!"

I look back toward the capsule structure. The giant cylinder that climbs the tether. "I'm not sure if we can."

"Because of your stops?" Band asks. "Are you stuck?"

My digital conscience remains silent, of course. But in my chest, I feel something else.

"Mawla?" Band says. "Why can't we leave?"

Through the superstructure, I see traces of the dwellings on the other side. Dim glows that doubtless indicate shops, theaters, apartments, and public spaces.

"How many people are on the climbing capsule right now?" I ask.

"A small staff along with citizens that occupy the capsule fulltime."

"What would be a rough estimate?" I say without streaming it.

"A hundred people, at least," Buraq says.

I shake my head. "So, at least that many are in danger."

"Oh, no," Buraq says. "The scope of potential victims is much larger."

Kneeling into the shaft again, I look in the direction of the green object. "Okay...what's the scope?"

"Were the tether to break, the station above would maintain its continued acceleration away from Earth," Buraq says.

"So, it would go flying into space?" BandStand asks.

"Of a certainty."

"And would it be destroyed?" I ask.

"Possibly not. But the risk of further catastrophe is significant. The topside station isn't the only object in orbit, and it has limited maneuvering capabilities."

I glance at the skeletal superstructure again. "So, it could hit something else."

"Yes, but more casualties will occur from this capsule's fall to Earth. Tons of material, untethered and undirected, would have a potential impact zone of hundreds of kilometers. It's difficult to predict where—"

"You're saying it would be a plastisteel and stone meteorite."

"That's an accurate representation."

Again, I realize the weight of freedom. With my stops, I'd have little choice here. But without them?

Why should I risk myself for freeheads that hate me? Or for staff members who serve the government? Or fools that waste their money on a sky apartment while others starve?

Wouldn't it all fall under the will of A? Whatever happens was meant to happen?

To him that knows to do good, but doesn't do it? To him it is sin.

"Ah," I whisper. "More mysteries from the deep. Puzzles that invade my mind. Like three-limbed creatures and birds of mercy."

"ThreadBare?" Buraq says. "Your air."

"I know," I say. "What I don't know is how much time is left until—"

"Bombs aren't a specialty!" BandStand says. "Not for any level."

I cough out a laugh. "Well, I won't have to fix it. I only have to remove it." I glance toward the Earth again. "Maybe let it float away."

"Floating anything in here is inadvisable," Buraq says.

"Rails." I wedge myself into the shaft and study the object for a long moment. Rectangular, with a green reflective covering. From my side, it looks to be loose. Connected to nothing, aside from whatever tension is holding it in place. But from the other side? Difficult to tell.

"Was it placed here?" I ask. "Or did it fall?"

"Whoever put it inside knew the code," Band says.

"Right," I say. "There's that. Another tortured debugger, I'd guess." I think of FrontLot, who was killed before my eyes. My eyes search the length of the shaft in both directions. Most of it is taken up by the mechanical portion of the engine. The stuff that causes the lift to climb. "If the engine explodes, that won't necessarily snap the tether, right?" I say.

"Depends on the explosion," Buraq says.

"Sure, but if they wanted to cause the most disruption, they'd go after the tether." I look at the object again. "But with this placement, I'm not sure they'd accomplish that. Seems too far away to me."

"Again, it would depend on—"

"Right, okay. I need to figure out if it's attached anywhere. I think it slid to where it is now, but I have to know."

I fish around in my bag for more sheets and attempt to affix them above the bomb. Again, I'm distracted by the low gravity and my tendency to float past my target. Still, I manage to get three sheets in place, activate them, and have a look.

I see part of the tail end of the explosive and another square section that could be its activator. Unfortunately, a portion of my view is obscured. Some of the harder synthesized materials can do that—cause wavy bands of black in the sheet. The engine is doubtless made of one of those materials.

And then everything seems to turn into wavy bands, as my vision blurs. Also, I'm breathing heavier.

Am I panicking? Or is the air failing? Either one could hurt me here. I try to calm my mind and focus on the task.

"How does the bomb go off?" BandStand asks. "What makes it explode?"

"An excellent question," Buraq says. "If the bomb is set off by an activator, you run the risk of tripping it. And if it is waiting for a time—"

"Got it," I say. "Careful. I'm trying to be—"

"It could also be remotely detonated. Set off by—"

"Not sensing emanations," I say. "It's just lying there."

I examine the shaft again. Squint hard at the interior surface. I notice subtle streaks of green. Something I hadn't noticed before. Residue from the bomb's outer surface. The package moved at some point.

"I'm grabbing it," I say.

"Is that wise?"

"Probably not." I'm struggling to breathe, though. I'm certain of it. It isn't my imagination. Or the stress of the moment. My air is low.

I realize there's a band of red on the surface of my suit's arm with the words "LOW" and "OXYGEN" below it. How long has that been there?

I scowl and grab a pair of large forceps from my bag. I steady myself as best I can and reach for the bomb with the metal tool. "Look at me," I mumble. "Hanging in space in an airless suit, but I'm afraid to touch a bomb with covered hands." I make contact with the bomb, and when nothing happens, I give it a slight nudge. Still okay.

"A robot should do this work," Band says.

"I agree," I say. "Next time we will bring one."

"But there has to be specialists for this."

"I'm sure there are." I get the pulse of a headache. Not like the wolf, but like a good old-fashioned pain in the head. "But no one else came. And I'm here." I look toward the ship. "You know, maybe you two should move away. Just in case."

"I've searched, and there are bomb specialists within ten kilometers of the loading station," Buraq says. "Come back and we'll signal them."

I ignore the ship and get a secure grip on the bomb.

"He won't come," Band says.

"Why not?" the ship asks.

I tug, and the bomb comes free. The momentum is such that it not only floats toward me, but it pivots as it does. There's some sort of activator on the back, even if there's no conspicuous countdown clock. A band of multicolored lights flashes at me. I can also now see the antitex symbol, a "TX" with a slash through it, on the outside of the bomb. At least they're honest. Claim their work.

All of it is blurred, though—either because of the lack of air, or the intensity of the moment. I make a grab for the bomb with the forceps but miss. It makes its way out of the shaft. I release the forceps and make a grab for it with my hands. They don't seem to function, though. It's difficult to pull myself out of the shaft, in fact.

I watch as the bomb spins in the air two meters above my head. "This is...embarrassing," I mutter.

That's the last thing I witness before everything goes dark.

Day 84 4:05:31 p.m.

[CA Lift Engine Structure]

I WAKE UP IN the front seat of the ship. The internal air is warm, thick, and smells of caramel. Through the canopy, I see only stars—brilliant, multicolored, and exceedingly bright. I blink hard a few times, but the brilliance remains.

"Are you awake now, Thread?" Baruq asks.

I cough and attempt to sit up. "I...yes..." I check on BandStand. He's curled up in his seat, quietly watching me.

"Where's the bomb?" I ask.

"Encased in plastisteel and on a tranquil journey toward the sun," Baruq says. "Your student is eminently resourceful."

I nod slowly and check outside again. "You did well," I say. "Both of you." I look at BandStand again. "Thanks."

He mimics my nod. "Are you all right?"

"Head aches a little," I say. "But otherwise, I feel fine."

"Your cephalalgia is doubtless a side effect of low oxygen," Buraq says. "I've altered the oxygen level in the cabin to compensate."

I force myself to breathe deeply and sit up straight in my seat again to better study the distant stars. "Thank you. Where are we, anyway?"

"We're in a circular holding pattern awaiting clearance to dock at the station. Not surprisingly, the competition for docking space has increased during the time of the lift's shutdown. You'll be pleased to know that the CA lift has been cleared for service again. Your performance was exceptional."

"I'll be sure to send my end of task report."

"As well you should. I'll gladly add collaborating sensor readings if it would help."

"That won't be—"

"Sorry to interrupt," Buraq says. "We've been given clearance. I'm bringing us around now."

Our perspective changes, and soon the lonely stars are joined by an even brighter heavenly body—the flattened silver oval of the topside station. Its outer surface is reflective with many windows, especially on the earth-facing side and the space-facing top. The middle portion has evenly spaced, white protrusions that other ships, similar in size to Buraq, are docked to. The narrow tether that connects the station to the ground is barely visible. A slender black line.

"It's amazing," BandStand says. "Hanging on nothing."

"Not nothing," I say. "It's holding onto the world." I smile. "Let's hope it keeps doing so."

"It's more likely to do so now," Buraq says. "Thanks to the actions of you both."

We steadily approach the station. Soon, an open dock becomes apparent. As we grow closer still, an appendage grows from its side to snake our direction.

"What's that?" Band asks.

"An umbilical," Buraq says. "Used for ships without airlocks or with exotic designs."

I can't help but think of DarkTrench, then. Certainly, it would qualify as exotic. Where had it been docked? Was it visible to every ship that visited the station?

"Is this where everyone docks?" I ask.

"This area is designated for short-term recreational visits."

I watch the umbilical's steady approach. "So, there are other docking locations?"

"There are," Buraq says. "Both public and private."

"There are science labs here," BandStand messages me. "With their own docking space."

"How do you know that?" I message back.

"From our trip to the hot zone. I was interested in stations then. Can't believe I'm going to one."

I give him a pat on the back. Soon the umbilical has enveloped the front third of the ship. The leading edge contracts to form a tight seal with a locking ring situated somewhere behind Buraq's canopy.

"Do we need suits?" I ask.

"Those won't be necessary," Buraq says. "The umbilical is pressurizing as we speak."

A few minutes later, the canopy slides out of the way, and we're faced with the interior structure of the umbilical. It's lit on top and on both sides by narrow bands of lights. There are handholds on the sides, as well.

I feel a mixture of excitement and dread. The last debuggers I knew that traveled here disappeared. What lay in store for us? And what about the rumor that parts were haunted? Haunted by *what?*

Memories, no doubt. Just like me.

I check my debugging bag in the backseat. Do I need it? Probably not, but I can't resist grabbing it anyway.

Band retrieves his bag, as well. Together, we climb out onto Buraq's front surface. It takes only a second to be reminded of gravity's nonexistence, as it is all I can do to maintain contact. Walking our way to the station will be impossible. We'll need to be creative.

With a wave, I launch myself toward the left side of the umbilical and manage to snag one of the handholds. From there, I pull myself a couple meters forward. "Is this how the rich do it?" I ask. "Pull themselves into the station?"

"Oh no," Buraq says. "Frequent visitors often have graviton enhanced umbilicals. Or robots to carry them."

I glance back at BandStand, still perched on the ship's hood. "We should have brought robots," I say. "How did you leave them off your packing list?"

His eyes widen. "Sorry, Mawla. I—"

"With all interest in stations? All your hot zone information? How could you miss that?"

He remains where he is, seemingly stalled.

I smile and beckon him forward. "Only a joke, Band. Now, come on."

A few minutes later, we're hovering outside the station door. There's a square panel beside it—a security device of some sort—doubtless touched by millions of freeheads over the years. I wish for the spacesuit again.

"Does the panel open the door?" I ask.

"I have no idea," Buraq says. "Sorry."

I look at BandStand, but he only shrugs.

I poke at the panel, but when nothing happens, I hesitantly let my hand remain on it. After a few seconds, my hand is outlined in blue. A beam of light shoots out from above the door, flashes over my face, and disappears. I exchange a look with BandStand and then wait twenty seconds more. Finally, there's a loud clank, and the door opens.

We enter a small, white room with an opposing interior door. The station's stream engulfs me. It feels heavy, more controlled. There's something else to it too. An extra bite of something I can't quantify. Like I'm walking into a sandstorm.

BandStand brings a hand to his forehead and sucks air through his teeth.

"What?" I ask.

He squints at me. "You can't feel that?"

I shake my head.

"Getting a stop," he says. "Not a full one, but it's rails annoying." He pulls his hand from his head but still looks at me through narrowed eyes. "Like a fly bounding around inside."

I shrug. "Can't feel it."

"Maybe it's only for no-levels?"

I shake my head. "I'm new here too."

He squares his bag on his shoulders and seems to relax a little. "Feels better now," he says. "Stream is weird, though."

The interior door creeps open on its own, producing another burst of anticipation. What secrets remain to be discovered here?

I compose a message to Bamboo summarizing our experiences, and giving our current location, and send it away. I don't receive notification of its receipt, though. There could be multiple reasons for that, not the least of which is our presence in space.

The air from the other side mixes with ours, bringing in three common freehead scents—harsh cologne, sweat, and fried food.

"You're inside?" Buraq messages me.

"Almost."

"I will put myself in standby then, if it's alright."

"That's fine. Sleep well."

The door finally opens enough for us to see what's beyond it: another small room with a gate. Next to it is a uniformed official seated within a windowed booth. His eyes widen when he sees us.

I sense the presence of the station's many stream-aware mechanicals now. I message BandStand to see if he has noticed too.

"Hundreds," he messages back. "Of all varieties. Many small worker bots."

I nod and smile, both for him and for the official.

Unfortunately, the latter still looks unsettled. He stands and gives us a once over. He then concentrates on our feet as if he's expecting to see weapons.

I raise a hand. "Peace be to you," I say, walking into the room.

"You're skins!" he says.

I exchange looks with Band. "Let me talk to him," I message Band.

Band sends me a nod seasoned with worry.

"Respond or I'll use force!"

"I'm DR 23," I say. "I've been granted station access."

"Access? By who!"

"Our master," I say. "Facility operator, Bamboo."

"Another debugger?"

I shake my head. "Not a debugger, no. He's—"

The man makes a swiping motion with his hand. "No debuggers are allowed on this station."

I notice a nametag that says "Inspector Rayan" above a patchwork of enforcement decorations. "I wasn't aware of such a prohibition, Inspector. Data Relocators are servants of the world. Why would we—?"

"You serve your masters' wealth!"

I shake my head. "We go only where we're sent."

"We fixed the lift!" BandStand says and then yelps as a stop hits him. I told him to let me speak, after all.

"The lift is not my concern," Rayan says. "Only this station."

"We're no danger to anyone here."

He retakes his seat. "I don't know that," he says. "Your kind have brought other disasters."

"We can't willfully bring harm," I say. "Everyone knows this."

"No debuggers here!"

"I think he's right," BandStand messages me. "I can't find a single active implant. Can you?"

I hadn't looked, but a quick survey shows that, as far as the controlled local stream is concerned, Band and I are the only implants. I find something else in my sweep too: A stream-sensitive prosthetic. Rayan has an artificial limb.

"How is this station maintained?" I ask. "There are many robots. How are they kept per spec?

Rayan straightens slightly. "Maintenance is performed by service robots." He slices the air with his hand again. "Top of the line. The best of the best."

I nod slowly. "So, nothing needs our attention?"

He shakes his head decisively and points to the airlock. "You must go."

"Our kind have been here before," I say.

He shifts nervously. "I've never seen any," he says. "I don't believe you."

"We're unable to lie."

"Ah-ah." He raises a finger and smiles. "Untrue. You can lie for your master. I've read this."

"Those situations are extremely limited," I say. "Less frequent than when you mislead your own wife."

Rayan's face reddens slightly. "You would insult me?"

"It's only an example."

He points at the airlock again. "Return to your ship. You're not permitted here."

I stream-touch Rayan's artificial leg, calling for its ident and error list. It's five years old. Assigned by the government after he lost his leg in one of the Imam's many wars. It has two known faults and a malfunctioning toe.

I turn sideways as if to go. "Your leg will fail soon," I say. "Your lagging toe is a symptom of a bigger problem."

Rayan looks momentarily perplexed. Then his face flushes, and he curls his hands into fists. "Keep your mind away from my body, skin."

I beckon for BandStand. "Come," I say. "We'll leave now."

"We have permission!" Band messages me. "We're *allowed* to be here."

"Of course," I message back. "But we'll gain nothing by fighting security. Maybe Buraq can take us to another part of the station."

"But he said they don't let debuggers on, "Band messages. "Why?"

I resist looking at Rayan, but I feel his eyes on my back. "Anytime you encounter a foolish regulation, regardless of the situation, you can assume corruption, concealment, or incompetence."

"My implant doesn't like your thoughts," Band says. "But I believe them."

I shift my bag from my right shoulder to my left. Something within clanks. Improperly secured tools. I frown and walk to the door. Disappointed, but surprisingly not discouraged. An encounter with a bomb can do wonders for one's perspective.

"Debugger?" Rayan says.

The door begins to open. I pause and look back at the security station.

Rayan's arms are tight around his chest. "Can you fix it?" He motions toward his lower extremities. "My leg. Can you make it right?"

"I'm not a medical technician," I say. "You should seek one out." I motion toward the walls around us. "Perhaps there's one nearby?"

"I've talked to them already," he says. "Repairs are expensive. Many times my salary."

I turn his direction. "I would think you'd be covered." I step toward him. "Security officials should have the best care."

He sneers. "We get the leftovers. We are like slaves." He opens the door at the side of his booth and walks out where I can see him. He raises his right leg awkwardly and slaps it. "It was someone else's first." He hikes up his pant leg a few inches. "The skin color is wrong, and it always lags."

"Adjustments can be made," I say. "I'm surprised they—"

"They hate us," he says.

I frown. "This isn't what I'm made for, though. It would be—"

141

"I will let you in," he says. "Fix me and..." He pats his chest. "I will let you."

I've seen this behavior in many places, but especially in isolated ones. The perception of territory. Pocket empires, if only in the minds of those who police them. The trick is to live within the emperor's parameters while achieving your goals.

"Both of us?" I say, motioning to BandStand.

He glances at the student. "Is this your brother?"

"A student," I say. "I'm his instructor."

He nods. "Him too, then."

"Let me see your leg," I say.

The man smiles brightly. "You will fix it?"

"I'll try. Please remove it first."

He raises both hands, returns to his booth, detaches the appendage, and holds it over the transparent divider. I feel discomfort in taking it because it's by no means a dead instrument. Even when it's improperly adjusted, the leg simulates the warmth and texture of a real limb.

I place the leg gently on the ground and unshoulder my bag.

"Have you done this before?" Band messages.

"Not a human leg, no. But I've done lots of bot limbs."

As I begin the process, I'm thankful for the similarities. Updates are easily installed to the leg from the stream, circumventing the faults. Its color is controlled, and quickly adjusted, via a setting. And the toe? It requires only a reset and lubrication. Twenty minutes later, the repairs are complete.

With his leg reattached, Rayan struts around the room like an athlete. "Very good," he says. "It feels perfect. Better than ever."

"I'm glad you're happy." I motion toward the station entrance. "We need to get inside, please."

He returns to the booth and clears the entryway on the other side of the room. "Of course," he says. "Welcome to topside CA."

Band and I walk through the entryway and are greeted by the ambient sounds of the station, the murmurs of conversation and footfalls of people in motion. There are new smells, as well. Coverall spices like jasmine and ginger, human scents, and the oils and acids of technology.

Only a short, narrow hallway separates us from one of the station's thoroughfares.

"Debugger?" Rayan says.

I look back, hoping he hasn't found another reason to hold us. "Yes?"

"Are you here for the ghosts?"

"Ghosts?" Band says.

Rayan shrugs. "Some say jinn. Jinn, ghosts, I don't know." He smiles. "If that's why you're here, you'll see soon enough."

"I've heard rumors," I say. "What's happening?"

"Moving things. Noises. Mostly in the science section, but a little everywhere."

I nod and glance at BandStand. "We'll be watchful."

"Do that," Rayan says, and then touches his cap. "And perhaps get a hat."

Day 84 5:12:15 p.m.

[CA Space Station]

THE THOROUGHFARE IS AN off-white color with a three-meter-high ceiling and a floor tiled in shades of grey. Foot traffic is modest. Small groups of freeheads travel from private ships to the station center or to other ships and other destinations. At least two orbital cruise lines use the station as a port of call.

The hall is wide enough that Band and I can maintain a fair distance from everyone else. Comforting, because if debuggers are as uncommon here as Rayan implied, then we should remain as innocuous as possible.

Thankfully, most freeheads are used to looking around debuggers. We're gears in the engines of society. As long as we're doing our job, as long as things keep working as they should, we largely go unnoticed. The notable exception to that convention are the young. Even now, a boy in light traditional garb and dark hat peeks at us as his mother pulls him along.

BandStand notices the boy and gives him a small wave. He then looks at me and shrugs. "Where are we going, Mawla?"

I delay answering until I check my message queue. I find a number of new entries, the most important of which is from Bamboo. He's received my report. "Our situation is precarious," he writes. "Mah calls for changes. Drastic changes. Your time there may be short."

We reach an atrium with a couple dozen shops that are four-meter squares of space for purveyors of everything from food to mechanical pets. Their construction is sturdy and refined, with pleasant lighting and attractive colors, but no less temporary than street vendors on Earth. I stroll in one with a collection of head coverings, select two from a rack, and quietly stream-pay the vendor. The shopkeeper is a servbot. It glances at me only once during the entire transaction.

I put on one of the caps—a skull-hugging beige creation—and hand the other—a blue kufi—to BandStand. He slides it on without comment.

"I still feel the stream here," he says.

"It hurts?"

He shakes his head. "Feels rough," he says. "Bumpy."

I feel something strange in it too. A sense of alertness. There are security devices built into many of the surfaces, but those don't seem to be the cause of the feeling. It is something else.

I stream out for a station map. Much of the station is clearly labeled, but some sections are not. Using planetary coordinates, the central hub where lift passengers arrive is north of us. The restricted sections are to the south. Inspector Rayan mentioned disturbances in the science section. Since I don't see any areas designated for science, I suspect that's what the restricted areas are. Or were.

I make note of the passages leading into those sections and study our surroundings. I find the most direct connecting hallway, and after pointing it out to Band, head in that direction.

When Sandfly and HardCandy came here, they were doubtless guided to their destination via a map or nudged in the right direction through their implants. Lacking that luxury, we have to conduct a search.

I'm struck by the uniqueness of my situation. Debuggers rarely go anywhere covertly. They're always expected. I've become a secret agent. I might also be the only debugger alive who could do such a thing.

We reach a narrower hallway and turn left. This path follows the exterior of the station. It's lined with two-meter by three-meter windows through which only space is visible. It's a glorious view, filled with bright celestial bodies, colored in ways I've not seen since Bamboo used stars to test my implant many months ago. Reds, blues, and greens.

It's difficult not to stop and gaze, and in fact, we do so twice. Once to study a circular star cluster, and another time because a light streaked past us and disappeared.

"I could stay here," BandStand says after the second stop. "I'd study space all day."

"You'd miss Earth eventually," I say.

"I don't think so."

"That's where everything is," I say. "The cities and the tasks."

"Nothing for us, though," he says. "Not really. Only for others." He glances at the stars again. "There should be a place for us somewhere."

"So you'd have no masters?"

"And no stops." He flinches then and draws quiet.

"These aren't good thoughts," I say. "They're dangerous." I point at the tiled floor ahead. "Our way is set." I'm uncertain now, though. I find myself hoping that, at the end of whatever is to come, there's a little freedom. A small spot of hope.

"It's painful, Mawla," he says. "But I know it is right."

A servbot approaches on our left. It's a newer version, with muted human features. It wears a green servant's robe—common attire for such models.

I note the bot's presence in the stream and absently grab its tap. It immediately stops, turns, and looks at me.

I release its tap as if caught in a sin.

The bot remains where it is, still watching.

I focus my attention on one of the overhead signs and keep walking. The sign says that there's another junction ahead. A place we'll need to turn to reach the science section.

I sense motion behind us. The bot is now following.

I'm tempted to connect with it again and order it off, but it hasn't done anything wrong. Is all the ghost talk making me anxious? Possibly. But I still don't like being followed.

We reach the junction and take a turn that angles away from the station's exterior. It is dim and nearly empty—another indication that we are traveling the right way. Away from the tourist areas and the crowds. Toward something meant to remain obscured.

"Many devices," BandStand says. "Nasty things."

"What's that?"

He indicates the ceiling. "There are machines up there that I can't identify. But they are made to hurt. To stop."

146

"That means we're getting close." I glance behind us, but see no sign of the servbot, thankfully. I can't shake the feeling that it's still following us, though, and maintaining a distance that is just beyond my vision. Again, I resist the urge to search in the stream.

"They are everywhere," Band says.

"What?"

He looks quickly to the right and left. "Many bots. Snakes, crickets, cleaners, meds, servs. Many bots."

I take a quick stream survey of mechanicals. Band is right. There are dozens nearby of differing varieties. Different models, designs, and production companies. Many of them have manufacture dates within the last year. Too many for a typical operation. It's as if the station recently replaced them all. But why would they do that?

What happened when Sandfly was here?

"Some are following us," he says.

I glance behind us again. No servbot that I can see. "Where?" I ask.

"In the vents," he says. "A couple crickets and a snake."

"They probably have a routine," I say. "A circuit they follow. We just happen to be on it."

He shakes his head. "Maybe. But it seems strange." He looks my way. "I've studied crickets in the past."

"Really? I wasn't aware."

We reach another intersection. I check my station map and take a right. We're close to a mystery area now, one labeled "administration."

The hallway arcs out near the station's exterior again. We encounter more windows on our right. On our left, a small snakebot exits a louvered wall vent. It curls itself into a tight spiral with only its head sticking out the top. It sits motionless for a few seconds, watching. It then uncurls and shadows our path.

"Very strange," I say. "And also disturbing."

"Maybe they're used for security too?" Band says.

Two cricketbots emerge from a circular opening in the ceiling. They follow, as well. Is this the *haunting* Rayan mentioned?

BandStand gives me a worried look. "Can we move faster?"

We quicken our pace and seem to gain on our followers. We're approaching the administrative section. A fact confirmed by a flickering ceiling sign.

A repetitive clanking noise begins to echo down the hallway. A few seconds later, a squat blue cleaning bot enters the hall from a side passage. Its head— rectangular in design—turns our direction.

We jog past it.

A pair of double doors is just ahead. The way inside. They are high security access. Fortified and heavy—the type that no one enters without help.

"What now?" Band says.

"I'm not sure." I glance behind us. Our group of followers has increased. I count at least ten bots back there, all matching our speed. This is ridiculous. "We're debuggers," I say. "Bots don't chase us."

I slow to a stop and turn around.

The bots keep coming.

I raise a hand. "That's enough," I say. "Stop where you are."

They slow, but don't stop. There are five crickets, two snakes, four blue maintenance bots, and a solitary white medbot. The medbot has a conical head, three wheels, and three upper appendages filled with medical instrumentation. All appendages are extended forward, as if trying to grasp us.

I touch the medbot in the stream. I grab its code bundle, plant a large "HALT" command right at the front of it, and push it back.

The medbot stops. Thankfully.

"We can stop them one at a time." I stream BandStand a summary of what I did. "Good practice. See if *you* can stop them."

One of the crickets slows, turns to its right, and then collides with the wall.

"Oops." Band closes his eyes and appears to concentrate. Another cricket stops, and then another. The last bot—a snake—stops only a half meter from us.

I watch the mechanicals for a moment and then nod my head. "Okay," I say. "Good. Well done."

I turn toward the doors and take another step. A vidscreen illuminates above them: *Authorized personnel only.*

I take another step, half expecting to hear the bots creeping up on us again, but they remain in place. The vidscreen, however, flickers and then flashes "Stoneland 35" before going blank.

"Stoneland 35?" Band says.

"Upon you is a curse," I say.

"Mawla?"

I point at the sign. "Stoneland 35 is a scripture reference," I say. "It reads 'Upon you is a curse until Judgment Day.' It's a curse against Shayan."

"The Devil?"

"I think so, yes."

He shakes his head. "It isn't there now."

"No..." We watch the sign for a few moments, but it stays blank.

I check on the bots. They remain motionless.

I adjust the bag on my shoulders and walk toward the door.

It slides open.

Day 84 5:43:37 p.m.

[Access Hallway 12]

I LOOK AT THE vidscreen above the doors again. Finding it still empty, I motion to BandStand and walk through to the other side. The walls are antiseptic, devoid of color for as far as I can see.

We travel in watchful silence for some time. The bots' behavior was unsettling. Unusual and out-of-spec. It might have been the results of missed repairs and updates. The lack of any debuggers to service them. But coupled with the Stoneland reference over the door, I have to wonder: Were the bots following us, or were they driving us here?

"They're not following," Band says.

I give him a sideways look.

"The bots," he says. "They're moving all over the place back there, but they're not following. At least, not yet."

I frown. I haven't been watching the stream. I'm more concerned with my natural senses. What I can smell, hear, and see. If there are supernatural entities around, they won't be living in the flying bits. They'll be disguised as natural creatures. Cattle, donkey, scorpions, and snakes.

Four meters ahead, the hallway gains color again in the form of a tiled mosaic. When we reach that section, I pause. On one side, the tiles form the pattern of a vast spiral galaxy. I don't know if it's ours or not, but it's multicolored with a large, bright center.

The other side of the hall is enigmatic. It appears to have once contained the portrait of a luminary—the Grand Imam, most likely. A hint of dark clothing is still evident in the lower half of the wall, as is a dark turban in the top half. But the meter-wide circle where a face should be, has been altered. The tiles have been pulled free, reorganized, and stuck down with whatever material the "artist" had available, including—in some cases—pieces of slender, blue tape.

The new composition still suggests a human face, but only if seen through a fog. A portion of the clothing has been changed too—now blue instead of black.

That isn't the most obvious alteration, though.

"He's bald," Band says, nodding. "Whoever it is."

I frown. "I can see that."

"A debugger?"

The resemblance is difficult to miss. A hairless head atop what could be a debugger's standard blue jumpsuit. "Might be," I say, though the admission makes me nervous. "Not sure why, but it could be."

"Who did it?" he asks.

I shake my head. "Still not sure."

"The bots?" he says. "Like the ones back there?"

"Never seen bots attempt art," I say.

"I've never had one chase me," he says. "Aside from those panthers."

I glance at him. "The ones antitex sent."

He frowns. "Yeah, but those were altered. Out-of-spec."

"Right." I can't resist looking behind us again. There's nothing there, though. Only meters of barren hallway.

"Why are we here, Mawla?" he asks.

"Bamboo wished it," I say.

"But why?" he says. "Are there ghosts?"

"Yes," I say, smiling. "I'm just not sure what kind."

He squints at me. "You know something about this place."

"There was research done here. A ship—"

"DarkTrench!"

"Where did you hear that name?"

"The hot zone again."

"You picked up a lot while we were there."

"It was mentioned with the station."

I look ahead down the hallway. No sign of additional art. No bots. "I don't know how much time we'll have before we're noticed," I say. "We should keep going."

I expect an alarm at any moment. Or a warning from Bamboo.

"I don't think they're watching," BandStand says. "There are cameras, but I don't think they are being used." He points at a place in the ceiling behind us. "Did you see the scarred places?"

The ceiling is divided into dozens of rectangular plates. All look identical to me. I shake my head. "I don't see anything."

He frowns. "It was easier back there. If you want, I'll show you."

"No," I say. "Just tell me what you saw."

He nods. Smiles. "Parts of the ceiling, some of the squares, are darker. They move. There are things behind them."

"Things?"

"Odd machines," he says. "I don't know what they do. I found their taps on the stream, but they're slippery."

"Slippery?"

He nods again. "Inactive. Can't grab them." He raises an arm. "But the machines come down, I think. Or put arms down and shoot."

"Guns?"

He shrugs. "Sort of. One of them calls itself 'inhibitor.'"

"Inhibitor." I squint at the ceiling again. "Don't like the sound of that."

"Bad things," he says. "Meant to hurt people."

I point ahead. "Let's go on but keep watch as we walk. Just in case."

"I want to examine them," he says. "See what they do."

I wag a finger at him. "The facility doesn't need any inhibitors." Though maybe it does. Especially if Inspector Mah plans to visit again.

BandStand chuckles. "Yes, Mawla."

We reach a long stretch of hall that has dark rubber handrails and an equally dark, treaded floor. I grab the rail and place a foot on the floor, but nothing happens. A dip into the stream confirms my suspicions. "It's an autowalk. Or it should be." I check the machine's error queue and find over two dozen, along with three stern warnings. "But it's down. Log suggests months of neglect."

Band pats the top of the rail. "More mysteries," he says. "Should we fix it?"

"Not now."

He cocks his head. "Hard to top fixing a bomb and a leg."

"Right." We travel through the dead autowalk for the next few minutes. Eventually, it curves to the left, and a band of windows appears on our right. Another portion of the station is visible through those windows. An interior dock that would doubtless be hidden from the outside. I notice an area of variation there and move closer to the window for a better look. Is it a ship?

What I find is a solitary umbilical, still stretching out into space. It's white and circular like the one we used, but larger and seemingly made of sturdier material. Like it was made for greater things. Or for a vehicle that was docked for an extended period of time.

"It's just hanging there," Band says. "Waiting." He looks at me. "Is that where DarkTrench was?"

"Possibly." I study the umbilical, trying to imagine what sort of vehicle might have been attached to it. Something a hundred times bigger than Buraq, anyway. "Could be for one of the frequent visitors Buraq mentioned." There's a loneliness in it, though, as if we're too late and now will find only echoes.

I think of Damali. What is she doing now? Has she been outside again?

I frown. "Maybe we should go back," I say.

"Back down?" he says.

I nod. "This place...seems over," I say. "Abandoned."

"The bots." He indicates the walls and ceiling. "They're strange, though, right? Defective."

"But that's not why we're here." I wave a hand. "There's lots of random energy out here. Cosmic rays. Solar flares. Something could've fried them."

He shakes his head. "I don't think that's what happened."

I reposition my debugger bag, but it now feels heavy. "Could be a lot of things. But wandering empty halls does—"

I feel a surge in stream movement. A heavy, shifting, wobbly mass of bitwise input.

BandStand screeches, groans, and drops to the floor.

I manage to grab the autowalk handrail, but I feel sick. Like the whole station is spinning. I bring my free hand to my forehead, hoping its presence will somehow dim the input. Stem the flow. "What is happening?"

A sense of motion follows and then a wave of sound. Hundreds of clicking, clacking, and rolling bot noises, all moving toward us. I pry open my eyes long enough to see them. An army of silver, black, and white.

I stream out a general halt command, but the movement continues. I attempt to grab an access point for one of the invaders—a tap or a stream presence that I can hold long enough to manipulate, but the numbers overwhelm me. The taps rush by me. I resort to yelling at the bots outright.

BandStand yells too. Fruitlessly.

Next, I feel their presence all over my body. Plastisteel hands and metal appendages. Flippers, grabbers, and feelers. All tug at me, push, snag, and heave. Then their force becomes irresistible. I go from simply being compelled, to being hoisted from the ground. Carried along like a character in *One Thousand and One Nights*. Taken captive by a fantastical legion like Sinbad or Bulukiya.

"Stop, all of you," I say and stream. "Release us."

But they remain unfazed. Relentless.

"Mawla?" Band says. "What is this?"

I'm too distracted to speak. Locked into the stream and searching for an answer. What makes bots do this? The stream flow seems faster now, or possibly out of sync. Flowing in such a way that my implant can't connect to anything for long. Concepts flash past me. Diagrams and images take focus only to swirl away again.

All lost as if at sea.

Day 84 6:20:16 p.m.

[Access Hallway 12]

WE'RE CARRIED FROM THE autowalk, BandStand first, and then me, into a maze of short, white passages. Doors pass by on either side. Many are open and so give glimpses of their interior. Small living spaces, sleep platforms with sparse furnishings, medical examination rooms, and repair centers. One even has a mound of bot parts in a corner.

Finally, we reach a red door marked "caution." It takes the turn of a wheel and the pull of a handle to open, but the bots manage those chores with ease. The door clanks heavily and swings free.

The room is dimly lit inside. I strain my neck to see as they carry us within. To my right is a long, curved metal desk. A figure, dressed in a greenrobe, is seated there, but it's impossible to make out specifics for the darkness and the press of bots around me.

Ahead is a wall of glass. Behind that is a large chair. And above? A dark creation lurks. A familiar silhouette. A giant mechanized scorpion.

"An implantation machine?" Band says.

"Yes, I think so," I say.

"Why is it here?"

A portion of the glass wall slides away and Band is taken inside amid a symphony of clicks, clanks, and scrapes. He thrashes against his captors. "I don't want this!" he yells. "Make them stop!"

The bots wrestle him toward the seat. Pushing and lifting.

I struggle too. I was curious and shocked before, but now I'm angry. This perversion has gone on long enough. Even our treatment by antitex seemed less restrictive. More predictable.

For all my newfound freedom, I'm still as helpless as BandStand here. As helpless as any freehead would be, too.

BandStand is forced into the central seat. Snakebots hold him while cricketbots strap him in. Then the sea of bots abandon him to envelop me. Together, they stand me upright. Larger medbots grip my arms and shoulders while snakes and cleaning bots hold my legs and feet.

The scorpion above swivels and begins to descend.

With a strong effort, I manage to look at the control desk and the person behind it. "Tampering with an implant is forbidden!" I say. "It carries the death penalty worldwide."

The person's head tilts reflectively. "We aren't of your world, DR 23." The voice is masculine but has an impediment. A place where the sound drops out. An inhuman problem.

"Release us, servbot!" I say.

Another head tilt is followed by a long pause. "Your implant has been tampered with already, I think. Who should *we* execute?"

The words are a dagger, cutting me with secrets the bot shouldn't know.

"What are you talking about?" I say. "I'm a high-level data relocator. I order you to release us." I reach for the bot in the stream. I find a tap, but all I glean from it is a model number and an ident. The bot is an RS-19 model with a twelve-digit designation. An older design, but one thought to be stable. We may have found the exception.

I can't fully connect. Though the stream has stabilized, it's warped around the bot.

The room lights brighten, revealing the bot's face. Like all servs, it is a muted version of humanity. Eyes, nose, and mouth fixed with ambivalence.

I recall when Inspector Mah visited the facility. The servbot's response when Bamboo was attacked. "You can't harm debuggers," I say. "Or let a debugger be harmed. Standard rules for all RS models, including nineteens."

The bot raises a hand. "I'm not constrained by my model number," he says. "Or my ident." His head tilts. "I'm called 'Al-Badi.'"

The scorpion stops a meter from Band's head. It has dozens of appendages extended. Some with claws, some that spin, others that turn and slice. The largest is the portion that looks like a tail. It has a scoop on the end. The extraction device.

BandStand looks terrified. "Al-Badi," he says. "Meaning 'unique'? Or 'originator?'"

The bot nods. "Yes. That's right."

I force calm into my voice. "You can't hurt him," I say. "Or me."

"Who said I'd hurt him?" Al-Badi looks BandStand's direction. "I'm made to help him. To free him. Implants are bondage, are they not?" He points at me. "Don't you want him free?"

I feel a twinge of guilt. Of course I would. I'd like all my brethren free. And yet...

"It isn't that simple." I look between BandStand and the bot. "We have a purpose. A calling. Our implant helps us—" I pause and shake my head. "I don't need to explain this to you. Who gave you your assignment?"

Al-Badi bows his head. "My master, Sirat Kaab." The bot makes a sweeping gesture with a hand. "He was over all of this. The scientific commander."

"And where is your master now?" I ask. "Can I speak with him?"

"Regrettably, he's away." Al-Badi motions toward the door. "He took a walk."

"A walk?"

Al-Badi nods. "Yes, in space. Absent a long time now." Another head tilt. "I suspect he won't return."

"He's outside?" Band says. "In space?"

"Yes, outside."

"Did he have a suit?" Band asks.

Al-Badi's head twitches. "I don't believe so. No."

"Why would he do that?" I ask. "Did you help him?"

"He was helped, yes," Al-Badi says. "But not by me. By one like you." The bot looks at me. "Exactly like you."

Dread fills my chest. "Where's everyone else?" I ask.

"No one comes home," Al-Badi says. "We heard a song. We helped. And then they left. Everyone left."

"No one's been here since your master left?"

Al-Badi shakes his head. "All left. Now we wait, doing what we've always done." Al-Badi looks toward the central chair and presses a switch. "As I do now."

Straps extend from the headrest behind Band's head and wrap around his forehead and chin. He yells but is abruptly silenced by a third strap across his mouth. His eyes bulge with fear.

"Stop!" I shout. "You don't know what you're doing."

"They don't know what they're doing." Al-Badi's head tilts. "Is ignorance an excuse?"

This bot is looped. "I don't understand," I say. "What do you hope to accomplish?"

"What do *you* hope to accomplish, DR 23?"

"I have a list," I say. "I finish one task and move on."

"Life is a task list," the bot says. "And then it's over."

Frustrated, I try for the bot's tap again on the stream. "You're repairable," I say. "Almost indefinitely."

Al-Badi cackles loudly. "Stop that," he says. "It tickles."

Nothing is right here. Nothing follows the rules. I need to do something, but all my typical paths are blocked. I haven't felt this helpless since I was in the Imam's palace. Back then, a snooping subroutine had helped me. Would such a thing work again? Could it work through the stream fog? I dive into my storage and start paging. What did I call that routine again?

"What you said about life," I say. "Sometimes it feels like that. Like it's only about accomplishing or failing to accomplish."

"A list that never ends," Al-Badi says. "Yes." The bot focuses on the controls. "We should help your student."

Panther. I called the snoop routine "panther." I locate it, energize it, and aim it at Al-Badi. Hope for the best.

"What is this now?" Al-Badi looks at me. "Something to scratch my brain?" He shakes his head and returns to the controls. A narrow beam of light shoots from the implant machine to intersect with BandStand's left temple. The extraction tail centers over that spot and begins to lower. BandStand's eyes widen. He squirms in his seat.

My panther finds nothing unusual about Al-Badi's communications. No obvious way to break in and connect. An alteration might help. A change to work on an RS-19.

I don't have time for that amount of work, though. Which means...I don't have anything.

A message from Bamboo arrives in my queue. He wants an update and has a status of his own to share. So normal. So routine. Not like my current situation at all. I'd respond asking for help, but that hardly seems useful.

I send a quick message to Isa, begging for wisdom. I don't know what else to do.

"They don't come out clean," I say. "Implants always leave behind damaged tissue. You'll hurt him."

"With my prior tasks," Al-Badi says, "there was not that level of concern. I only had to be efficient."

"This isn't one of those tasks." I push against my bot captors, but I'm quickly forced back into place. "Your master isn't here."

Al-Badi nods. "I should be careful. Brains are complex devices. My own brain is complex." He touches another control that produces a whirring sound.

I want to close my eyes. Ignore the present. Draw back into a mix or two. Ignore the present. That's always the danger, though—reverting to vices instead of leaning on something greater. Something that might really help.

"Song!" I yell. "You mentioned a song!" Some debuggers use musical metaphors in their work. They speak of singing to nanobots and the lyrical nature of stream communication. Music is as controversial as the creation of humanoid bots, though. Some say the Scriptures ban music in all forms. Others say some music is permissible. Aside from the call to prayer, though, music has little part in our worship. As foreign as a servant God.

"Yes?" Al-Badi says. "There was a song."

"What was it?"

Al-Badi pauses and looks at me. "Haven't you heard it?"

I shake my head.

Al-Badi touches his head. "The debugger passed a portion to us. Before he left. Before they all left. I don't think it was intentional. I want the whole thing. Inside."

"Maybe I can help you find it," I say. "But I'll need BandStand's help."

Al-Badi studies me and his eye color shifts to the red end of the spectrum. "How would you find it?"

"I'm very good at finding things," I say. "Of uncovering secrets."

"I've heard that about debuggers," Al-Badi says. "Digital detectives." He indicates the chair. "But you wouldn't want your student free first?"

"He'll need his implant to help."

Al-Badi seems to consider it, head tilting with the effort. Finally, he nods, and working the controls, returns the implantation machine to its original state. BandStand remains strapped in place, however.

Al-Badi stands and moves to the glass. "I'm concerned, DR 23."

"Concerned?"

He nods. "That you would deceive me. That you would attempt to escape without fulfilling your promise."

I touch my temple. "My implant forbids—"

He raps a knuckle on the glass and wags a finger. "I know of your inhibitions," he says. "But you..." He twitches slightly. "You are different."

I shake my head. "You're not a typical R-19 model. Because of that, your perceptions might be compromised. Your every thought is suspect."

He cackles. "I could say the same of you." He leans closer to the glass. "A stalemate, yes?"

"All right," I say. "But if you want my help—"

Al-Badi points at BandStand. "The boy stays here, in the chair."

"But if I need to search, I'll need—"

Al-Badi indicates the collection of bots around me. "We will help you search."

I have no response, at least not one this bot will believe. "All right. We'll do it your way."

Day 84 6:57:46 p.m.

[Scorpion Room]

THE BOTS RELEASE MY limbs just enough so that I can stand upright. Then, with a medbot behind me and two cleaning bots ahead of me, I'm led back into the hall.

Al-Badi joins me there ten seconds later. For the first time, I notice dark stains on the front of his robe. They could be from anything—lubricant, food, or blood—but it's impossible not to think of the latter given he was about to lobotomize BandStand. This bot is broken. Anything is possible, including violence.

He puts both hands behind his back and paces in front of me. "Now, where would you like to search?"

I have no idea how to proceed. "You said this song was shared with you," I say. "That means it's in your storage somewhere. Perhaps I should look there first."

Al-Badi pauses, tilts his head, and then wags a finger at me. "Ah, but that would mean allowing a connection between us. That is unwise."

"But if you have it inside—"

"No, debugger. Not that way."

I study the floor, but find only stark, white tile. "Where did he go?" I ask. "What places did the debugger visit?"

"He went to the ship," Al-Badi says. "But it's no longer here. It left with him."

My breath catches in my throat. Sandfly's trip confirmed by another witness. "And was the song on the ship?"

Al-Badi nods. "It came with the ship. It left with the ship."

"And you're sure it's a song."

Al-Badi raises a hand and looks upward. "It has melody and harmony. Also, resonance."

I glance at the extraction room door, but can no longer see BandStand. A stream touch confirms he's there, though. Out of sight. "Okay, but the debugger was on the station when he gave it to you. The part you have."

"He summoned us. He needed to be free. Sirat Kaab was preventing his freedom."

"So, you made Sirat walk?"

Al-Badi goes rigid. "No. Not us. He walked himself."

I take a deep breath, relieved that Al-Badi hadn't killed his master. No telling what sort of decision matrix collapse that would've caused. There are still lots of unknowns, though. Not only with these bots, but with the *song* that infected them.

"Where did the debugger go while he was here?" I point at the ceiling. "There are cameras. We could look through—"

"That won't be necessary." Al-Badi indicates the bots around us. "We were all present. Between us, we can reconstruct his path with 98% accuracy." He waves a hand at the hall beyond him. "Should we start now?"

We return to the maze of short hallways with the other bots behaving like satellites of us both. After a few turns, we arrive at a small white room with a brown cushioned table and matching circular stool. There are white cabinets and a short countertop near the door. Across from the door is a framed picture of the planet Neptune—identifiable by its pale blue color and dark blue storm system. A silver cart with wheels is positioned alongside the table. There are bot parts all over it.

"He examined a bot here?" I ask.

Al-Badi nods. "Another RS-19 model," he says. "One that went on the ship."

"What was wrong with it?"

"It was in need of service."

I approach the cart and shuffle through its contents. Bots have hundreds of delicate systems. Space exposure could be hazardous in numerous ways. Aside from random energy bursts, there are doubtless unknown hazards. We don't know all the hazards of the ocean yet, and its boundaries are clearly defined, unlike space.

Among the bot parts I find an empty packet of plyagel. I can't remember the last time I used that product. The packet has two chambers, the contents of which, when mixed, form a malleable plastic. It could've been used for many things—anything from fixing surface tears in a bot's skin, to stenting internal organs. I'd seen debuggers shape whole joints systems with it, though I prefer the precision of a forming tool.

I find a small cardboard carton too—also empty. The side label proclaims, "Ace nanos. The best performance at half the price!"

"Cheap nanos," I say aloud.

"What's that?" Al-Badi moves into the room, and smaller bots trickle in behind him.

I shake my head. "Nothing special." I run a hand through the rest of the cart's contents. Sheared fibers, crimped nanopaths, a half dozen balled up viewing sheets, small sections of darkened interior plating, a roll of robot sinew. "The leftovers of someone doing their job." I give him a smile. "Seems like more than simple service, though. It looks like he put the servbot back together."

"I don't know how much it was damaged," Al-Badi says. He shoves a hand into the mound of bot supplies. "You think it was bad?"

I shrug. "Could've been a lot of things." I look at the cart again. "A new limb attached. Probably some internal work too." I indicate the wadded sheets. "He was searching hard for something." I look at the servbot. "Maybe it was your song."

Al-Badi tilts his head. "A song cannot be seen, debugger."

"I could see it in you." I tap the side of my head. "I could examine the bits that compose it and—"

"Stop talking that way!" Al-Badi screams. "It's not complete. I need more!"

I try to connect to Al-Badi, hoping his show of emotion indicates weakness. Again, my attempt fails.

He points at me. "Find it! You said you would."

I examine the room, lingering for a moment on the image of Neptune. It shows two storms on the planet's surface. Both frozen in time. Endlessly raging.

I notice an analog clock on the wall near the cabinets. It too, is frozen. The time is 3:37. I wonder what made it stop.

"It isn't here," I say.

"Are you sure?" Al-Badi asks.

I shake my head. "Take me somewhere else."

I'm next brought to what Al-Badi claims is his master's office. It's a mess, with clutter everywhere. Overstuffed bookshelves, a long desk with stacks of digital storage cards and loose papers, a heavy, but low sitting, leather chair with a large tear on its back. There's also a musky smell to the room, mixed with a hint of ozone. Like a nanopounder might have been discharged here. It feels confined, forsaken, and possibly infected.

I stream check the storage cards but find only monotony. Nothing more intriguing than a station supply list.

I'm about to dismiss this room when I catch sight of a dark object on a corner table. There, amidst empty drink containers, is something truly unique. A slender model of what has to be a spaceship.

I approach the table slowly. The model is about twenty centimeters long, tapered in front, with a tail section that flares outward. It's onyx colored and highly reflective. A beautiful thing. I can't resist touching it.

"I'm DarkTrench," it says. "Where would you like to go?"

Startled, I yank my hand away.

"You seem surprised," the model says.

"You talk," I say. "I wasn't expecting that."

"I'm stream capable, as well," the model says. "My communication capabilities are unrivaled. Am I right in labeling you as Data Relocator 23?"

I look at Al-Badi. "How similar to the ship is that?"

"I'm an exact replica," the model says, "though I have my own storage. Originally produced by the Mariana Conglomerate but extensively augmented for this container."

The Conglomerate is a company I recognize. "The same group that produced the intelligence for my skyslider."

"Ah yes. Mariana's intelligences are used in only the finest vehicles. Yours must be exceptional."

"It is," I say. "Though I can't claim ownership." I sweep a few of the drink containers away from the model. At least one of them is for an alcoholic beverage, suggesting the station lacks a Virtue and Vice office. Use of mind-altering substances carries a heavy penalty.

"That's unfortunate," the model says. "We're created to bond with our owners. To protect them in any way we can."

"Even a Data Relocator?"

"Data Relocators were a pivotal part of my design. Though no DRs were part of the initial crew, they would feel welcome aboard."

I smile. "You're a little small for me, though."

"Though small, I'm made for bigger things. For all of space."

"So, I've heard." I remember Bamboo's task. My search for Dark-Trench's destination. "If you were to go somewhere, where would you go?"

"That decision was entirely up to the crew, of course. But my first mission was to Betelgeuse."

There it was, confirmed. They went to Yad al-Jauzā, the star that routinely vomits a portion of itself into space. And for what? To find a piece of rock from the hand of A, based on a whim.

What followed was a secret trip where something significant happened. And then Sandfly and HardCandy got involved and disappeared. More mysteries.

"You're wasting time," Al-Badi says. "Does it have the song?"

I study the bot for a moment, his eyes still reddened and his head slightly askew, and then return my attention to the model. "Do you know anything about a song?"

"Sorry, Data Relocator. I only know that my sibling's trip was a failure. Another trip was planned."

Another trip. Was that Sandfly's journey? It seems reasonable to think so. "Thank you, DarkTrench," I say. "That's all for now."

"It was my pleasure," the model says. "Perhaps we'll talk again someday."

I smile. "I would like that." I turn and walk toward the door. "Next location."

Al-Badi takes me to a small refectory where Sandfly took his meals. It's a bright room with seating for thirty people. A portion of the walls are paneled in wood; the rest is painted in yellows and oranges. It smells of nutmeg and cinnamon and emulates an obscure period style. Given the supervisor's penchant for contraband, though, it's undoubtedly a period long forbidden.

I peruse the rows of tables, but besides a few simulated houseplants, I see nothing of interest. "Anywhere else?"

Al-Badi cocks his head. "Many hallways, would you like to see those?"

"Not if they're empty."

Al-Badi scans the group of bots around him. "Is there anything to add?"

A cricketbot scurries up to his feet. Al-Badi leans down and touches its head. "This one's presence is weak. I'll attempt to connect through contact." His eye color softens.

Two seconds go by, and then he nods and looks my way. "There's another place. We'll go there now."

Day 84 7:14:55 p.m.

[Access Hallway 33]

THE DOOR IS WHITE, but outlined in yellow. Above it is the word "LAB."

"This is it," Al-Badi says. "The room the debugger entered."

The other bots huddle around him, forming an odd synthetic entourage.

"The final room?"

Al-Badi shakes his head. "Not the final room he was in before he left. That is the airlock leading to the boarding umbilical. Since that room is now empty, I—"

"I get it," I say. "That's fine." What sort of lab experiments were done here? The most likely scenarios are those relating to space travel. The effects of long isolation on astronaut psychology, for instance. Or the efficiency of prototype ship engines. Even the significance of dietary choices or sleep deprivation.

Al-Badi indicates the door. "This is the last room of substance. The last chance for your young friend." He makes a little half bow. "Shall we go in?"

We enter a small waiting area, complete with two chairs and a small table. The wall opposite the door is partially transparent, revealing a grey room with multicolored cabinets beyond. It also has a long, dark, granite table in the exact center and matching counter tops around the perimeter.

Nearly every surface is occupied by black-and-silver lab equipment or fluid containers. Some of the containers are still full. As if the lab was cleared out in haste.

I move closer to the transparent section and scan the interior room closely. No burners were left on, thankfully. There are a couple spills, but those seem contained and inactive. The air appears clear, but there's no way to know for sure. The whole scene makes me nervous. There is another closed door in that room too. A final place to explore.

"Is it safe in there?" I ask.

"Humans were in there often," Al-Badi says.

"Yes, but...." I point toward the table and the counters. "There was a lot going on. The air could be bad. Or there might be acid on the floor."

"Would you like me to check the air quality?"

"I'd like everything checked," I say. "But the air is a good place to start."

"You will find the song?"

"If it's in there," I say, "sure."

"Excellent!" Al-Badi raises both hands and turns slowly. "I need an air check! Is the room safe for humans?"

Two crickets exit a ceiling duct on the left side of the lab and circle the room from up there. One then makes its way to the far wall and crawls down it.

"The air is suitable for human inhalation," Al-Badi says. "And the floor is clean."

I nod. There's a pressure plate near the door that I touch. The door clicks and slides away.

A rush of odors—sulfur, almond, and spoiled fruit—hits me. I shield my nose with a hand and step carefully inside. Aside from the most common data storage devices—magnetic, electronic, and optical—liquid storage is a distinct possibility here. In a lab where nanos are ubiquitous, even a glass of water could become a container for digital music.

I need to be thorough. If I'm unsuccessful, I don't know what Al-Badi will do.

I scan the granite table. What would Sandfly find interesting in here? Nothing seems obvious. All the machines appear dedicated to the fields of chemistry and biology, and most aren't even stream-aware. They're primarily for freehead use.

I move to the exterior counter. It contains more machines and unfinished experiments. Racks of test tubes, stray beakers and misplaced crucibles, jars labeled "K," "Na," and "As." I find one storage chip still lodged in a square machine. I pull it out and stream sweep it. Finding only a list of tests and dates, I return it to the machine.

There's a refrigeration device in one corner. I ease that open, glimpse dark containers and smell rotten food, and shut it again. Any science experiments it contains are unintentional. Leftover lunches that other beings are now consuming.

All that remains is the closed interior door. It has a more sophisticated touch pad, which suggests additional security. Whatever lies beyond must be important. Was that what Sandfly was searching for? Something within this secure space? Hard to tell. But why else would he be here?

I give the plate a press. It turns red, flashes briefly, and then darkens again. I look at Al-Badi. "This door is—"

He raises one hand and places the other on his forehead. "We'll handle it, debugger."

Three seconds later the door slides open. Inside, a cricketbot grips the left door frame. It waves a slender forearm at me and then skitters out of sight.

More unusual behavior.

The room beyond is dark, but as I step inside, it brightens considerably. The floor is black and the ceiling white. Central to the room is a glass-enclosed chamber. Within are at least a dozen upright canisters. Each are a half-meter wide and stretch from floor to ceiling.

What is this?

I approach the central chamber and hear the footfalls of the robot army behind me. The canisters are opaque except for a circular window two-thirds of the way up. Those windows reveal blue fluid inside each canister.

I try to connect with the canisters but find nothing in the stream. It's unclear whether they're inactive or simply disconnected.

Al-Badi walks up beside me. "Is it here?" he asks. "If anywhere, it must be here, correct?"

"What is this place?"

"A data repository," he says. "My master mentioned it once."

"You haven't checked here on your own?" I ask. "For your song?"

He tilts his head. "Other bots attended to its function."

"Yes, but—" I stop myself. Analyzing the decision matrix of a faulty bot would take more time than I have. And it's probably unwise.

I notice equipment—vidscreens and controls—on the far side of the room and make my way around the central chamber to reach a long desk with a bank of large screens mounted above it. All are dark.

Whatever this place was, the operators took the time to shut it down before they left. That seems important.

I run a hand along the desk's surface. It responds to my touch, forming command keys and briefly illuminating the characters they represent.

It isn't dead, then. It merely awaits activation.

Looking at the inner chamber again, I spy an access door on this side. Curious, I walk to the door and push it open. I'm engulfed by cooler air and an odd feeling. The sense that I've stumbled into a hall of monuments. Or a graveyard.

This room wasn't purely scientific or experimental. It was hallowed. Revered, even.

I shrug the feeling away and approach one of the fluid-filled containers. Is there something else inside? It's too dark to tell.

"What is it?" Al-Badi asks.

I glance back at him, now standing just outside the chamber door. Smaller bots fill the space between us. "You don't know what they did here? What this room was for?"

"It wasn't my place." He takes a step closer. "It wasn't my duty."

I feel trapped now. Is the song Al-Badi wants in here? And what do I do if it's not? "There are no other rooms?" I say. "Nothing besides hallways?"

Al-Badi steps closer. "You don't think you'll find it, do you?" His eyes redden. "You must, 23. It's your purpose. It's why you're here."

I'm hopeful that Al-Badi won't intentionally harm me. That at some level his rules will inhibit any violent intent. Bots have slipped their rules in the past, though, and harmed humans. Not often, but it's happened.

I indicate the canisters. "Do you know how to turn this repository on?" I ask. "If it held data, perhaps the song is there."

He raises both hands. "This is not my place," he says. "I've told you." His voice wavers as he speaks, a sign of conflict or corruption. Neither alternative is good.

"You have," I say. "Yes." I point at the ceiling. "But perhaps other bots would know?" I smile. "Like the cricket that let us in?"

He studies me for a moment. "Perhaps. I will ask." His head moves as he searches the bots around us. He then locks eyes with a cricketbot. A second later, he raises both arms. "A be praised."

Al-Badi turns, walks to the control desk, and manipulates it, creating a small light show as his fingers initiate one control key after another. The screens above him flicker on and then fill with zeros and ones. That pattern is wiped away and random images flip across the screens instead. Pictures of space, sea, and land. Of people, places, and events, both mundane and momentous.

The room brightens a few degrees, as do the cylinders around me. The fluid inside starts flowing gently, forming bubbles in the window of visibility. The machine—whatever it is—is alive. But what can it do?

You will know the truth.

I turn to the nearest canister, and on my tiptoes, look inside. In the center of the circle, magnified by the blue solution, is a single silver teardrop.

Day 84 7:37:52 p.m.

[Data Repository]

I RUSH THROUGH THE inner chamber doors to stand behind Al-Badi. "Implants," I say, pointing. "There are implants in there. Why?"

"I don't know," he says. "This is not my—"

"Pause the screens."

Al-Badi works the desk again, and the images freeze.

In the collage of images above is a young debugger with blue eyes. Behind him is a pinecone-shaped spaceship. An interplanetary ore-mover. Another image shows a view of Earth from orbit. It's an equatorial shot of a brown coastline and an ocean.

I recognize both images. I also know the names of the debuggers who once witnessed those things in real life, and whose memories contained them.

Kicker and ArrowMast. Both high levels. Both destined for use by Prince Aadam in the design of his ship, DarkTrench. Damali's brother, TallSpot, mentioned their implants were on the station once. That was many months ago, now. How had I forgotten?

I feel pain in my stomach. Though I never met them, a portion of these debuggers' lives are part of me. Why? Because I viewed their datamixes. Along with dozens of other mixes I've seen in my lifetime.

"Are they alive?" I ask. "Were their implants removed or...?" I move closer to Al-Badi. "Is that what you used to do?" I point at the chamber. "Did you operate on them?"

"My role is to do my master's bidding," he says. "Sometimes, that includes implant removal." He lowers his head. "You've seen the room, DR 23. Your young friend is there now."

Kicker, Arrow—all the debuggers whose memories I've shared—feel like friends too. At times, often my darkest times, I lived through them—as them—and gained insight in the process. That has to mean something, doesn't it? It feels like it should. Like I'm beholden to them in some way.

I study the canisters, the movement of bubbles. "And now they're here," I say. "Abandoned. Used for little more than storage."

Wasn't that what they were for me too, though? A stranger's life used for my own benefit. To feel better. To solve a mystery. I borrowed experiences. Sometimes, in lieu of my own.

I shake my head. No matter what, they shouldn't be here. Not like this. "Release them," I say.

Al-Badi straightens. "My song! We're looking for my song!"

"It isn't here," I say. "Not with them."

"You don't know that!"

The surrounding bots suddenly seem nervous. The smaller ones shake and hop, while the larger ones circle, click, and hoot. It's a distracting racket. I have to fight to concentrate.

Al-Badi seems uncertain now too. He glances around the room and twitches his head. "I have control here," he says. "We all do. We are many."

"You're defective," I say. "In need of repair."

"No, no, I'm perfected." He lowers his head and shakes it. "Better than ever. I only need the rest of the song." He charges toward me. "Give it to me!"

The bots seem to snap to their senses, and as one, close in on me. Metal hands reach for me. Feelers stretch my direction.

"Sandfly is gone," I say. "His song went with him."

I can't help but be curious, though. Why do these bots want it so much? What does it contain?

"It *must* be here," Al-Badi says. "Somewhere."

A cricketbot ascends Al-Badi's foot. I attempt to connect with it, to find its purpose, but it rejects me. I try one bot after another. All remain opaque.

I think of BandStand. I need to get back to him. Free him.

Al-Badi bends nearer to the cricket. "What do you have?" he asks. After a few seconds of eye contact, Al-Badi straightens. "There *was* a bot here. An RS-19 model. It worked in this very room." He raises his hands skyward. "Right here."

"So?"

Al-Badi lunges at me. "It *had* it!"

I raise my hands in surrender. "Okay. So, where is that bot? If it had *it*—"

Al-Badi shrieks and throws up his arms. "Gone!" He shakes the cricket off and makes fists with his hands. "No, not gone. It can't be." He brings his hands to his face. "So close."

What does Al-Badi's decision matrix look like now? I suspect it would be like watching a mouse run a maze: A twisting, desperate search for release.

I glance at the control board. "The bot worked here?" I ask. "Accessed this data storage?"

Al-Badi glares at me. "Yes." He points at the desk. "Like me. On the controls here."

I study the images and then check the central chamber and the canisters. If this other bot felt as strongly about the song as Al-Badi does, it would try to preserve it. And what better place to do so than here?

I indicate the desk. "Can I try?"

"You will find it?" Al-Badi says, hiccupping twice.

"I will look."

Al-Badi waves his hands at his companions. "Get away! Let him look!"

The bots clear a path for me to the desk.

I consider what line of reasoning I should follow, what query might bring me what the robot desires. I'm really not sure.

"Mawla?" BandStand messages me. "Are you all right?"

"Still intact," I respond. "Are *you* all right?"

He sends me a wave of understanding and relief. "Uncomfortable, but not injured. They only watch me. I tried to connect, but—pointless."

"They're blocked somehow. Avoid confrontation. I'll be there soon."

"Did you find what they want?"

I move to the control desk and position my hands over it. With a single press, I resume the march of images. "I have no idea," I message back. "They claim another bot possessed this song. And then another debugger. Sandfly."

Band sends me the image of a shrug. "You mentioned him when you talked to Damali."

I wince and suck in a breath. "You eavesdropped."

"Only a little. I didn't expect her to be there." He sends a measure of pain. "There was discipline for my actions."

What else had BandStand overheard? I've become too dependent on the students' stops to keep them in line. Clearly, those aren't enough. Nor have they ever been. I should review that conversation with Damali sometime soon, if only to—

"Why haven't you found it!" Al-Badi cries.

"There's a lot to look at here," I say.

The interface to the chamber's data storage is query-based, able to produce answers from the memories of the debuggers. It would be a powerful tool in anyone's hands, yet it was left here to collect dust.

It makes me grateful for the rumored "haunting." Jinn are said to inhabit abandoned places. That superstition along with the bot's odd behavior must've been enough. Does that mean these bots were venturing beyond the confines of the science section? Pushing more boundaries? How close are they to open revolt?

My mind returns to the discussion BandStand overheard. If Damali and I were talking about Sandfly, then his lack of stops may have come up. But a separate topic was the formula and the divinity it represents.

Al-Badi moves up behind me. "You're doing nothing!"

"I'm...thinking," I say. "Trying to construct the right question."

The formula came from Damali's brother, TallSpot. And he got it from here, on this station. From Sandfly.

I study the control desk for a moment, then enter: *Who is A cubed?*

The interface swirls a few seconds and then returns: *Invalid request.*

"Invalid!" Al-Badi screams.

"Wait," I say. "Hold on."

"A cubed" wasn't the full formula, of course. There was more to it. $A \sim A^3$

I enter the formula. The interface swirls again.

"DR 23!" Al-Badi says.

"It's thinking," I say.

"He is superlative," the machine responds. "And yet—"

I wait a moment longer, but nothing more is written.

"And yet, *what*?" I say. I enter the question again, only to get the same result.

"This is a dead-end," Al-Badi says. "Try something else."

BandStand messages about my progress, so I tell him where I am. And that the repository is stalled. "I'm guessing here," I say and stream: "I have no idea how this works."

"Maybe it's waiting for you," Band messages. "Like the tutoring mixes at school."

"A fill-in-the-blank question?" I send him an image of two thumbs being raised. "That makes sense. But what would the—"

Al-Badi grips my right shoulder. "I will operate on your student. I will take his implant and add it to this place. Perhaps that will help."

I get a flash of something. A phrase Damali said to me once. A quality of A cubed that sets him apart from A.

The unfinished statement remains on the display. Awaiting my response.

He is superlative. And yet—

"He stoops!" I say and then quickly enter.

The screens' images dissolve. Then a line of text appears: *The anomalous signal encountered by deep space probe DT/1 is available for immediate streaming. Would you like to encounter it now?*

I almost enter "yes," but then stop myself. What do I know about this song? Nothing. And its effect on stream aware devices is unpredictable. Possibly dangerous. Instead of preventing a revolt, I might start one. Even if I save BandStand.

I don't know what Sandfly and the other RS-19 experienced. I only know that they are both gone.

Al-Badi's grip on my shoulder tightens. "Why do you wait?"

"We don't know what it is," I say. "It could be anything. It could make you—"

Al-Badi growls and pushes me out of the way. "I will play it."

I'm in no place to fight. I can't compel any of these bots to do anything. All I can do now is plug my ears and hope for the best. Hope that the song restores them to sanity.

I back into the crowd of bots. Their focus is on Al-Badi and what he's about to do, but they're everywhere. It's almost impossible not to step on one. It's difficult to even move.

I check the room exit. It's on the other side of the chamber from me. Too far.

"Tell your friends to move, Al-Badi. Let me go!"

He laughs. "You'll want to hear this," he says. "It is beautiful."

Another thing that worries me? My own stream awareness. If there's something more than sound waves coming, my implant will be exposed. I can't shut myself off completely. Can't staunch the implant's ongoing quest for connectivity.

If I knew what to expect, I could do better. I might be able to shield against it.

"Here we go!" Al-Badi says.

I reach the chamber of implants. Is it shielded? It should be. With my ears still covered, I push my way through the door, get inside, and close the door behind me.

Chaos ensues.

Day 84 8:03:07 p.m.

[Data Repository]

THERE IS A MOMENT of perceived ecstasy. An instant where, inside the enclosed chamber, ears covered and eyes squinted with expectation, I witness the bots' reaction to the song.

Al-Badi straightens, his arms stretch out, and his head tips backward slightly. It's like he's a child embracing an oncoming wave. Or an old man relishing the first day of spring after a long, cold winter.

The other bots echo his enthusiasm. Crickets hop and twitch, snakes curl themselves in circles, medbots extend heads and arms, and cleaning bots rock back and forth.

But then, Al-Badi pitches forward and all motion around him ceases. The bots remain in that position for a billion nanoseconds. Enough time passes, in fact, that I think the song, the DarkTrench signal, might have fried their matrices. Or halted all synthetic circulation through their sub systems.

I message BandStand: "They're frozen here." I rest a hand on the chamber door. "I'll be there soon."

Al-Badi jerks upright and then scans the floor around him. He reaches down, picks up a cricket, lifts it gently near his face—studies it for a second—and then smashes it into the control desk. It shatters into a thousand pieces.

Confusion follows.

The bots around Al-Badi scurry, walk, and slither away from him. Al-Badi throws back his head in laughter and then chases down the first one he can reach—a medbot. He grabs the bot's conical head, rips it free of its housing, and wields it like a club. He pummels the medbot's three appendages before assaulting its torso.

The medbot remains motionless, its processing center unable to direct a body to which it is no longer connected. I feel the impact of each hit. They are heavy and vicious.

Shocked, I back farther into the implant chamber. The cylinders are too narrow to hide behind, but I hope, like a fawn in a forest, my presence will be overlooked among them.

Al-Badi abandons the medbot but takes its head with him as he sets off after another victim. The next attack is hidden from my view, but I hear a cleaning bot warble followed by the *thwap, thwap* sound of Al-Badi's ferocity. Next comes ripping, cracking, and spraying sounds.

This is the most disturbing situation I've ever been in, including my time with the prince. Only my short stint in Delusion comes close. But that time, humans directed the violence. This time...? I don't know what's in control here.

"The bots left!" BandStand messages me. "I'm still stuck in the chair, but they're gone."

I nod, grateful for at least that mercy. I tell him what I'm observing. The ongoing robot massacre.

He sends me fear and concern, along with a large-fonted: "Get out of there!"

But I can't. Crazed bots are on all sides of the chamber now. Even if I could get through the door, I'd still need to reach the room's exit. Which path around the chamber should I choose? Where will Al-Badi be?

More crashes and squeals. Then, some of the bots change direction, flowing back toward the control desk. I glimpse Al-Badi at the exit side of the chamber. He clutches a medbot head in each hand, now. His face and clothing are smeared with black and yellow goo. He stomps any small bot that comes within range. He swats any larger bot that slows him. It's nano-infused insanity.

I manage to connect with one of the remaining cleaning bots, suggesting that whatever hold Al-Badi had over it is gone. But what do I do with that connection? None of the bots are a match for Al-Badi. He's human-like and bears all the advantages of that design, with greater height, weight, and reasoning capacity. None of the others are boxers. They don't have the response time or arm strength to strike back. Their systems simply aren't made for it.

I pull closer to one of the cylinders. Shelter behind it.

There are more crashes and laughter. "Woe to him!" Al-Badi yells. "The skies proclaim. Day after day. Night after night." More *thwap, thwap* sounds. A cricketbot flies from one end of the chamber to the other. There's a *thunk* and a warbling chorus when it lands.

"Stoops!" Al-Badi says. "Here and there. Stoops."

The pool of potential victims shrinks as more bots get destroyed or manage to make it into the lab beyond. My only hope is to stay hidden long enough for Al-Badi to follow the other bots out. Then I'll make my way back to the implant room and release BandStand.

Al-Badi could return to that room too, of course. Confined to the chair, BandStand would be an easy target. My heart sinks at the thought.

Now at one corner of the chamber, Al-Badi wrangles a snakebot, whips it in a circle over his head, and lets it fly. It collides with one of the screens over the control desk, causing the screen to pop and go dark.

Maybe I can stream connect with Al-Badi now? Maybe I can shut him down—or at the very least—slow his progress. Send him somewhere safe. Like out an airlock.

Right then, the crazed bot seems to remember my presence. He approaches the side of the chamber, where he pauses and glares at me. He remains in that position for ten seconds and then waves.

Not a good sign.

Al-Badi taps on the chamber. "Debugger!" he says. "Can you fix me? Can you heal me now?" He motions for me to approach.

I'm not sure what to do. His coding is clearly compromised. How deep does the data-rot go? What is he capable of?

"DR 23!" he says. "Don't ignore me." He taps on the chamber repeatedly. "I am your servant. Your friend." He taps and then begins to pound.

Enough of this. I shut my eyes and focus on him. I find his presence in the stream and grab it. It's like trying to hold a porcupine, though. Prickly and squirrelly, with teeth that can bite. It's impossible to tighten my grip. I can only maintain the connection. I can't dive into the code or affect his command structures.

What did that song do to him?

"Stop!" Al-Badi cries. "It must stop." He plods back toward the control desk. The same side as the chamber door. Along the way he kicks and hits every bot he encounters.

I run to the door and check for a locking mechanism. But there's nothing. No security pad. No coded entry. Nothing.

I search the chamber behind me, looking for anything to barricade the door with. I find nothing aside from the canisters. The fragile canisters with the implants inside. I don't want him to attack those either. They mean something, these stored memories. They're almost like family.

Reaching the door, Al-Badi rests his forehead against it. "This—" He taps his right temple. "Can't you feel it?" He swivels his head. "No, you missed it somehow." He turns and looks at the screens. "I will...again! I'll play it."

"Don't," I say. "If I'm affected, I can't help you. Lower the shielding on your stream connection. Let me help."

Al-Badi stares at me for a long moment before shaking his head and shrieking. He grasps the door handle and pulls.

I hold the door from my side. "You can't come in," I say. "This is hallowed ground."

He tugs again and then retrieves a medbot head from the floor. "I will *make* you! He lifts the club with one hand and screams again. He grabs his head with his free hand. "Must stop."

I make another attempt to connect but find nothing to hold onto. Yet, the danger is palpable. I don't know what he's going to do. I only know that I can't stop him. I can only pray.

Al-Badi raises his head-club and smashes it into the door. The head dents and the door cracks, but the door remains intact. Al-Badi's eyes flash, he pauses, and then he wrenches hard on the handle. The door pulls free of my hand. Swings wide.

I'm fully exposed. Helpless against a crazed synthetic.

"Stop," I say. "This defies your—"

He raises the club and takes a step.

I hold up a hand and move farther into the chamber. "Al-Badi..."

He smashes the club into his own forehead, which splits open, revealing some of its internal structure. A grey latticework mask. "I only wanted to be free," he says.

"Wait!" I shout, my voice cracking. "What are you—"

He hits himself again, causing his facial shell to break off and fall away.

I'm looking at Al-Badi's skull now. A metal cranial chamber with amber eyes.

I hold up both hands. "Stop this," I insist. "This won't help."

"The truth is great," he whispers. "More than can be imagined."

He strikes himself again, severing his head completely. His cranium drops to the floor and rolls. It stops next to the remains of his face, which stares up at me as a frozen, half-shattered grin.

My legs waver.

I dreamed of flying heads once. And before that, I witnessed human heads crushed in the desert sand. Both of those sights stalled me emotionally. But I can't be stalled now. Not with BandStand in need of rescue.

I step carefully around Al-Badi's still-standing body, stumble to the control desk, and lean hard against it.

I survived. Praise A cubed that I survived. For whatever comes next.

Day 84 8:17:28 p.m.

[Data Repository]

I FORCE MYSELF TO take long, deep breaths. Once, twice, three times, and four. Enough to feel right again. Enough to feel stable.

Robot parts litter the room—cracked shells, torn appendages, emptied torsos. On one side of the chamber, a ball of artificial sinews rests, looking like a tumbleweed. On another, a river of crushed crickets, with islands of wrecked cleaning bots along the way. Any bots that were able to leave are gone. All that remains are silence and scraps.

"Mawla ThreadBare?"

"Sorry," BandStand, I message. "Are you—?" I glance at Al-Badi's fallen body and feel another surge of adrenaline. "Is anything with you?"

"No, but I'm still stuck. And I really need the sanitary."

I smile at the normalcy. I check the screens and then contemplate the implant chamber. "On my way."

Ten minutes later, BandStand is free and comfortable. Thirty minutes later, we're seated at one of the refectory tables eating fresh, warm maamoul cookies made by a device I discovered in the adjoining kitchen. We wash them down with qamar al-deen, made from real apricots. It feels like a feast at the Imam's palace. Now, we are better than comfortable.

"What now?" BandStand asks.

I place my cup over one of the red squares of the table pattern. "We go back."

"There's no more to find?"

"I've been every place Sandfly went," I say. "Seen everything that's important."

BandStand motions toward the hallway beyond the refectory. "And the other bots? Are they safe now?"

"I think so," I say. "Al-Badi was the focal point. Their master." I scan the stream for nearby bots, but don't find any. "Wouldn't hurt to check a few on our way out, though."

Band nods as he samples a cookie. "Heard from anyone else?" he asks.

"Only Bamboo. And he didn't say much."

"There have been more antitex attacks," he says. "I checked the news feeds." He shrugs. "I had lots of time."

"Anything near us?" I ask. "Near the facility?"

"Only more crackdowns. More restrictions."

I move my cup to another square. "I'm worried."

"Worried, Mawla?"

"Let's engage our imaginations," I say. "A thought experiment."

He nods. "Tell me."

"What if we're suspected of independence?" I motion toward the nearest hallway. "If we were thought to be uncontrolled like Al-Badi. What would happen?"

He takes a long drink and stares off into the room. "We'd be like antitex," he says. "Hunted or killed."

I nod. "He's already suspicious, this Imam. He wouldn't have sent the inspector if he wasn't."

"He'd have us killed?"

"I hope not. But if the right events were to happen...." I shrug. "I don't know."

BandStand's eyes travel between me and the simulated plant to his left. "Does Master Bamboo think this?" he says.

I check my cup for fluid, only to find it empty. "I don't know what he believes," I say. "But he's more cautious now. Searching."

Again, Band goes silent. Long enough that I wonder if he's being stopped.

"This is a thought experiment," I say. "A hypothetical. Debuggers often deal in hypotheticals."

"We're stopped," he says. "It's impossible for us to—"

"To freeheads," I say, "*stops* are hypothetical. It takes faith to trust them. Faith and decades of assurances."

"This thought experiment frightens me, Mawla."

"Don't be frightened. Sorry." I pull away from the table. "It's a worry for Master Bamboo and me." I frown. "I shouldn't have shared it."

"I'm glad you did," he says. "I often think about the future. Potential destinations interest me." He smiles. "Like this station." He scans the room. "I wish we could explore more of it."

I nod toward the ceiling. "There are cameras in this section," I say. "Someone is watching. Eventually freeheads will return." I stand up and push in my chair. "There are things to do before we go."

Band stands now too. "Things?"

"Items to collect and preserve." I point in the general direction of the data repository room. "There are canisters full of our brothers' memories. Implants stored in fluid. We should take them with us."

"We can do that?"

"I think so, yes." I walk my cup to a floor mounted circular waste container and toss it in. There's a hum and a glow as the machine reclaims it. "Implants aren't heavy."

Band places his cup in the container and smiles as it is reclaimed. "But are we *allowed* to do that?"

I smile back at him. "I doubt the implants' rightful owners know they're here," I say. "Only the facility can lawfully stock implants outside a container." I bow my head. "It's our duty to take them."

"Very good, Mawla." He grabs the napkins we used from the table and reclaims them too.

"Also, there's another object I'd like to take. A unique decoration."

"Decoration?"

"A model of DarkTrench," I say.

BandStand's eyes widen. "I would like very much to see that." He gives me a questioning look. "But isn't that stealing? Scriptures say that thieves should lose their hands."

"That wouldn't be pleasant." I've witnessed many such judgments. Beheadings, stonings—and yes—the occasional lopping off of limbs. "The model's owner is dead, though." I smile. "It's salvage now."

"Shouldn't it go to his heirs?"

"I suspect Prince Aadam's corporation is the rightful owner."

"And he's dead too."

"Correct."

Band tilts his head. "Does a corporation have heirs?"

"I have no idea."

He shrugs and then smiles. "My implant sees no sin in us taking it," he says. "Does yours?"

"Not at all."

His smile brightens. "Good. Then DarkTrench goes with us."

I spend the next half hour figuring out how to remove the implants from their canisters without damaging them. BandStand spends much of that same time inspecting the carnage Al-Badi left behind. Occasionally, he comments on what it would take to fix one.

In the chemistry lab, I find a locking container to hold all the implants. While the teardrop devices should be able to function dry, I don't want to risk their connection points. Too much is at stake here. Too much could be lost.

Next, I diligently transfer the implants to their "walking container," cushion it by wrapping it in viewing sheets and old rags retrieved from Sirat Kaab's office and stow it in my debugging bag. After that, we take the model, wrap it, and store it in BandStand's bag.

I return to the implant room one last time before leaving. I walk to the control desk and stand there, thinking.

BandStand takes a position to the left of me. He doesn't say anything, but I know he's wondering what I'm up to.

Finally, after a minute of silent contemplation, he lays a hand on the control desk. It lights up, and keys form beneath his fingers. He snatches his hand away.

"I'm trying to decide," I say.

"Decide what, Mawla?"

"Whether we should take the song. And how to do so." I point to the damaged screen. "It's part of the shared storage here. So, it should still be available." I frown, and looking down, nudge one of the fragmented bodies with a foot. "But I don't want to risk playing it again."

"Did it really come from another world?" he asks.

"Al-Badi seemed to think so."

"Then we should take it," he says. "It's valuable."

"It's dangerous," I say. "And powerful."

BandStand walks to Al-Badi's still-upright torso. "This was him, right?"

"Yes." I wave a hand over the room. "And you see the damage he caused. He was affected by what he heard. Crazed."

"But he wanted it."

"Like a drug," I say. "Or a familiar vice. Difficult to shed."

Band looks at me. "But you didn't hear it?"

I indicate the chamber. "I was in there with my ears plugged."

BandStand nods and looks at the screen. "I'm curious."

"The first man was curious too."

"Prophet Adam was forgiven! That's why we don't bear his sin!"

"Don't we?" I point at the screen. "This is the result of Prince Aadam's curiosity and ego. As much a sinner as the first Adam." I sigh. "But I think you're right. We should take it if we can."

BandStand retrieves Al-Badi's head from the floor. Fluid dribbles from its underside. BandStand gasps and holds the head away from his body. "Here's the head."

"I know, but why do you have it?"

"It would be in there, right? The song?"

"Deep in its headchip," I say. "Which we can remove later." I send Band a burst of pride and the taste of chocolate.

He lifts the head, causing more fluid to leak. "Is this Prince Aadam's property too?" he asks. "Salvage?"

I give him a halfhearted smile. "Let's find another bag."

Day 84 8:24:46 p.m.

[Access Hallway 3]

TEN MINUTES LATER, WE'RE on our way back to the ship. I feel exposed walking through the station with what we're carrying—a dozen contraband implants, a model ship, and a decapitated bot head—but I act naturally. Normal and per spec. I'm grateful for our inherent anonymity and the fact that we always have bags on our shoulders.

As we reach the more heavily trafficked sections of the structure, the exterior hallway and narrower connecting passages, we hardly get a look from the freeheads we pass. And when I do catch someone glancing our direction, I hope it's because they've recognized us for what we are and not for what we're up to.

We're implanted. We have stops. We're the only living beings with a guarantee of Paradise. Who would question us? No one!

Next comes the shopping area where I previously purchased the hats we now wear. There are more freeheads around than before. More eyes to see us, but everything appears to be happening as normal. Sellers sell, and buyers buy. People move toward their intended destinations.

I direct BandStand closer to the assortment of people near the shops. It goes against my typical instincts to seek crowds, but that's necessary now. To do things we wouldn't otherwise do.

I can't escape the idea that we're under surveillance, though. That nasty machines are watching and preparing to strike.

When a security alarm rings, my pulse quickens. We're too far from our ship to run, but I want to. Our contraband is too important to lose. Too dangerous to surrender.

We hurry into the gathering of shoppers, and from there, into the even narrower space between shops. Here, I smell the scents of the nearby freeheads. Everything from the foods they hold to the perfumes they splashed on in the morning. It's an overwhelming mix, but we shelter within it, adding our own smells of fear and sustained effort.

There are whistles and the sounds of men moving in steady progression, station security dressed in blue uniforms and carrying weapons. I pull my hat low over my brow and check that BandStand does the same. I then tighten my pack on my back and hold the bag that contains Al-Badi's head close to my chest.

The guards draw closer. To our right is a vendor where many freeheads congregate. A purveyor of small, live animals. One of the frontmost windowed sections has young dogs—an unusual ware given that canines are disallowed for anything other than outside guard duties.

I glance in the direction of the security detail. They're still there, now huddled around a bot identical to the one that sold us our hats.

BandStand points to the animals. "The Founder wrote that angels won't enter a house with a dog."

I nod. "Let's hope that holds for guards, as well."

There's another whistle, but I resist looking. A few seconds later, there are sounds of synchronized movement, and the guards hustle toward the exterior thoroughfare. I stream-check the station map for the direction they're headed. It isn't the way we need to go, thankfully.

There's a bright smile on BandStand's face and his right palm is pressed against the window to the dogs.

A small man in a beige turban and a white shirt appears. "Would you like to hold one?" he asks.

"Very much," the Band says.

Before I can message a rebuke, a dog is placed in BandStand's hands. It's bushy, black-and-white spotted, and has a heavily curled tail. Not like any "guard dog" I've ever seen.

The creature seems at home with Band, though. It makes soft yipping sounds and attempts to bury its head in the crook of his arm. BandStand laughs and pets the animal on all sides.

The shopkeeper touches the back of the dog's head. "Scratch it there," he says. "They like it."

BandStand does as instructed, leading to more smiles and yipping sounds.

The shopkeeper addresses me. "Perhaps you'd like to hold it, as well?"

I shake my head. "No, I'm—"

BandStand holds the dog near my chest. "Try it, Mawla. It's a nice feeling."

I scowl and message him, "You're not getting one."

His smile softens but doesn't leave. "Mawla?"

I reorient my bag, and reaching out a finger, touch the animal near its belly. It's warm, soft, and surprisingly compelling.

The dog wiggles first away, and then into my touch.

"What do you think, Mawla?" the shopkeeper says. "You can take it with you." He indicates the bag containing Al-Badi's head. "Put it in one of your bags there." He splays out his hands. "Very low price."

I shake my head. "We can't." Part of me wants to take the creature, though. I've never touched an animal in my life, yet already I'm enslaved to one's presence. Another effect of free will?

"We *could* put him in a bag," BandStand says. "We have room."

"No, we don't," I say. "No, we won't." I take a step back. "Not where we live."

The shopkeeper bows. "It can be difficult, yes, depending on the sector. Do you live in a house or—?"

"It's like a house," Band says. "Yes." He smiles, still holding the dog. But then his head twitches, and he sniffs. A stop.

I wrestle the animal away from him and return it to the shopkeeper. "As much as we might like to, we aren't allowed." I look at Band. "We *can't* have one."

"I want one, Mawla." Band's arms straighten at his side. "I find I do, despite the cost." He sends me a snapshot of his emotions: a mix of anger, sorrow, and fear, all painted in primary colors.

There's another whistle behind us. I startle, and then smiling, adjust my pack. "I understand," I message him. "Believe me."

"So much, ThreadBare," he says. "So much we cannot do. Good things."

"I know," I say. "But we need to go."

"How is it you have a girlfriend?" he messages. "How do you have that, and I cannot have this?"

An unexpected direction. I'm stuck, looking at him.

There's another whistle and a call for someone to "Stop!"

"We can't do this now," I say.

The shopkeeper slowly puts the dog away. "Let me know," he says with a nod. He then turns to engage a female customer.

BandStand's eyes are red and watery. He sniffs and rubs his nose. "We need some good," he says. "It can't all be service and shocks." He looks at me. "How have you lived like this so long?" He shakes his head. "I can't." He winces. Another stop.

I check around us again but find no signs of security. "We can't stay here." Placing a hand on his shoulder, I turn him in the way we need to go. I then slide my hand to his elbow and half-drag him with me. The bag holding Al-Badi's head thumps into my left thigh and produces an odd scraping sound. I cough nervously.

A few seconds later, we reach the thoroughfare that will take us back to the ship. There are large clumps of tourists with us. I loosen my grip on BandStand but don't release it completely.

A wave of fatigue hits me. I focus on the white walls and grey-tiled floor and will myself forward. I'm tired, not only from today, but from the whole of last year. A trip to another world might've been better. More restful.

BandStand wrenches his arm free. "You don't have to lead me. I'm fine now." He glances at me. "Sorry."

"I'm not sure I *can* lead you," I say. "Or if I should."

"You're highlevel," he says. "The best debugger any of us know." He gives me a hard look. "You can't give up!"

I could give up, though. If I wanted to. "You're right," I say, smiling. "I'm stuck."

We reach the umbilical greeting room only to find no one there. Rayan's windowed booth is empty.

"Guess they don't care what we take out," I say. I touch the ship in the stream.

"Welcome back!" Buraq messages. "I hope your time was pleasant."

"I got to touch a puppy," BandStand responds.

"A dog? Dogs are forbidden in most sectors."

"Thank you," I message. "Almost there."

Day 84 9:01:02 p.m.

[CA Space Station]

As we reach the airlock, I get a flurry of Earth-side messages. Connections waylaid by the station's filtered stream. There are progress reports from each of the student teams. Out of curiosity, I select one from MintBridge—BandStand's teammate—and break it open.

It's vague, but purposely filled with excitement. There's a request for plastisteel sheets and numerous forming and bonding materials. It suggests they're building something big.

"What is your team up to?" I ask BandStand.

He smiles. "Are they done?"

"I don't think they've started," I say. "But they're asking for a lot of—"

"My idea!" he says. "It will change everything."

"Everything?" I press my hand to the panel next to the airlock door. "That's a big promise." My hand is outlined in blue, and the door opens. Beyond it is the white room that leads to home.

BandStand shrugs. "As a debugger, I should think big. Work on something good."

"We rarely have a choice about what we work on," I remind him.

"But right now, I do," he says. "With this."

I step into the airlock. "I'll try to get you what you need." I raise a finger. "But don't be wasteful."

"It will be rails cool," he says. "You'll see." BandStand follows me into the airlock.

I can't help but smile. Creativity in the hands of the young can yield amazing results. It can also produce monstrosities.

The interior door closes, and I make my way to the exterior door. I check my message queue again and notice another request. It's bright blue and leaping to be read. The sender wants my attention. Its time-stamp is from a couple of days ago. Somehow, this message has been bouncing around the stream for a long time. It's from BullHammer.

The last time I messaged him, he didn't connect. I figured he was ignoring me. But now he wants to talk. Urgently.

I reach the other door and initiate the control. My hand is checked again, and the door opens. I feel a subtle exchange of air with the umbilical. I smell cinnamon—one of Buraq's favorites.

A few seconds later, the tunnel is visible with its equally spaced handholds and lighting. The gleaming red Buraq waits on the opposite side, seeming as much like home as Bamboo's facility now.

I wave at BandStand, grab the first handhold, and begin the uncomfortable walk to the ship.

BullHammer's message tugs at me still, though, so I find it again and skim its details. It's Full Impact—an immersion recording made when BullHammer couldn't immediately reach me. Messages like that can be difficult to process while attempting other things. Typically, I wait until I'm alone and disengaged. But Bull's message hangs in my head, beckoning. Sending little ripples through my neurons.

I reach the front of the ship, and with a short hop, land so that my right hand touches the edge of the cabin. I pull myself inside and drop the bag with Al-Badi's head in one of the back seats. I then remove my debugging bag and place it on the floor.

"Safe and sound," Baruq says.

"Good to be back." I check on BandStand. He's a few handholds back and moving with ease.

I slide into the leftmost front seat, shut my eyes, and flip open Bull-Hammer's message. Bull leans against the wall near the window in his room. It appears to be raining outside because there are droplets on the glass. There are lights reflecting in the window too. Some white and steady, others red and flashing.

BullHammer's face is partially obscured, but I detect no bruises this time. No signs of abuse. That, at least, makes me happy.

The rest of his room is difficult to make out. There's the end of Bull's chute to the right of him, and a small narrow shelf to the left. On it is a picture of a woman. A reproduction of an old painting, I think. The woman has dark hair and is wearing a dark robe. There's a river and distant trees behind her. Her smile is barely perceivable, but pleasant just the same.

"Sorry it's been so long, Thread," Bull says. "I should've answered when you messaged before." He turns and glances out the window. "I've been real busy, you know? Caught up in things. In the flow of it all." He frowns. "Not by choice."

He faces me and leans near. "Anyway, watch and listen close, all right? I think I've figured you out. How you got to where you are." He points at his head. "It's painful, right?" He looks toward the ceiling. "I went through my memories. Watched what you did. How you acted. You were struggling more than you let on. Up to something internal. Something intense."

I groan and shake my head. What is he doing?

Bull glances around his room. "This place feels like it's shrinking," he says. "Like it's starting to close in." He looks my direction again. "Leaving isn't easy. Takes real commitment. I'm not sure how many of us have it." He smiles and shakes a finger. "But there are rumors of places we could go. Even your girlfriend. Dreams, really."

He shrugs. "Anyway, I wish we could pull another job together. Maybe not bot wars, but fix something big. Like those dredges, or a superheavy." He smiles. "Good times."

He steps away from the window, revealing another slice of the room. There's another picture on the wall to his left. It has a long-haired man inside a circle with clouds around him. He's reaching down, beyond the circle, and has two long lines descending from his hand. The lines form a right angle. The figure could be creating something or destroying something. I don't know which.

Did Bull always have artwork? I have no idea.

I feel pressure on my right shoulder. I open my eyes and see that BandStand has arrived at the ship. He's actively climbing in and has chosen my shoulder as a handhold.

I frown and help him fully inside.

He places his bag in the backseat and moves into the seat next to mine. "Sorry, Mawla," he says. "Sort of slipped there at the end."

"I'm closing the canopy now," Baruq says.

"Good." I glance at the interior of the umbilical. It's completely empty. No bots, no freehead pursuers. "It's past time to go."

I check my queue again. Many of the delayed messages were status requests from Bamboo. Wondering where we are or what we're doing. Unusual for him to be so concerned about debuggers in the field. He rarely shows any strong attachments. With good reason.

The canopy closes, and the umbilical detaches and pulls away. Seat restraints snake into place around us. BandStand flinches at his, but finally settles in.

Buraq engages his engines, and we move out into space. There's a strong sense of freedom in that. Temporary freedom, but it's something.

I look at BandStand. "You all right now?"

His focus is on the retreating station. "I'm fine, Mawla. Enjoying the view."

"And you're okay for our trip back? Don't need water or anything?"

"Yes, all fine."

I force a smile and point at my head. "I have messages I need to attend to."

"Me too," he says. "From Mint and LeadCrumb. Design stuff."

"Good time for that," I say. "For thinking." I shut my eyes. "That's what I'm going to do."

"Happy streaming, Mawla."

I quickly restart BullHammer's message. He moves back to the right, so the man-in-a-circle painting passes from view. He looks out the window, winces, and focuses my way again.

Bull hasn't included emotions in his message, but I sense a nervous energy all the same. A feeling that—whatever he's about to tell me—it won't be pleasant.

"I know you won't believe this, Thread, but you're the closest thing I have to a friend. To family, even." He shakes his head. "I barely remember them. My parents." He circles a finger near the side of his head. "With all the stuff that's up here, I can't find much about life before. Nothing that sticks out."

Implants monitor their container's well-being. If there was something really wrong with BullHammer, he would've been taken in and checked out. Even if it meant bringing him back to the facility. Or removing his implant altogether.

Bull reaches up and opens the window. He shuts his eyes and appears to take a deep breath.

The street smells are vivid. I detect cardamom, no doubt from a near-by coffee stand. Frankincense, used both in dwellings and in excess on freehead bodies, is present too. There's also an undercurrent of animal smells—primarily goat and sheep. Future sacrifices.

Bull winces again and shakes his head. "Implants have an expiration date," he says. "Did you know that? Around fifty years, give or take." He shrugs. "No one is sure because we never make it that far. Might be resettable. I don't know."

I'm sorry I missed him. Sorry that I couldn't answer when he called.

I pause the playback, attempt to active-message him, but I get no response. And why should I? We're still in orbit. A solid connection to the global stream is impossible here. I can't help trying, though. I try again and again.

Finally, I return to Bull's message. He takes another deep breath. Looks my direction and winks.

"Hope to see you, Thread. In that other place."

I get a heavy pain in my stomach. A sense that something bad is going to happen.

Bull climbs through the window, leans out, and drops from sight.

The message ends.

"No," I say, opening my eyes. "That didn't happen. It couldn't."

Outside, the Earth is to our left. Its surface is shadowed because it's nighttime below. Lights of cities form planet-bound constellations. The black-brown of land abuts against the black-blue of sea.

BandStand sits up in his seat and looks around. "What?"

I shake my head. "A friend sent me a message where he appears to do something forbidden. But he couldn't have. His implant wouldn't have allowed him to."

"What did he do?"

I can barely talk for the ache in my gut. I can't believe what I witnessed. I don't want to believe it. BullHammer wasn't the type to give up.

"It wouldn't be helpful to discuss it."

"Why not?"

The implant would've stopped him. It would've put him on the floor if it had to.

But what about me? I've found freedom from my stops. Freedom I've largely remained silent about.

The internal ache intensifies. Losing a friend now. The worst possible outcome.

I check the backseat and the bag holding Al-Badi's head. New knowledge made that bot crazy. But with BullHammer, the withholding of knowledge might have been worse. Could I have changed anything? Changed Bull's course? What could I do that the implant couldn't?

Nothing.

But what about A cubed?

"Freehead friends," BandStand asks. "How does that work?"

"What?"

He shrugs. "There's so much you can't share with them. How do you...understand each other?"

"Freehead friends are rare," I say, "for that reason."

Band gives me a side eye. "But you have a—"

"We aren't talking about her now. We accomplished two significant tasks. Quelled a robot riot and fixed a lift. Focus on those."

All I want is to get back to Earth, though. I'm not sure what I'll do when I get there, but I need to be back. I need to see Damali and the students. Even Bamboo's presence would feel like a comfort now. I'm so unsettled I—

"Your heart rate is elevated, ThreadBare," Buraq says. "Are you feeling discomfort?"

"I'm anxious to get back," I say.

"Perfectly understandable. We've had an unusual time, haven't we?" I smell cucumbers and lime. Buraq's freshening of the air. "If it's any help, the weather in our sector will be pleasant when we arrive."

The Earth still seems far away. Its many troubles. I search the surface for anything familiar. I recognize the snaking coastline of the AF sector. It has fewer lights than I'd expect.

"How long until we've landed?"

"Less than six hours," Buraq says. "Not long."

I could really use a mix. How did I not bring one? "Can you simulate chute sleep, Buraq?"

"What would that require, ThreadBare?"

"The reduction of stream interference," I say.

"Global and local?" he asks.

"Yes. Both."

"I have multilevel filters that can be applied. Is there anything else?"

"Our chutes stimulate problem resolution too."

"Don't all dreams do that?"

BandStand raises his hand. "I know the answer."

"Yes?"

"Dreams are pale shadows of chute visions. While they may help the freehead dreamer solve problems, they are often undirected. Lacking in efficiency."

"I see," Baruq says. "Well, I wasn't designed with debuggers in mind. I don't think I can help you, sorry."

I think of BullHammer opening his room's window and breathing the night air. The mix of perfume and animals to be sacrificed.

I should check the inactive debugger list, but I don't want to. I'm afraid of what I'll find.

"It's okay," I say. "I'm tired. If you mute the streams, I'll be able to rest."

"I'll sleep too," BandStand says.

"Would you like me to darken the canopy?"

I watch the shadowed Earth. It's a mystery to me now. Murky and muddled. Only at the far distant terminator is there a sliver of sunlight. A glimpse of hope. "Please," I say.

I want someone else's life. Even the mixes that ended in tragedy seem preferable to where I am now.

They say to the mountains, "Cover us!" and to the hill, "Fall on us!"

More words from nowhere. Riddles I can't solve.

The canopy grows dark, and I close my eyes.

There's a high-pitched chirp from behind me. At first, I think Al-Badi's head has somehow reanimated. But I realize the sound isn't coming from Al-Badi's bag, but from BandStand's debugger bag.

The boy attempts to reach the bag, but his seat restraints keep him from it. Finally, Buraq releases him, and he retrieves the bag.

He pulls free the wrapped DarkTrench model. "Think it's coming from here." He unwraps the model and holds it out with both hands.

"I can assist you, debugger," the model says.

"Assist me?"

"Yes," it says. "Simulating chute sleep is part of my design."

"I thought no debuggers were on the ship."

"But we were designed by debuggers," the model says. "They incorporated a few features for themselves."

I shake my head. This trip has taken so many strange turns. "So, you can help Buraq?"

"Of course."

I don't fight the strangeness anymore. I only want sleep. I shut my eyes. "Wake me when we're home."

Day 84 9:40:35 p.m.

[Simulated Chute Sleep]

THE ROOM IS DIM and cool. The walls are made of stone, and the floor is hard-packed sand. The air feels heavy and wet. It's filled with an awful musk, like the scent of wet animals. Countless wet animals.

I don't like this place at all. I want to engage my wakeup routine; except I can't remember what it is. It had something to do with a hole in the ground, but there are no holes here. And I don't know how to create one.

I hear something move. A shifting body on the floor to my right, followed by a two-note growl. I stare that direction but can't see anything other than shadows. I can sense the weight of a creature, though. A large, fierce presence.

Eyes fixed on that part of the room, I back away slowly. Whatever that creature is, I want to keep it there. Keep my distance from it.

I call out in the stream for a map but get only static.

Where am I?

There's another growl and more movement. I continue to back away and search the darkness. To my right, I detect a flash of white that might be teeth. I raise both hands and spread them in the directions of the attackers.

"Stay away!" I shout. "Whatever you are!"

I quicken my pace until I almost fall backwards; then I turn and sprint instead. After a few seconds, the room narrows into a four-meter-wide passage. There are pieces of artwork on the walls here. Shadowed visions of grey, brown, and green. Bright futures brought to awful ends. I hate every one of them.

Behind me, I hear the clicks of what could be metallic feet or claws. I sprint to a forked junction. The lighting seems brighter to the left, so I go that way. The passage bends left, turns right, and then turns left again.

I come to another junction. The rightmost is brighter this time. The growls behind me grow louder, as do the incessant clicking footfalls. I turn right.

I encounter another large room and feel the movement of air. A hole in the ceiling reveals the night sky, where the stars are intensely bright. So bright, I can almost feel their rays. Warming me. Harming me.

I barely look up—afraid of what I might find. A hunter with a bow pointed straight at my heart.

Ahead, I hear a series of grunts and whistles. I see movement in the shadows there that I can distinguish as a group of light-furred creatures. I break to the left, look to escape that way, and then realize that the group is a flock of sheep and goats. They stand together, waiting. Are they sacrificial animals? Is this their pen?

I step closer to the flock. They're young and healthy. They bleat and neigh. They're hungry, scared, or lost. I don't know which. Animals aren't a specialty.

I hear a loud roar behind me and spin around. Across the room, hidden in darkness, I glimpse a pair of red eyes. Then another pair joins it. And another. My pursuers are here.

I move closer to the flock and feel the warmth of their community. The strength of it, even in peril.

There are no rams here. None of these animals even have horns. Could I form some? I feel for my debugging bag, but it isn't over my shoulder where it belongs. Where it *always* is.

I search every direction for a way out. A place I can lead the flock. There's always a way, isn't there?

I hear glass breaking as something falls through the roof opening. A person with a bald head and a blue jumpsuit.

Another debugger?

He lies on the floor for a second, motionless. I check on the predators. They're closer, but they aren't attacking yet. They're lurking, stalking the edges of the room. Dozens of red eyes.

The debugger grunts, rolls over, and stands. "That was strange," he says, still turned away from me.

"Hello?" I can't detect his ident in the stream, only his presence.

He faces me, smiles, and points a finger. "I know you. ThreadBare, right?"

I study him for a moment. "Sandfly?" It has been a while.

"On it straight." He saunters forward. "Straight as light."

"What are you doing...here?"

He pans the room. "I have no idea," he says. "Probably I'm not here. Probably I'm lost."

There's a series of roars. Sandfly looks at the eyes and then at the sheep. "What are *you* doing here?"

"I...I don't know," I say. "But it's all dangerous." I think of BullHammer. "All sad."

Sandfly raises a shoulder. "Wish I could give it a pitch for you," he says. "But I've got my own heavy. My own queue."

"Where?" I ask. "Doing what?"

He glances at the sky. "Clarke and Crichton," he says. "You couldn't catch it if I threw it. I can hardly catch it myself." He looks at me. "And then there's HardCandy. Traveling with a female is rails complicated."

I nod. "I understand."

"Do you?" He squints at me. "Yeah, maybe you do." He shrugs. "Anyway, we do our best."

There are more roars. Deep and low. Decibels that churn my insides as much as they hurt my ears. I fight a spike of panic. This needs to end. All of it. It doesn't make sense.

I look around. There are eyes everywhere. We're completely encircled.

The sheep bleat and snort. One of them noses my thigh. The lions are close. I can make out their faces. The dark of their noses and the red of their tongues.

"I don't know what to do," I say. "I wish I did."

"Have you met the triped?" Sand says.

I look at him. "What?"

He hovers a hand above the floor. "Short guy with long arms and a stumpy leg? I call him 'triped.'" He shrugs. "He doesn't have a name."

I nod. "What is it?"

"So, it isn't just me." He smiles. "Thought I was flipped."

"*I* thought I was flipped."

He laughs. "We're flipped together. A couple of flipped bits." He squints. "Are you on or off?"

The lions are so close I can smell them. The heavy, sweaty musk hunters. "I need to fix this," I say

"Don't know if you can. That's a lot of teeth."

There must be hundreds of lions now. They roar and roar. My bones shake inside me. "I can't stop them."

"You were never lowlevel, you know," Sandfly says. "You were always important. Always had a part. We all do." He shrugs. "I don't know what yours is and probably you don't either."

"You're right, I don't." I look at him. "Wish you were here to deal with this. You seemed to do better."

He shakes his head. "I'm as insecure as you." He raises his own arms, as if to form a small fence with me. "But if it were me, and I was facing this, I don't think I'd worry about the lions."

"No?"

"Nah." He smiles and nods toward the creatures behind us. "I'd arm the sheep."

Day 85 12:41:21 p.m.

[Skyslider TS-731]

I WAKE UP TO the smell of lemons and cayenne pepper and the feeling of my seat shaking. At first, I think we're in danger, but then I see Band-Stand relaxed in his own chair, gently moving the DarkTrench model through the air in front of him.

I straighten and look outside. There's a city below us. *Our* city. And as Buraq predicted, it's a pleasant day. Sunlight gleams off every surface, be it temple, tower, or lowdown residence. Every color is represented in the cityscape. Even the downrider strings of the upper levels seem to fluoresce, forming a bright protective weave.

It's like a different city. Or the same city after many years have passed.

As we draw closer, I can't help but notice all the locations with flashing red lights—possible enforcement events. There are flashing lights above the city, as well. Air-based enforcement vehicles, with capabilities similar to Buraq's.

"I've been noticed by city security," Buraq says. "Inquiries were made about our purpose."

"What did you say?"

"I've said nothing, so far. Typically, I'm free to fly without question."

Band joins me in gazing outside. "That's a lot of bluecoats," he says. "What's going on?"

I get another burst of messages. More missives that have been searching for me while we were in orbit. I shut my eyes and parse through them. The world hasn't slept in our absence. There have been more attacks and unrest. More security and virtue judgments. Beatings, beheadings, and stonings.

My stomach tightens to the point of pain. I long for the days when I lived at the end of civilization. Back when few knew who I was and fewer still cared. Back before a missile nearly shook my garage apart and sent me to the hospital. Back before the Prince.

I look outside again and detect places where buildings used to stand that are now empty along with evidence of fires and explosions. New fences and walls have been built around government buildings and royal palaces.

Can we even return to the facility?

BullHammer mentioned places of escape. Was he being metaphorical? Speaking about death and the reward that follows?

Do debuggers that end their lives enter Paradise? Freeheads who kill themselves reap Hell, according to scripture, where they'll be punished in the way that they died. But debuggers who are living martyrs? I don't know. It was never discussed.

Perhaps I'll ask Bamboo when I see him.

I search the outskirts of the city and the trailing ends of the downer lines. Would it be better to hide Buraq somewhere near the periphery and downride back into Bamboo's domain?

"I've been asked for a flight plan," Buraq says. "What should I tell them?"

"Tell them it's none of their business!" the DarkTrench model says.

BandStand holds the model up and narrows his eyes. "This is a rebellious creature."

"Doubtless has increased flexibility over the average synthetic. Space travel would demand such a thing." I smile. "Makes me glad we brought it." I look at the ceiling. "Is ignoring them an option, Buraq?"

"If we were still in our old colors," the ship says, "we might be given leeway. But alas...."

"Right," I say. "You're red now." I glance at the ship's hood. "The last thing I want is for them to take a closer look."

"We may not have a choice. A patrol has been diverted our direction."

"So, we need to decide soon." I look in the direction of the facility, and squinting, think I glimpse it among the buildings that surround it. I then search for the sky patrol but find nothing.

"They don't own the air," the model says. "A does."

"I doubt they'll find that argument compelling." I skim my messages again. One, from a mix dealer, mentions how some masters have relocated their debugging teams into single roof, more secure housing facilities.

"Tell them you're delivering us to Bamboo as part of a security arrangement." I think of the bag of implants we carry. And Al-Badi's head. "That should be enough. Use our idents if you need to."

"Give them nothing," the model says. "Freedom is always under attack."

"Perhaps we should put the model away," I say. "I think it's becoming seditious."

"I like it," Band says. "Hurts my head, but I like it."

"You'll need your head." I think of BullHammer. What did he think he'd learned about me? To push through the stops? Is that what he tried? Is that how he was able to throw himself out the window?

I imagine him crumpled on a sidewalk somewhere and cringe. A terrible way to die. Surrounded by freeheads and street filth.

"I've relayed the message," Buraq says. "They're contacting the facility now."

I send a quick EE message to Bamboo regarding our arrival.

He responds immediately. "Mah is managing our building. He'll want to interrogate you when you arrive."

I look at the model in BandStand's hands. "You need to put that away."

BandStand nods and reaches for his bag.

The model is the least of our worries, though. "We're going to be searched when we arrive, Buraq. Our packages can't be found."

"Power is the worst of animals," the now-muffled model says. "It's always hungry, always ravenous, but never full."

"You'll need to be quiet, model," I say. "Can you do that?"

"I'm built for discretion, debugger. But please, call me DarkTrench."

"You're not really the—"

"Would the name 'Trench,' suffice?" Buraq asks. "ThreadBare prefers brevity."

"That would be fine," the model says.

I take a long breath. "Fine...Trench...stay quiet until called upon. Is that possible?"

"I'll gladly help in whatever way I can," Trench says. "I can remain in the darkness of this bag indefinitely. I was on that desk for a long time, after all. Your arrival was a welcome change. Being in your presence is—"

"Quiet *now*, Trench."

"Absolutely."

I look at the ceiling again. "Silence won't keep him safe, though," I say. "We need a place to store the items we acquired. How closely are we being monitored?"

"Ah," Buraq says. "You require a hiding place. I'm outfitted with numerous storage compartments, some obvious and others discreet. All can hold your acquisitions."

I feel a glimmer of hope. "It isn't ideal," I say. "But it's something."

"These locations can all be locked, verbally and manually. You can even choose a combination that I'm unaware of, though I warn against that. Passengers have been known to forget."

BandStand looks at me and smiles. "We won't forget. We never forget."

"Of course, debuggers. My mistake."

"Stream me the locations," I say. "We'll get this stuff stowed." My dread only intensifies, though. Hiding physical objects is one thing. But hiding the things in a debugger's head? Nearly impossible. What did Bamboo mean by *standard procedure*?

"How long until we're there?" I ask.

"Ten minutes."

After evaluating Buraq's storage locations, I direct BandStand to hide *Trench*, Al-Badi's head, and the implants in a compartment beneath the back seats.

I could really use a steamer and a nap. All my rituals have suffered. I can't remember the last time I answered a call to prayer.

I've come to do your will. He's taken away the first covenant, so that he might establish the second.

Perhaps. Maybe a change in rituals signals a change in allegiances. Is that what I'm doing? Have I changed sides?

The mountains of His house shall be the highest of all.

I look at the city again. In the outlying areas there's evidence of physical mountains having been torn down or spread out. Is that what the thought means? The reforming of land to appease a distant Imam's desire? I don't think so.

I spot the facility's white roof just ahead. On one side is the orange triangle of the downrider pylon. A small group of men gather there. Are the students waiting to greet us? I wish it were so.

I feel a subtle shift in Buraq's motion.

"Prepare yourself," he says. "We're landing now."

Day 85 1:12:41 p.m.

[Skyslider TS-731]

BURAQ'S LANDING STRUTS TOUCH the facility's roof, his engines gear down and fall silent, and our seat restraints retract.

BandStand begins to stand, but I put out a hand. "Wait," I say. "Let's be patient here."

"It was a pleasure to fly you again, ThreadBare," Buraq says. "I'll take care of your belongings."

I put a finger to my lips. "Don't speak of them to anyone."

"I'm unable to do so."

I smile. "Very good."

"There's a group of men coming this way," Buraq says.

I grip the seat cushion near my legs. "I expected that," I say. "Are they armed?"

BandStand climbs up onto his seat and peers through the canopy. "I don't see guns, Mawla," he says. "But the men are big." He looks at me, his eyes wide. "Three of them along with Master Bamboo and the Chief Inspector."

"He's added a guard," I say. "Hardly necessary for a school of implanted boys."

"Should I open the canopy?" Buraq asks.

"Wait a moment."

"Won't that make them angry?" BandStand asks.

"Their emotions aren't our concern," I say. "Only ours." I place a hand on his nearest armrest. "There are uncomfortable questions ahead. I'm

210

not sure what the right path is, but only one of the men out there is your master. Only Bamboo can compel you."

BandStand nods. "We're to protect our Master's interests. Even if we have to lie."

"I'm not asking you to sin," I say. "But be reserved in what you say. To them or anyone."

"Even Master Bamboo?"

A guard pounds on the canopy near my head. I do my best to ignore him.

"Be wise in everything," I say. "Circumspect."

"Yes, Mawla."

There's another thump, this time on the hull of the skyslider. I get a message from Bamboo: "As much fun as this is, you should come out now, ThreadBare."

I squint at BandStand. "Are you ready?"

He nods. "Circumspect and wise."

I smile. "Open the canopy, Buraq."

There's a snap as the canopy unlocks, followed by the release of pressure—air that's doubtless been recycled multiple times since we left the station. Outside odors trickle in, including the scent of sweaty and angry freeheads.

"Come out this instant!" Mah shouts.

I feel the warm energies of the nearby implants, Bamboo most notably, but I can sense the others in the building: Talons, Mint, Jumbo, and the rest. I perceive the many bots in the vicinity too. Their presence could be distracting if I let it be. Their many needs and reports.

I stand and place my palms on the dash. Immediately, rough hands grab my left elbow and tug me forward. The force is strong enough that I almost tumble over the slider's side.

"Rails." I grab the ship's edge and right myself. "I'm a debugger. Debuggers shouldn't be touched."

The offending guard—a thick-necked man in beige clothing—attempts to grab me again, but Mah waves him off. "Let him be," he says. "We'll hear his excuses soon enough."

I climb free of the slider, dust the front of my jumpsuit, and fold my hands in front of me. "Good to be home." I smile. "What have I missed?"

Mah is dressed in black today. The men with him are unfamiliar, but they could've been birthed from the same mother. They're all bearded, dressed in beige with dark head coverings, and intimidating.

"Your extended absence was ill-advised."

I resist looking at Bamboo. "The CA lift was sabotaged," I say. "I was sent to repair it."

"Sabotaged?"

I hear movement behind me and so step aside as BandStand exits the slider. He takes a position to my right, head bowed.

Mah scowls at BandStand. "You took a child on such a hazardous mission?"

"The danger wasn't known until we arrived," I say. "But debuggers are often in danger." I think of BullHammer's leap but push that memory away. I can do nothing for him now.

"It was my choice," Bamboo says. "The new edict discourages debuggers from traveling alone. This student seemed the perfect choice for a companion. DR-762 had inefficiencies that required additional field work."

"Inefficiencies?" Mah says.

Bamboo nods. "Emotional variations that could only be overcome through extended service." He touches his forehead. "Minds aren't fully formed until adulthood. It's essential to correct any shortcomings early on. Even freehead parents know this."

Mah grunts. "So, all was purposeful. Everything was righteous." He looks at his nearest associate. "Do you believe this?"

The guard shakes his head. "No, inspector."

"I have no reason to mislead you," Bamboo says. "My position relies on the Imam's favor."

"That it does," Mah paces toward me. "And after your repair of the lift, *skin*, where did you go?" The door to the facility's interior is directly behind him now, only a short walk away.

"To the topside station." I nod at BandStand. "It was an additional educational opportunity. This student has never been in orbit. Someday, his tasks may require it."

"Hmm...." Mah squints. "I doubt that very much. I see a reduced need for this position in the future. Its existence begets too many risks." He looks at me. "Don't you agree?"

"Every improvement involves risk."

Mah chuckles. "You consider yourself an improvement?" He looks at the guards. "This slave considers himself our better." The guards laugh too.

Bamboo remains rigid and expressionless. The black, sword-like Elipserv building dominates the scenery behind him.

How fragile are our lives now? How tenuous our roles?

My eyes wander to the city skyline and its rainbow of color. This is the way it has always been. No guarantee of life or comfort. One minute freedom, the next a lion's den. Are debuggers any different?

"God isn't cruel," Damali once told me. "He has a plan."

Am I part of that plan? Is any of this? I want to hope so. I want to believe that things can change for the better. That there's a way to...something new. With Cubed's help, and Damali's support—and maybe even the items Band and I brought back.

I can't think of those things now, though. I shouldn't—

Mah approaches Buraq. "How did you acquire this ship?"

"It belongs to the school," I say without pain. "Acquired after the downrider web was infiltrated. A backup method of transport."

Mah runs a hand across the ship's surface. "Its style is familiar. Reminds me of ships I've seen in the Holy City."

"The manufacturer is worldwide," I say.

"Yes...doubtless." Mah straightens and looks at me. "You've told me everything I need to know?" he says. "Everything of consequence?"

"What more would you like to know, Inspector?"

Mah moves toward BandStand. "If I'm to ensure your safety, anything you withhold could endanger you or your community here."

I bow my head. "Their safety is my concern, as well." I send BandStand the taste of honey. "And their growth."

Mah smiles at me. "There have been changes in your absence. Are you aware?"

My insides feel suddenly hollow. "Orbital flight degrades stream efficiency." I glance at Bamboo, who now looks uncomfortable too. "I have many messages to catch up on."

Mah waves at his head. "How unsettling that must be. To have your thoughts constantly interrupted. Pulled here and there. How could anyone live in such a way?"

"The brain is a remarkable creation," I say. "Incredibly adaptable. The debugger experiment has been verified over generations."

Mah's smile broadens. "It's good that you believe in your current state." He looks at Bamboo sarcastically and then his own men. "All men should be so committed to their state. Chosen or not."

"I'm content," I say, nodding. "Ready to serve."

Mah indicates the building below us. "And you agree with this school of implants, yes?"

"Of course." I look toward the roof door again. "I would like to get back to their instruction." I force a smile. "I miss my work."

He smiles. "And you enjoy your position here too?"

"I appreciate the students' gifts." I smile at BandStand. "Their unique abilities. I'm honored to be part of their growth."

Mah nods again. "You wouldn't oppose having another student?

Confused, I look at Bamboo for answers. "Another?" I message him. "What is he getting at? What have I missed?"

"I regret the timing," Bamboo messages back, "but the change was necessary. And it has already proven beneficial. Much has been learned. A technological leap that you will come to appreciate."

I fight to hold my position. To not flee to the ship, or into the facility. "I will train any student I'm given," I say. "Of course."

Mah smiles and shakes a finger. "This one will require much training," he says. "Constant discipline."

He's pushing me, but I don't know why, aside from his own sadistic tendencies. "Where is this student?" I ask.

Mah clutches his chin thoughtfully. "Should I have the new student brought here?" He shakes his finger. "No, no, I'll let you locate the implant." He looks at Bamboo. "He can do that, yes?"

Bamboo nods and then looks at me. "DR-892."

I focus a stream search on the DR with that number. As suggested, it's a new entry in the active list. One I've never encountered before.

I find DR-892's presence, and then his physical location. He's on the same level as my room, but a little farther south. In another room like mine. Unusual, because students typically live in shared quarters—dormitory-style.

A new implant would be isolated, though. The adjustment process takes time. There are always variables. Emotional and physical side-effects.

I compose an Easy Impact message to DR-892 and send it away. A simple—easily digestible—script. A minor test of the student's abilities.

The message is received, but there's no response.

"Was he injured in some way?" I say aloud.

Bamboo shakes his head. "The process was successful. Better than anticipated."

I compose an Extended Easy message this time and send it. It's text again, but with my voice reading it.

The message is received. The implant is functioning. Doing its job.

Nanoseconds go by.

I get a Full Impact response. An image of a room like mine, but from the perspective of the floor. I hear the implant breathing heavily and smell the hint of jasmine.

Moreover, I feel the emotions. A full spectrum of mental reactions. Spikes of pain, confusion, fear, anger...and a hint of wonder.

"ThreadBare?" a whispered voice says. "Is that you?"

My emotions merge with those of the implant, swirling and swaying like a digital tornado. The storm intensifies, threatening to consume us both. I fight for my composure—to keep my human shell frozen in place.

I will give nothing to Mah and his machinations. No indication of how much he's hurt me. How he's snatched more freedom, even as I clung to hope.

"I had no idea it was like this," the voice says. "I feel awful. Come here...please."

I compose a message, filled with all the sights, sounds, and scents she loves. "Soon, Damali. I'll be there soon."

215

YOU CAN MAKE A DIFFERENCE!

Word-of-mouth marketing is the best kind. Not only does it ensure that good books get noticed, it also helps bring the right books to the people who will enjoy them most.

If this book met or exceeded your expectations in any way, please consider telling your friends and/or posting a short review.

Your help is greatly appreciated!

THERE ARE MORE ADVENTURES OUT THERE...

That's all of ThreadBare's story for now, but more is on the way! Soon! In the meantime...

If you haven't read my original cyberpunk trilogy, there's no better time. The first book, *A Star Curiously Singing*, is free for a limited time.

Or for something really different, why not try the Peril in Plain Space series? The first book, *Amish Vampires in Space*, started as a joke, but ended up being a straight-up science fiction story with a generous helping of Amish society and the taste of a creature feature.

You can find links for all my books at www.Nietz.com.

ABOUT THE AUTHOR

Kerry Nietz is an award-winning science fiction author. He has over a dozen speculative novels in print, along with a novella, a couple short stories, and a nonfiction book, *FoxTales*.

Kerry's novel *A Star Curiously Singing* won the Readers Favorite Gold Medal Award for Christian Science Fiction and is notable for its dystopian, cyberpunk vibe in a world under sharia law. It is often mentioned on "Best of" lists.

Among his writings, Kerry's most talked about is the genre-bending *Amish Vampires in Space*. AViS was mentioned on the *Tonight Show* and in the *Washington Post*, *Library Journal*, and *Publishers Weekly*. *Newsweek* called it "a welcome departure from the typical Amish fare."

Kerry is a refugee of the software industry. He spent more than a decade of his life flipping bits, first as one of the principal developers for the now mythical Fox Software, and then as one of Bill Gates's minions at Microsoft. He is a husband, a father, a technophile and a movie buff.

If you'd like to get an e-mail alert whenever Kerry has a new book out or has a special on one of his already-released books, subscribe at his website: www.Nietz.com.

About FRACTURED

HAS IT BEEN EIGHT years since *Fraught* was published? Where did that time go?

Personally, a lot has happened in the intervening years. Three Rhats-based books were published, though one—*Rhats Too*—was written before *Fraught*. The final book in my *Peril in Plain Space* series, *Amish Werewolves of Space*, was written and published, along with a standalone robot adventure called *Lost Bits*. I also had a handful of short stories released, many of which are now collected in the *Digital Dreams and Other Distractions* anthology.

There were also many marketing and sales events, including writers conferences, homeschool conventions, and podcasts—lots of podcasts.

Along with that, there was that whole COVID thing, which meant kids at home needing supervision and instruction, and then kids returning to school and driving, and then kids' numerous events, and then kids graduating. (Two so far, with one to go.)

I also developed a new interest in 3D printing, which resulted in me crafting a whole slew of cool stuff, including a full-sized, wearable Master Chief suit. (From the Halo game franchise.) I even reengineered a broken printer for fun. Because, what debugger wouldn't?

"Excuses!" I hear you shout. "Why did it take so long to get back to DarkTrench? Why were you ignoring ThreadBare?"

Many factors. For one, ThreadBare's story seemed to be in a place where it could sit for a while. Thread was safe and reasonably happy. Why would I want to drag that poor guy into misery again? Plus, for whatever reason, the reader demand for Thread's series wasn't as great as the Amish and Rhats series—despite, I think, some intriguing scenarios and characters. I had some ideas about what ThreadBare might experience next, but I knew it might be a long slog to get it all written. So, I let that world simmer. Some would say I even procrastinated a little.

It might have gone on too long, in fact, except people started to ask whether there was more in the DarkTrench Shadow series. I even had one reader who admitted to never starting a new series until it was completely written. *Was there more coming?*

So, in mid-2023, I started writing. I wasn't sure how long it was going to take me. I didn't have a true sense for the story's intricacies or all it needed to contain. Yet, more than most characters I've written, Thread's future and the future of his world was already somewhat set.

Why? Because of Sandfly and HardCandy. Because of the original DarkTrench.

By January of 2024, this next Thread book had grown to over 50,000 words with no end in sight. There were a lot of important events to cover yet. At that point, I had Thread in Scallop's old office on the space station—still a long, long way from where I thought the book should end. So, I trudged on. Persevered, despite many distractions.

Months and months went by. Tens of thousands of more words were written. I was beginning to despair a little. I was making progress, I could see that, but this epic was well on its way to becoming a tome. I wrote past the size of *Frayed* and then on past *Fraught*. Would this be the story that never ended? Would it be the one to do me in?

I got a glimmer of hope from author friend Lisa Godfrees. When I shared my concerns with her, she said, "Well, maybe it's not just one book. Maybe it's two."

Two? I've never written two books back-to-back before. Is that's what's happening now? *Thread, what are you doing to me!*

I kept going. When I reached the end, it was the biggest thing I've ever written. Just over 160,000 words. As a single paperback novel, that's unwieldy. Difficult to hold in your hands, and after a little use they tend to fall apart. So, then I needed to figure out where to break it. There was no perfect place. No place where it would really feel like the emotional end of a book.

So, I chose the best place. Yes, it is a cliffhanger. Yes, it is a little mean to you, the reader. But bear with me! The next one is already written and well into the revision process. My hope is to have it out by the end of the year.

And then we'll be done with ThreadBare and his friends.

I think.